He sensed that Marjory Barrowman needed a sympathetic ear, which might or might not lead to an actual job, but considering the balance in his bank account, it was worth the time.

"Why don't you start at the beginning?"

She sighed, and her eyes welled up with tears. From her handbag she pulled a fresh tissue, dabbing at the tears before launching into her dilemma. "It's my daughter, Stella. She's missing."

David pulled a lined pad from the top drawer of his desk and started taking notes. This sounded like it might actually amount to something. "Go on. Give me the details about her disappearance. How long? Her age? What makes you think this is something to worry about?" He tried to keep his tone neutral and warm, hiding the natural enthusiasm he had for such situations. It'd been a while since something like a missing persons case had come to his attention.

"Stella is twenty-three years old. She's been missing for about two months." Her lips set in a firm line, and he could see she was struggling with the information about to be shared.

"Two months is a long time," he prompted.

Marjory's eyes searched his face, starting an ache in his bones that told him something serious was going on. An air of defeat came into her demeanor, knocking her well to-do status down a few notches. It was obvious she was deeply troubled. "Stella has been in trouble for the better part of the last ten years. She has a drug problem, she's run away in the past. She usually turns to stealing or prostitution to maintain her drug habit, which is how her family gets back in the picture. We get called in when she's been arrested or taken to the emergency room. This time seems different. She always calls to try and con me out of money, but there hasn't been a peep from her. I'm worried that this time she's finally gone too far, and she's lying in a morgue somewhere."

About the Author: Liz is an author and screenwriter from SE Ontario She loves true crime, horror movies, cats and ancient history.

MISSING DAUGHTER, SHATTERED FAMILY

BOOK ONE OF DAVID LLOYD INVESTIGATIONS

BY LIZ STRANGE

JUNE 10TH, 1995

When David stepped through the back door of McBurney's Bar & Grill, his life changed forever. From the way Jeremy had watched him through the night he'd figured the man had finally decided to put his comments and innuendo into action. Walking to that door, he'd expected a confrontation, even a physical altercation of some kind, but never in a million years would he have expected the deliberate and vicious attack that waited for him.

The door to the alleyway stood open, an unusual circumstance in itself, but when he heard his name called he knew this was it. He'd either have to put up, or resign himself to countless years of harassment and alienation. He'd never been one to run away from a fight.

The sole of his shoe just touched the damp concrete when the first blow took him in the gut, the power of a large and fit man behind it. The impact forced a grunt of air from his body. David turned in the direction of the hit, wanting to strike back, but a second attacker came at him from behind. A heavy, solid object struck him in the back of the skull, and he went down. Bright pinpoints of light flashed before his eyes as agony exploded out and down through his torso. He hit the pavement, feeling a strip tear open along his cheek, and tasted dirt. The boot coming toward him caught him under the chin and spun him onto his back.

A large man landed on top of him, and a brutal series of punches smashed into his face and upper body. His left ear began to whine, then went numb. Another man joined the action, and when his foot connected with David's knee there was a sharp cracking sound that seemed to reverberate through the narrow alley. Hot pain screamed from his knee, and as he instinctively reached out his hands to cradle the injury, another kick crushed his fingers. He wasn't sure at that point if there were only two attackers or more.

He slipped into shock, the grey wave of unconsciousness filtering in past the pain. As he was about to pass out, he heard a voice that he recognized. He forced his eyes open, zeroing in on it.

At least he would live.

CHAPTER 1

Crumpled balls of paper littered the carpet around the wastebasket, the castoffs of the better part of an afternoon spent playing office basketball and daydreaming of a vacation in the Caribbean. Business in the previous few weeks had been slow, nothing more than a few background checks and the surveillance of a possible cheating spouse. The background checks turned up nothing remarkable, and the wife had indeed been cheating—with the best friend of her twenty-two-year-old son. David had been glad to collect his fees on that one, thus wiping his hands of the messy situation. He just established the facts, he didn't deal with the aftermath of the painful (but truthful) revelations. Thank God.

The freezing rain beat an annoying tap-tap-tap staccato against his office window, an irrefutable reminder that winter still lurked outside, and there weren't any white-sand beaches or palm trees in the foreseeable future. Only dirty slush, bitter winds and chapped lips awaited. Truth be told, he rarely wandered far from Toronto's borders, and the only time he'd left North America had been for his honeymoon, almost ten years ago. David didn't like to think about that trip, as it inevitably led to thoughts of the subsequent dissolution of the marriage and the downturn his life had taken in the wake of that particular failure. *One day,* he thought, *I'll be on a beach somewhere, drinking a cold Corona with a slice of lime and none of that shit will matter.*

A peek at his watch told him it was creeping up on four o'clock, and being a Friday with no appointments on the books, it seemed an ideal time to call it a day. Setting his own hours and workload was one of the few perks of being his own boss. An intense workout at the gym and a pizza with the works beckoned.

He went about the usual closing shop procedures—locking files away, turning off the coffee pot—and was just about to pick up the mess of paper on the floor when there was a hesitant knock at his door. He took a swipe at the pile and dumped an armful of the paper balls into the wastebasket before answering. Just before his hand touched the handle he stole a quick glance down at himself, glad to see his shirt was still tucked in and his socks matched. First impressions could make or break a deal, and he was in desperate need of a new gig.

The door opened to reveal a nice-looking woman, small, but soft in a motherly sort of way. She had sandy brown hair, shot through with generous streaks of grey, which she wore shoulder length and parted on the side. Her makeup was subtle but accentuated her features, in particular her cool blue eyes. She was dressed in a high-end wool coat, and he would bet money that her handbag cost more then his monthly mortgage. She offered her hand in greeting. He took it, pleased to find her handshake firm. Nothing irritated him more than a weak handshake, something he equated with wilting lettuce.

"Hello. Are you David Lloyd?" the woman asked, waiting for acknowledgement before stepping into the office.

"That's me," David said. "Please come in."

She moved past him, leaving a lingering aroma of expensive perfume and clean hair. She took the seat meant for clients, and he moved his lean, six-foot-two frame around the side of the walnut desk to his usual spot. His chair let out a soft creak as he sat. The woman waited until he made eye contact before speaking again.

She cleared her throat. "My name is Marjory Barrowman. I'm sorry for stopping by without an appointment. I pass by here often, and today I thought I'd just take my chances." He tried not to look at her hands, which were fluttering about like anxious butterflies on her lap, a telltale sign of discomfort. He smiled to offer reassurance that she should continue.

"I'm not interrupting anything am I?" she asked, stalling

the point of her visit, as many new clients did. Pleasant circumstances generally didn't bring people to his office, and he'd learned to be patient with clients as they meandered their way to the purpose of coming to him.

"No, you're not interrupting." She looked about the space, taking in everything the room contained, including the small amount of paper still on the floor. She didn't comment. He was thankful the carpet had been recently cleaned and the furniture was good quality. Her presence reeked of money and affluence, and he felt psychologically demoted to a lower status because of it.

"Obviously I'm interested in your services...but now that I'm here I don't know if this is such a good idea. My husband is against hiring a private investigator, but this is more than I can handle on my own. And the police don't seem to be taking the situation very seriously." Her hands picked up tempo, a distraction difficult to ignore.

David leaned forward on his desk, giving her his undivided attention. He was a handsome man, he knew. It was just one aspect, but one that often worked to his advantage. It made men feel he was capable, a strong leader. With women, he just needed to put a little effort into making them feel as though their particular problem was the only thing that mattered to him, and then they were able to relax and trust that he could solve their problems. A little harmless flirting didn't hurt either. He sensed that Marjory Barrowman needed a sympathetic ear, which might or might not lead to an actual job, but considering the balance in his bank account, it was worth the time.

"Why don't you start at the beginning?"

She sighed, and her eyes welled up with tears. From her handbag she pulled a fresh tissue, dabbing at the tears before launching into her dilemma. "It's my daughter, Stella. She's missing."

David pulled a lined pad from the top drawer of his desk and started taking notes. This sounded like it might actually amount to something. "Go on. Give me the details about her disappearance. How long? Her age? What makes you think this is something to worry about?" He tried to keep his tone neutral and warm, hiding the natural enthusiasm he had for such situations. It'd been a while since something like a missing persons case had come to his attention.

"Stella is twenty-three years old. She's been missing for about two months." Her lips set in a firm line, and he could see she was struggling with the information about to be shared.

"Two months is a long time," he prompted. Marjory's eyes searched his face, starting an ache in his bones that told him something serious was going on.

An air of defeat came into her demeanor, knocking her well-to-do status down a few notches. It was obvious she was deeply troubled. "Stella has been in trouble for the better part of the last ten years. She has a drug problem, she's run away numerous times in the past. She usually turns to stealing or prostitution to maintain her drug habit, which is how her family gets back in the picture. We get called in when she's been arrested or taken to the emergency room. This time seems different. She always calls to try and con me out of money, but there hasn't been a peep from her. I'm worried that this time she's finally gone too far, and she's lying in a morgue somewhere."

That was a quite a bit to absorb. "How can you be sure she hasn't just run off again? Maybe she's found someone who's keeping her in drugs, or to take a positive spin, maybe she's drying out somewhere." David mulled over a few plausible scenarios in his mind.

Marjory blew her nose and managed a weak smile before answering. "She's tried stopping before. We've put her in a few different rehab programs, and she's tried going cold turkey, NA, you name it, but it never lasts. She's an addict, and there's more."

"Tell me."

"Do you know what a borderline personality is, Mr. Lloyd?" she asked. Her tears had stopped, but her eyes were tired and red-rimmed.

David had a rudimentary understanding of the term from the mental health and addictions courses he'd taken in college. It had been a mandatory part of the curriculum for the Law & Security program he'd completed in his early twenties. After that he'd wasted a few years as an armored car driver, before getting his act together and applying to the police department. Again, that was a time he didn't wish to dwell on. His hand rose to touch the small hearing aid he wore under his shaggy dark hair before he could stop himself.

"I have an idea, but please fill me in if this has some bearing on the case."

Marjory gave a humourless chuckle. "Oh, I assure you it does. Stella was diagnosed as a borderline personality at seventeen. Borderlines are known to be manipulative, unstable in relationships, quick to lash out in anger. Their behaviour affects everyone around them. They are impulsive and have a poor self-image, which often leads to thoughts of suicide or inflicting injuries on themselves. Stella liked to cut herself, and often complained about how ugly she was, even though she was a gorgeous girl, and I don't say that just because I'm her mother." She rummaged about in her handbag, pulling out a photograph, which she pushed across the desk's surface in David's direction.

David looked down at the picture. Stella was sitting in what looked like a dance studio, dressed in the typical attire: black leotard, tights and pink ballet slippers. Her sandy hair was pulled back, highlighting a face that could have been on the cover of any fashion magazine. Her lips were full and pouty, her cheekbones high. Bright blue eyes regarded the photographer. She wasn't smiling though, and her posture was tense, as though she were very conscious of how her image would appear.

"She's beautiful," he said, after examining the picture for a few minutes.

"Yes. She's sixteen there, a few months after her first round of rehab, and she was still more or less keeping her nose clean. As far as I was aware anyway."

"But she relapsed?"

"Yes, very shortly after that picture was taken. This had been after a number of troubled years, when we'd been to various counselors, and dealt with endless problems at her school. Stella had been hit by a car when she fourteen, and that was really the start of it all, the drug problem anyway. She came through it fairly well, but it did cause some damage to her knee, which was a tough thing for a girl like Stella. Sorry, I'm not telling this right. I'm jumping all over the place. I should have mentioned that she was a dancer. It took a few months of therapy, but she got back to dancing. Truth was, it hurt her more than she led on, and she became addicted to the pain-killers she was prescribed. This led to her looking for relief from other sources, which unfortunately she found."

"Street drugs?" he clarified, starting to see where this was heading.

"Yes, which cost money. At first she got by on her allowance, but then the drugs became more than just relief from her pain, she was addicted. She stopped eating, had trouble sleeping, and it all took a toll on school, her relationship with her family, and she starting failing classes. It was a mess."

"And the borderline personality?"

"Well this came out in the second rehab we sent her to. She was enrolled in an intensive inpatient program to deal with her addictions and get her the counseling she needed to repair relationships, get her life back on the right track. She was diagnosed by the psychiatrist she worked with."

"And did the diagnosis help?" he asked.

"Not really. It just seemed to give her free reign to be even more difficult than she'd already been. It did explain a lot of things about her behaviour though, from even before the accident. Stella had always been difficult, never seemed to keep friends for long. She was very self-centered but also overly sensitive, and often thoughtless. I used to think it was because she was spoiled, but her brother was never like that, and he had the same advantages that she did."

"So there's a brother? Can you give me some information on him? And yourself, your husband, anybody else you feel might be helpful."

In the discussion that followed, he learned that Christian, the brother, was twenty-seven and had recently finished his Social Work degree. He worked for a non-profit agency in Toronto that counseled troubled youth. He and Stella had been close as children, and Marjory felt that Stella's problems might have influenced his choice of profession. He was hard-working, had a long-term girlfriend, had never been in any kind of trouble. In other words, the polar opposite of Stella.

George Barrowman was a high-ranking executive with the Canadian Imperial Bank of Commerce and provided a very nice income for his family. He had a good relationship with his daughter, according to Marjory, but worked a lot, so he was not always available to deal with the day-to-day issues. She also mentioned that he was a just a few years from retirement, which led David to assume the man was quite a bit older than his wife, who didn't look any older than her late forties. He made a note to check out their relationship, to see if any family stress might have been adding to Stella's already numerous problems.

The family lived in an affluent neighbourhood, the kids attended private schools, and the family vacationed in Europe and other places that David had never been. Outside of Stella's drug addiction and mental health issues, there were no family heath issues. Marjory was a program director at nearby York University, a position she'd been in for a number of years, and an organization she'd worked for since her mid-twenties. On the surface, nothing struck David as odd or sinister, but many families were adept at hiding the skeletons in the closet.

David took down a list of relatives and family friends, work associates of both George and Marjory. He asked about teachers and counselors, dancers, school friends, people Stella may have met in rehab, even any names or places associated with her drug connections and other illegal activities. For the most part, Stella tended to stick around the Toronto area, though she had gone to New England once, following a boyfriend to Vancouver, even ending up on the streets of New York City for several weeks.

When the name of a certain detective who'd picked up Stella on a number of occasions was mentioned, David almost snapped his pen in half. The Barrowmans had spoken with him when they'd filed a missing person's report the month before, and he'd been dismissive, assuming Stella had simply run away again. Since she was an adult, it wasn't a priority matter for the police. Marjory didn't think they'd put any effort into finding her daughter.

It was a name he loathed to think about, a face that had

haunted his dreams for more months than he cared to admit, and hearing it out loud was a slap to the face. He started to sweat.

Jeremy Black.

"Are you all right, Mr. Lloyd?" she asked, taking in the flush rising from the neck of his dress shirt.

"David, please, and I'm fine. I think I have all the background I need for now. I guess we just need to discuss the fees." David pulled a form from the lower drawer of his desk and started filling in the standard information. When he'd done all he could he handed the form over to Marjory. "If you can make sure to fill in any and all ways to contact yourself, your husband, your son, and the numbers or addresses of any of the other people we've discussed."

Marjory took the paper and skimmed over it briefly before filling in the missing information. Her hands trembled.

"As for the fee, I charge sixty dollars an hour plus expenses. Any out of the norm costs, like say having to fly somewhere, I would discuss with you beforehand, of course. Now, for a case that could take anywhere from a few days to many weeks, like this one with your daughter, I'd require a five-thousand-dollar retainer. Any money not used would be returned in full, but be clear that it may take two to three times that if she doesn't want to be found, or if something bad has happened to her."

Their eyes met and the implication was clear. "I understand, and money is not an issue. I just want my daughter back, or, if the worst has happened, I want to lay her to rest. I will stop by the bank Monday morning and get a draft for the retainer, and I'll drop it by for you about this same time?" She handed back the completed form.

"Perfect." He looked over the paperwork, then offered his hand across the desk. They shook. Marjory Barrowman fumbled with the bag in her hand for a few moments, looking like she wanted to say something else to him, but instead turned to leave.

At the door, she looked back. "Thank you, David."

"You're welcome." The door made a loud click as it closed.

He sat down to re-read the notes he'd taken, trying the gauge the best place to start the investigation. The drug associates seemed key and any friends Stella had remained in touch with since her school and dance days. Time and time again his mind wandered back to Jeremy Black, to the point that anger throbbed through his arms and legs and anxiety tightened his chest. He needed to take a break, eat, and refocus. Hearing the name out of the blue like that had been a definite shock.

He was walking down the stairs to his car when his cell phone rang. The caller ID told him it was his younger brother Sean, and he smiled as he snapped the phone open.

"Hi."

"Hey Dave, what are you up to tonight?"

"I was just about to head to the gym, and then I was thinking pizza and a couple of beers, try and find a hockey game or something on the tube. Where's Cheryl?" he asked, pleased but surprised to hear from Sean on a Friday night. Cheryl was Sean's live-in girlfriend.

"She's out at some Pampered Chef party or some shit. I don't get why girls go to stuff like that and then complain about cooking dinner. Know what I mean?" Sean was a nice guy but clueless sometimes.

"Okay, so you're free for the night then?" The wind slapped him with gust of arctic air as he stepped out of his office building. He pulled the collar of his coat up to protect his naked skin.

"Yep. How about I meet you at your place around seven? Unless you have plans with Jamie?"

"Nope. Seven sounds good." The snow, having fallen with enthusiasm all afternoon, had turned to freezing rain, making the streets an icy, slushy mess. His shoe sunk in a freezing pocket of water, sloshing over the edge to the inside and leaving his socks damp against his skin. He rushed as quickly as he could without falling on his ass to his nearby car, the pellets of ice sharp against his face. By the time he was unlocking the door, tears were streaming down his face from the bitter cold.

In the locker room of the gym he slipped on the knee brace he'd been using for working out since the bar incident some years before. His bum knee and the partial hearing loss in his left ear were a constant reminder of what he'd gone through and survived. It could have been a lot worse, and would have been if Sean hadn't come looking for him. His whole life David had always looked out for his younger, smaller brother, but the one time he really needed someone himself, Sean had come through.

David was a strong, athletic man, having grown up playing hockey and football. He'd gotten into boxing as a teenager and belonged to the track team in both high school and college. He liked to lift weights, and he still ran as much as his knee would allow. He'd been a good student, a good kid, never getting into more than the usual adolescent escapades: missing curfew, school pranks, or an occasional drinking bout with his buddies. Once his dad caught him with a bag of pot, and he'd been grounded for two weeks. He decided it wasn't worth the risk after that, and truth be told, he hadn't had that much fun smoking it anyway.

Sean was a few years younger and always trying to keep up with his big brother. He'd tag along whenever David would let him, copied his hair and clothes. He worshipped the ground his brother walked on, even after David's secret was out in the open. In fact, Sean had been one of the first ones he confided in, and to this day the brothers remained close.

As he went through the various exercises of his routine, memories of different people churned through his brain. Hearing Jeremy's name had scared loose a bundle of odd memories. He thought of Dana, his ex-wife, who despite the awful pain he'd put her though, still remained a friend. He thought of his parents and the long six months he hadn't spoken with his father. He thought of his buddies from the police force, most of whom had disappeared after the assault and subsequent investigation. He thought of his eighty-five-year-old grandmother whom he had dinner with every Wednesday night, remembering her support and confidence that his dad, her son, would eventually come around.

Eventually his thoughts drifted to Jamie.

CHAPTER 2

The Bay Street corridor was a mecca for drug dealers and their buyers, prostitutes, and troubled youth. The same problems existed in Danforth Village, Morningside, Glenfield-Jane Heights, or any number of suburbs; this just happened to be the part of town Stella liked to come to for her drugs. The street where David parked his car was all bars, fast food, and hock shops. The storefronts were dingy and dated, and the whole area reeked of neglect. If a neighbourhood watch group ever formed, they had their work cut out for them.

A couple of suspicious characters lurked in front of Joe's (an original name if David had ever heard one), the pub where Stella made some of her connections.

David took a seat, hesitating a moment before leaning his elbows against the surface of the bar. He could tell without even touching it that the surface would be sticky and would leave marks on his coat. The bartender watched him take his seat, his macho bravado wavering under David's scrutiny. He ordered a Coke and decided to let the guy sweat a while before asking some questions. David thought he might be more open with answers once he realized the focus wasn't on him. When deflecting attention away from themselves, people are often inspired to divulge the dirt on everyone else.

He took a sip, swirling around on the stool to once again survey the bar's patrons. No one met his eye, most trying too hard to seem as though they hadn't noticed his arrival. David was sure that if he poked around in the background of any of the people before him, more than a few secrets would rattle loose. He imagined scenes of abuse, neglect, poverty, and brushes with the law. The fact that they were in a bar in the middle of the day reeked of unemployment and trouble.

"Who ya lookin' for?" asked a grumbling baritone voice. David knew without looking that he'd worn the bartender down.

"Leland Makowski," David answered without missing a beat. When he turned back the bartender was right in front of him.

The men were now only separated by less than three feet of bar top, and by the way the bartender was leaning forward, he'd narrowed that distance in half. His hands rested on top of the slab of wood, the biggest set of mitts that David had ever laid eyes on. Despite the man's unkempt appearance, his hands were very clean, and his nails clipped short.

"Lee ain't here right now. He don't usually make it in till after eight or so."

"I see. Any idea where I might be able to find him in the meantime?"

The bartender leaned forward and lowered his voice. "What are you? Parole officer or cop?"

David pulled a card out of his pocket and handed it to the much larger man. "Neither. Just looking for some info on a friend of Lee's. Nothing to be concerned about." The man was so focused on the card that David started to wonder if he could read. He stuck his hand out. "David."

The man looked up then down at the hand held out to him. "Gregor," he offered in return and shook David's hand. His touch was light but firm, not the bone-crushing mauling he'd expected.

"You and Lee buddies?" David asked.

A dark look flickered across Gregor's face. "Not really. We chat sometimes in the bar, but what he does outside of here I don't want no part of, know what I mean?" He was still leaning in David's direction, and the effect was a little threatening. David fought the urge to lean back, thus taking the submissive role in their interaction.

"I do." He nodded to emphasize his agreement. He decided on a new tactic. "Maybe you might be able to help me. You know a girl named Stella? Young, really pretty. Might have seen her in here hanging around with Lee?"

The man's stony expression never wavered, though his good eye did shift away from David's face. "I might know who ya mean. Why you wanna talk with her?" He straightened up and leaned against the back wall, his hands clasped before him.

David decided the truth was the best approach. "She's been missing for a few months now, and her family's worried about her. You know how it is."

"Not really. Never knew my dad, and my mom OD'd when I was ten."

Shit. "Tough break. Sorry about that. But you can imagine how a mother would feel, couldn't you?" He should have expected something like that, had taken the chance, and would now have to ride it out.

A man who bore an uncanny resemblance to his Uncle Lester indicated he wanted another drink with a wave of his glass in Gregor's direction. He filled the glass and took the guy's money without comment. When he returned his demeanor was less defensive, and David took that as an encouraging sign. He poured himself a shot and snapped it back with a quick jerk. The empty glass sat between the two men, sweating a ring of dampness on the counter.

"Listen, I know the girl ya mean. She goes through phases, you know? Sometimes she practically lives here, and sometimes I don't see her for weeks. She's a junky. Sometimes she *works* for Lee."

"Works?" David questioned. He didn't imagine that work meant she was scrubbing Lee's floors or walking his dog.

"Yeah, work. You know, selling for him. Sometimes Lee makes connections for her, arranging for her to spend time with guys looking for a little action."

"So she sold drugs and worked as a prostitute?" He was starting to like Lee less and less, and he hadn't even met the guy yet.

There was a loud crack from the closest pool table, and Gregor shot a hostile look in that direction. The bartender shook his head when raucous laughter broke out.

"Dumb shits," he said. "I know I made some bad choices in life, but some people never learn, you know what I mean? Anyway that Stella, she was a quite the character. I tried to help her once, offered to call her folks or a friend when she was having it rough, and she told me to stick it where the sun don't shine. That's what happens when people get on the rock. They get mean, and they want nothing but the next hit."

"So Stella was doing crack?" *Perfect*, David thought.

"That was her first choice, but she'd take whatever she could get her hands on. And when she didn't have the cash, she traded sex. Last time I saw her, prob'ly about two or three months ago, she looked like shit. She was skin an' bones. Dirty and shaking. Could barely hold a glass without dropping it."

"So this was back in September?" David asked, pulling out a small book to make a note to himself.

"Yeah, that sounds right. She came in, wanting drugs. She and Lee got into it. She had no money, and Lee told her there was no way anyone would pay to fuck her looking like that. She stormed outta here and I haven't seen her since."

David let that sink in. He turned to look out over the patrons again, and this time found a few looking in his direction with cautious interest. One man in a sleeveless denim jacket was flicking nervous glances in his direction while his buddy took his turn at the pool table. The man looked young but rough, like life had given him more than a few hard knocks. David would have been surprised if he'd made it further than ninth grade. He left shifty eyes to his game and returned to his conversation with Gregor.

"Any of these other yahoos I should be talking to?"

Gregor looked over David's shoulder to the small group at the back of the bar and shrugged. "Not really. Just a bunch of whores and lowlifes come in here. Maybe Ritchie? He's the one in the jean jacket." He gave a toss of his head in the direction of the pool table. *Shifty eyes.* "I think I seen him with Stella before, but not sure if it means anything. Coulda just been looking for the same thing."

"So why are you still here if you can't stand the clientele?"

"'Cause I own the place."

David was surprised. "Who's Joe?"

Gregor snorted. "No one. Just sounded better than Gregor's. Makes the place sound Russian or something. Don't know what my mom was thinking."

David thanked the man and left. It looked like he'd have to make another trip back to talk with Lee. In the meantime, he thought he'd stick around and wait for Ritchie to come out. Turns out he didn't have to wait for long.

As David sat in his parked car with a classic rock station turned down low, his mind wandered. He thought about the people in his life, the ones who would notice if he suddenly disappeared, and realized how lucky he was to have the relationships he did. He'd had more than his fair share of tough knocks over the years, some completely his own fault, but he could not imagine being so estranged from friends and family that two months without contact wouldn't give anyone a moment's pause.

Of course Jamie's face swam to the surface of the collection, looming large and central over all the others. They'd met about five years ago, not too long after David had finally come to terms with the issue that had caused so much turmoil in his life. He'd been harbouring a secret, denying a truth to himself that still somehow managed to leak out, often in ways that made no sense to him, less so to the others around him.

He'd met Jamie at court. He'd been a detective then, called to testify in a fatal hit-and-run that he had come across one unforgettable evening. Jamie was a prosecutor in the Ministry of the Attorney General's office, there to make sure the responsible party lost their right to drive and would spend a number of years behind bars. It had been the man's third DUI, and the accident had killed a young mother and injured two children.

David never forgot the way Jamie's face had looked as he questioned the defendant, or the way his loathing for the man had been so apparent though he had never raised his voice or been insulting in any way. He would also never forget how good he'd looked in his navy suit.

That was the moment, as he sat watching the lawyer from

his seat on one of the courtroom's hard, wooden benches, that he'd finally accepted he was gay. He'd come out, as people liked to call it, to friends and family, even a few colleagues he was close to at the police department, but had yet to give himself that complete, unrestrained permission to find another man attractive and be all right with the knowledge. He'd had a few encounters with other men, always rushed, hidden moments that had often left him embarrassed and frustrated. Most of his life he'd hidden behind his own self-induced pressure to be straight, passing years in relationships with women where he was little more than a shell. He knew then things had to be different.

Jamie had made eye contact with him a few times during the course of his day at court, and when he'd been on the stand himself, the proximity to the man had given him a colossal case of the butterflies. He was sure he'd been blushing, and several times had realized he was smiling, not an appropriate response in such a serious proceeding. Afterward he'd waited for Jamie to come out of the building, leaning against his car in the back parking lot of the court building. By the time the man had appeared the place was all but deserted. When he'd seen David he'd paused, then came to his vehicle.

"Officer Lloyd, right?" he'd said, looking David right in the eye. He noticed then that Jamie Brennan was as tall as he was and that his eyes were an odd shade of green.

"David," he'd responded, holding his hand out. When Jamie took it, giving a firm shake, fire raced up his arm.

"Jamie." He took a quick perusal of the parking lot, finding it empty. "Are you waiting for me?"

"Yeah, I though you might want to grab a bite to eat, or maybe a drink?" Now that he was in the moment, asking the man out, he felt his nerve slipping. Had he gotten the wrong impression?

Jamie took another look around, this time seeming a little nervous. "Are you asking me out?" His voice was even, like in court, but touched with a different tone.

"Yes, I was. Sorry, maybe I thought I picked up on something I didn't. I didn't mean to make you uncomfortable." David was stammering, poise crumbling. He started to turn away.

Jamie touched his arm. "It's fine. I'm just surprised, no one here knows about me, and I like to keep it that way. This is a tough business already, but having everyone know my personal business would make it impossible. I'm sure you know what I mean, being a police officer."

"So far so good for me," David had answered, the *incident* still a ways in the future.

"Well, good for you. I've heard the attitude of some of the men in this office, and unfortunately I don't think any of them would take too kindly to working with a homosexual. And believe me that's not how they would be referring to me."

"Right. I get it. There's still a lot of prejudice."

"So where did you want to go?"

"I guess that's up to you. I don't want to take you somewhere that you might have to explain something you don't want to."

"As far as anyone's concerned, we'll just be a couple of colleagues winding down after a tough case."

David was feeling much less enthused than he had minutes before. His first foray into an open lifestyle and the object of his affection was still in hiding. Figured.

"Now I'm sorry. I'm not making myself very appealing, am I? We can go wherever you want to."

David went with that. "How about the Italian place just down the block?"

"Sure, should we take both cars?" Jamie looked uncertain.

"That's a waste. Come with me, and I can drop you back off at your car after we eat."

That had been their beginning, and despite the trials and tribulations of having a relationship like theirs in the overly machismo world of law enforcement, they were still together. They were good together on many levels, but were always overshadowed by Jamie's need to keep his personal life hidden from his colleagues. Sometimes it made no difference, other times it chaffed at David like a sore that would not heal.

Ritchie sauntered out of the door, slapping on a pair of sunglasses even though the day had begun to slip into night. Little of the snow that had fallen the week before remained, the temperature jumping below and over zero without any rhyme or reason. He got into an older sports car parked up the next block and pulled into traffic. David followed at a discreet distance. Soon enough Ritchie made a turn onto a street lined with dingy apartment buildings and townhouses. He parked the car, and as he got out tossed a still-burning cigarette to the ground.

David parked behind him, drawing Ritchie's attention. He stared David down as he exited his car, lips pulled back in a sneer. Years of smoking, and David guessed a lack of brushing, had produced a mouthful of yellow-brown teeth. There was not enough money in the world to have made David get anywhere near that mouth with any part of his anatomy. The thought of it literally made his skin crawl.

"Aren't you the dude from the bar?" Ritchie asked with a surprisingly girlish voice.

"Yes. I need to ask you a few questions. You got a minute?"

"What's this about?"

"Stella."

"Whatcha want to talk to me about that stupid bitch for?" He changed his stance, as though trying to seem bigger and tougher than he really was.

David didn't buy it, but it did alert him to that fact that Ritchie had something to be defensive about. Good tip on Gregor's part. The fact that David had at least four inches and thirty pounds on the guy also made him secure in his own safety.

Getting to the truth was an entirely different matter.

"You want to talk here or inside?"

Ritchie's left eye began to twitch, and his overly done machismo faltered as he flicked his gaze in the direction of the nearest townhouse. He motioned with his fingers for David to come with him and began walking down the street, away from the building. David followed until they turned a corner, where Ritchie came to an abrupt stop.

"The old lady's home. Don't wanna talk about this stuff in front of her," Ritchie said, words rushed and defensive.

David took the understated route, seeming to agree with Ritchie's attitude to gain a sense of camaraderie. "Got it. What you do when she'd not around is none of her business, right?"

Ritchie smiled, exposing David to the unwanted view of his

teeth once again. "That's right. So whadya want to know?" He lit up a cigarette, taking a deep drag.

Something useful. "You and Stella friends? What kind of relationship do you have?"

Ritchie snorted. "I wouldn't call us friends, and we definitely don't have no kind of relationship, but I've hung out with the girl you know. Shared some goods, got some action. You get me?"

"So you and Stella have done drugs together and had sex?" As the words left his mouth, he thought of the picture of the beautiful, young dancer Stella's mother had shown him. He could not imagine a lovely girl like that letting Ritchie come anywhere near her.

"Sometimes when she didn't have enough dough, I'd let her suck me off. Win-win for both of us." Ritchie closed his eyes as though remembering, and David shuddered as the image flashed in his mind.

He tried not to sound as angry as he felt when he spoke. "So like charity? Just helping a girl out?"

Ritchie gave David a playful punch in the arm. "Exactly. That's the nice kind of guy I am. Besides before she got all cracked out she was a sweet piece of ass."

Bile burned at the back of David's throat. It took everything in him not to knock the guy's teeth down his throat. "She was a beautiful girl, no arguments there. So you know her through Lee, then?"

The defensiveness came back. "Yeah, I guess that's how I met her."

"You and Lee are buddies?" David asked with as much casualness as he could muster.

"Thought you wanted to know about Stella? Look I gotta get back. If JJ sees the car there and I'm gone, she'll be pissed. Plus it's friggin' freezing out here."

"Sorry, just a couple more questions." Ritchie looked down the street briefly and then nodded. "Okay, so when was the last time you saw her?"

"Dunno, must be a couple months. Been a while now that you mention it. She always seems to turn up at the bar or party or something, you know, looking to score."

"So this seems strange for Stella? To be gone this long?"

"I guess, but like I said we ain't best buddies or nothing. Maybe she found a new place to score. Or she took off somewhere. Girl could be crazy."

"So I've heard. Is there anything else you can tell me? Like was she having trouble with anyone in particular?"

Ritchie paused, eyes cast downward. Then with a shrug of his shoulder he said, "I don't think so. But she was a junkie, I'm sure she pissed off lots a people. I really gotta go." He started to walk back in the direction they'd come from, and David decided to drop it for the time being.

As he followed Ritchie along the street he wondered if there was any dirt on the man that he could use to make his lips a little looser. He seemed to be hiding something, but David didn't have enough insight yet to guess if it was just a matter of his own actions against Stella, or if he knew something about Lee. It could be any number of things with the lowlifes Stella had gotten herself mixed up with. He decided to put in a call to someone at the station he was still on good terms with.

Ritchie entered the house without so much as a wave goodbye. David drove away, feeling anxious and annoyed. Finding answers about where this girl had gone, or what may have happened to her, was not going to be easy.

Twenty minutes later he was pulling into the driveway of the house he had lived in for the past decade. Jamie's car was in the driveway, a nice surprise. His partner worked long days, often not available for many hours after David had closed shop. They tended to be hit and miss throughout the work week, better able to find time together on the weekends. He waved to Mr. Albert across the street, a man well into his eighties who liked to sit outside in the afternoons despite the heat or cold. He waved back, smiling. Jamie and David had both helped the man on a number of occasions, and he had never once questioned them about the nature of their relationship.

He came into the kitchen, dropping his keys on the counter. He had just opened a beer when his better half appeared, hair damp and body wrapped in a towel.

"To what do I owe the pleasure?" He waggled his eyebrows and gave an appreciative "woo-hoo."

"Give me one of those," he said, indicating the beer in David's hand.

"What are you willing to do for it?"

To his complete surprise Jamie dropped the towel. He walked naked across the kitchen to give David a deep, lingering kiss, then snatched the beer from his hand.

"Sucker." He picked up the towel and wrapped it about his waist again.

"Whatever, that was totally worth it."

David grabbed another beer from the fridge. He twisted off the top, chugged it down, then tossed it to Jamie. His partner easily caught it, putting it in the sink. Jamie was a neat freak, something that David liked to play on.

"No seriously," he continued. "How come you're home so early?"

"I had a meeting cancel, and so I decided to hit the gym instead. I thought we could go to a movie or something." He polished off the beer, then placed the bottle in the sink with the other.

"Sure, sounds good. Still can't convince you to come to my gym, eh? Would be fun working out together."

Even after all the years they'd been together Jamie still had his hang-ups. The people he worked with had no idea he was gay, let alone that he had a long-time boyfriend. He maintained a membership where many of the men at his office belonged, a fancy, over-priced establishment that catered to the lawyer-doctor-business mogul types. David went to the YMCA, where they had all the same equipment at a quarter of the price.

"David, why are we having this discussion again?"

"I know, you don't want your associates to see a couple of homos working out together. Scandalous."

"Please, I don't want to fight about this."

Jamie looked at him, his expression pained. David knew Jamie loved him, was faithful to him. He didn't want to start an argument either.

"I can think of a few ways you can convince me of your

sincerity." He let his gaze wander over Jamie's firm body.

Jamie smiled. He gave David a look that made his nether regions tighten. "Follow me."

Maybe they wouldn't make it to the movies after all.

CHAPTER 3

The Davenport Centre for Addictions and Mental Health had once been an imposing, three-story residence, built in the early part of the twentieth century. The house sat almost a kilometre back from the road, the drive winding through what David imagined would be an impressive expanse of green lawn and well-manicured gardens in the warmer months of the year. A towering wrought-iron fence encircled the property, and small groves of trees dotted the landscape. The only visible sign of life on that particularly cold Thursday morning was a small commune of squirrels chattering and darting across the thin layer of snow.

With the car parked as close to the building as he could get, David stepped out into the cold and made a beeline for the front door. Ten-foot-tall double doors stood in the centre of a wide veranda; heavy, beautiful pieces of wood showcased an era of craftsmanship that didn't exist any longer. Inside, the large front foyer had been converted into a reception area, with the requisite desk and smiling secretary. A set of couches had been arranged under a stained-glass window, through which the bright winter sun cast a flickering rainbow across the beige carpeting.

"Hello," the secretary offered as David took a look about the space.

He came to her desk, removing his scarf and gloves. "Hi. I'm David Lloyd. I have an appointment with Dr. Garfield for ten."

A quick glance at the appointment book confirmed his statement. "If you take a seat I'll let him know you're here."

She already had the phone to her ear before he could reply,

so he did as instructed. The table before him was lined with neat piles of magazines, none of which would have been his first choice in reading material. Instead of idly leafing through pages, David let himself become accustomed to the space; the sounds, smell, and sight. Like most high-end businesses, whether it be selling goods or healthcare, the place was immaculate and decorated with soothing colours and clean lines. There were faint murmurs of conversation in the distance, some light music set at a very discreet volume, but other than that no other sounds intruded. The building was far enough back from the street that the presence of the never-ending traffic did not intrude.

When he thought he might finally break down and grab a copy of *Golfer's Digest*, a man entered the lobby and, after a thoughtful nod from the secretary, came to where David sat. He extended his hand, which David took, finding the skin warm and the grip firm.

"Hello David, I'm Dr. Garfield."

The doctor was of average height, with dark hair softened at the temples with grey. A droopy mustache concealed most of his upper lip. He appeared to be in his fifties, dressed in khakis and a dark sweater.

"Thank you for agreeing to meet with me," David said.

A red file folder was tucked under one arm, the colour catching David's eye. The doctor extended his arm in the direction of the hallway leading to the left-hand side of the building. "Let's go to my office where we can chat in private."

As he followed the doctor down the hall David became quite intimate with the beginnings of a bald spot on the back of his head. He also took in a slight limp and a gold band on the man's left hand. Most of the doors they passed were closed, though one space held a small group of young people who appeared to be participating in some type of group session led by a frizzy-haired woman. The woman glanced up as they passed before returning her attention to the group. Dr. Garfield didn't comment on the nature of the session.

At the end of the hall was the doctor's office. A massive dark wood door opened to reveal his private work space. The room was large but cozy. One wall was a large stretch of windows, the blinds drawn to reveal a backyard that held several more gardens, a pair of gazebos, and a tennis court. An antique desk sat in front of the stretch of windows, a chair for visitors before it. The farthest corner from the door contained a couch and another chair, which David assumed was for sessions with patients.

The doctor took his position behind the desk, hands loosely clasped on the top. The many degrees and awards the doctor had received were discreetly displayed on a narrow strip of wall to one the side of the desk. After the attack, David had gone through a year of therapy, and he felt that strange combination of unease and relief filling him, the same feeling he'd had at each counseling session. He forced himself to relax.

The doctor began, "I must say I was quite upset to hear about this turn of events. I always have the highest hopes for my patients once they leave my care, though I know that relapse will be inevitable for some of them." His voice was smooth and sincere.

"So you remember Stella Barrowman then?" David pulled his notebook from his coat pocket and flipped through a number of pages. "Her mother says she was a patient here about six years ago. Stayed for several months for intensive therapy. Is that correct?"

"That sounds right." He pulled a pair of glasses from the case on his desk and opened the red file he'd brought in with him. "Stella was here for five months of inpatient care, then continued on with private and group counselling for almost two years."

"Did you treat Stella personally?"

"I did. I like to have some direct involvement with all the patients that come through this facility, stepping in on a larger scale if the nature of the case requires it. Once Stella had been diagnosed as a Borderline Personality, her primary psychiatric care came to me."

"Why is that?"

"Personality disorders are my area of specialty. I have been treating and involved in the research of personality disorders for the better part of thirty years." His words were not boastful, simply a statement of facts.

"What type of treatment did Stella receive?" David asked, though he was sure he would not fully understand everything the doctor might share with him.

"I must respect the client's privacy here, even though the parents have given me permission to discuss their daughter's care while she was still a minor. I'm happy to speak in generalities, but specifics need to remain confidential unless I see an urgent need to pass this information along. You understand my position on this?"

"I would like to assure you that our conversation will be held in the strictest confidence, only to be shared with Mrs. Barrowman, as my client."

"Of course. Please believe me this is no judgment on you personally, I wish only to do what I can to help while abiding to the regulations of my profession. I should start by clarifying that in addition to the Borderline diagnosis, Stella also had addiction issues. I understand that Marjory has already spoken to you about this. She self-medicated for both her physical and emotional pain, using whatever she could get her hands on. It was a complicated course of treatment, involving both individual and group therapy. I felt the best chance for relief of symptoms for Stella was the use of dialectical behaviour therapy and cognitive behaviour therapy, combined with medications for her depression and anxiety."

Whatever that meant. "Did this help her?"

"Stella responded very well when she was here, and even in the year after she returned to her parents. Now that's not to say that her behaviours ceased altogether, but she was better able to cope and manage her emotional responses. After high school she left home, and her participation in therapy dwindled and then stopped altogether. I understand from her parents that she had a few short hospitalizations after this time, usually stemming from an emergency room visit or an arrest. I would assume that she has not been on proper medication or working with a therapist of any kind for the past few years. With her condition untreated, compounded with the use of drugs and alcohol, Stella would have been in quite a state, susceptible to suggestions of others, engaging in impulsive, even criminal behaviour."

David let the information sink in, trying to decide the best avenue for further questioning. "Are there any particular incidents from her time here that stand out for you? Anyone she might have been close to?"

"In the early part of her stay she did run away with another patient. They were only gone for a few days, they returned on their own when they couldn't find anywhere to go with no money. I always thought the pairing was odd, and they did stay close during the rest of their time here." The tone of the doctor's voice hinted at more than just a mismatched friendship.

"Can you give me any more details? A name so I might follow up with the person directly?"

"I would have to get permission from the patient before I can do either of those things. I will follow up and get back to you."

"What about any of the other people who worked with her?"

"Stella really enjoyed the art therapy class. I could let you speak with Roberta, the woman who leads the class. She might have some more insight of a non-clinical nature."

"Okay. What are your feelings about the family? Often times the people that cause the most pain are the ones closest to us."

Dr. Garfield gave a pained smile. "I know it well. Now, as for the Barrowmans, they were genuinely concerned for their daughter's well-being and did their best to follow prescribed treatment plans. I believe that Marjory was more invested in the hands-on care, but I suspect that had more to do with time, rather than a lack of concern on the father's part.

"The brother came to several family sessions, seemed pleasant and well-meaning. I understand the siblings were not particularly close, but not enemies either. There was resentment on Stella's side for the attention her brother got, but it didn't seem to me to be an overt favouritism from the parents, just that he was a successful young man. At that time he was on the honour roll, in the drama club, and ran on the track team. He had a long-term relationship with a young woman the Barrowmans liked. His success and the ease with which the success came rubbed Stella the wrong way. It made her feel that much more a failure, an outcast."

"But you didn't pick up on anything like abuse, marital problems, drugs, or alcohol, anything like that?"

"No, nothing of the sort ever came out in any of my talks with the family, or with Stella. I think there was some distance by the father from the family that caused some issues. He worked a lot of hours, was often away on business trips, not the type to be demonstrative of his feelings. I think Stella wanted more from him, and the lack of attention fed her insecurities. But I don't believe he ever hit her or anything of that nature. You have to understand how hard this would have been on the whole family. Borderlines are notoriously hard to get along with, and dealing with any type of mental illness or addictions issues can be very stressful for those close to the sufferer. I believe the family managed better than most."

"Is there anything else you'd like to share?"

The doctor was quiet for so long, David started to wonder if he'd said something wrong. "I will say this. I believe Stella's struggles to be lifelong, meaning though she might do well under certain care and by taking medication, it would be something she would always have to work at. I wouldn't be surprised to find out that she had kept things from me that might have been beneficial to her recovery. She is a troubled girl."

"So you think it is a possibility that she's runaway or worse."

"It's definitely a possibility. I hope you find her soon."

David wasn't sure where else he should be going with this line of questioning. He decided to keep any further questions to the follow-up session he would be sure to have with the doctor, after speaking with some of the other staff and associates that Stella had from that time. "All right then, maybe we can speak with the art teacher if she's available? Or anyone else that might have come to mind?" He left the question open, but it didn't seem that the doctor was biting.

"Of course. Roberta should be in the studio. She has a series of classes today, for both inpatient and outpatient clients. She's always a favourite with our clientele." The doctor stood as he spoke, moving toward the door.

David once again followed along the hallway, this time trying to absorb more details of his surroundings. The group session they had passed on their way in had dispersed, only the facilitator remained. She was hunched over her desk, scribbling madly in a large notebook. She didn't look up as they passed.

Once back at the reception area, Dr. Garfield led David down the other hallway. This passage had several connecting hallways and short offshoots leading to offices, studios, and other meeting spaces. Several rooms were in use, people talking, exercising, reading, or just hanging out. A large room with the door open wide waited at the end of the main hallway. Soft music wafted out.

"Here we are," the doctor announced.

David followed him through the door into a bright, open space where the nearly floor-to-ceiling windows stood unadorned, allowing a rush of sunlight to fill the room. The chocolate brown floor had been made from wide, knotty planks of wood, gleaming from an impressive bout of polishing. Every bit of wall space was covered with overlapping works of art, watercolours and charcoal sketches, abstracts and still lifes. Every conceivable colour and pattern assaulted David's senses. He felt awed and overwhelmed, as though suddenly trapped inside too many people's pain and emotional triumphs.

David allowed himself a few moments to adjust from the more sombre, muted environment of the rest of the building to the entirely different feel of the art studio. After the initial shock of the varied representations put to paper and canvas, David took in the warmth and freedom the space offered; it was a cheery, otherworldly sanctuary of sorts. It was no wonder that so many clients enjoyed the class.

Roberta, or the woman he assumed to be her, stopped as the men entered, looking up from the impressive array of art supplies she had been unloading from a large cabinet. David's first thought was that she seemed stern, possibly even suspicious, but then she smiled, changing her appearance entirely. Long auburn-brown hair had been pulled back in a ponytail, a complement to the clean lines of her face. The high cheekbones and straight nose gave David an impression of an Eastern-European heritage, and her eyes were as clear and bright as a spring sky. Dark jeans, boots, and an oversized t-shirt bearing a caricature of Salvador Dali covered her lanky frame.

"Sorry to interrupt, Roberta. I have someone who'd like to speak with you about one of our former clients—Stella Barrowman," Dr. Garfield said, coming into a conversational distance with the woman.

"What's this about?" Long silver earrings jangled as she came around the side of the desk, drawing David's attention to ears that had been pierced numerous times.

She offered her hand to David, in the process displaying several tattoos along the inside of her lower arm. "I'm Roberta."

"David Lloyd."

"Mr. Lloyd is a private investigator working for Stella's family. She's been missing for some time now, and the Barrowmans are concerned about what may have happened to her," Dr. Garfield explained.

"I see. I'm happy to answer any questions you have, Mr. Lloyd."

"David, please."

"All right then, I'll leave you two to it. I have another appointment in about ten minutes." The doctor smiled, shaking David's hand before leaving him with Roberta.

"Why don't we take a seat, David?" She pulled out two chairs from the line along the wall by her desk, offering one in his direction. He took it and sat down.

"Well, first of all, thanks for taking the time to chat with me. I appreciate it."

She was still smiling, giving him a very direct look. "It's really no trouble. I like Stella. I know she was difficult and impulsive sometimes, but if she lets you in there is something very magical about her. She is very bright and imaginative, she just didn't always use it to her advantage."

This was one of the first positive things he'd heard about the girl, aside from comments on her beauty and dance talent. "Sounds like you were close."

"We are, but it wasn't an easy road. At first she didn't even want to come to my class. She used to sit on one of the chairs and refuse to take part in any of the activities. Then one day she just joined in. After that we started to build some trust, she would stay after class to help me clean up, and we'd chat. Sometimes she'd help with other classes, even after she'd left full-time care."

"Anything come up in any of these chats that might help me find out what happened to her or where she might have gone?"

Roberta laughed, but not as an expression of humour. "Lots of things came up, stuff that literally blew my mind. I don't know how much I can or should tell you. Stella has disappeared before, sometimes for weeks."

"Are you afraid of the confidentiality rules or breaking a personal confidence?"

"Both. Like I said, Stella and I became close. Even after she stopped coming here, she kept in touch. I feel strangely protective of her, like a little sister. We were kindred souls in many ways, having gone through similar things. The difference was how we dealt with the shit that got thrown our way. Sorry."

"Please, feel free to express yourself. I just want to get the facts and help bring Stella home if I can."

"I don't think Stella's felt like she had a home since she was a young teen." The statement came out with more force than anything she'd said up 'til that point, and she seemed to realize it. She looked away.

"What do you mean? Are there issues at home that perhaps her mother and Dr. Garfield aren't aware of?" He tried to infuse a heavy dose of concern into his words, so as not to seem pushy.

"I think there were many things that both of them didn't know, or didn't understand the scope of, at any rate. Some things I think they brushed aside, not understanding how hard it was for Stella to deal with."

"I feel like we're talking in riddles here."

Roberta stretched her long legs out in front of her, her movements fluid and pleasant to watch. Her eyes drifted closed. David assumed she was trying to work out her explanation and he patiently waited. "I'm sorry, I'm not trying to be difficult. Stella is complicated, but I understand at least some of why she acts the way she does. She desperately wants to escape."

"Escape from what or whom?'

"Herself. She wants to remove herself from all the things

that have made her the way she is and be someone new. A different, better Stella. It just seemed that the harder she tries, the harder the next fall becomes."

"Do you think someone might have hurt her?"

"It's possible." She paused, clearly conflicted. "It's also possible that Stella has hurt herself, and I mean overdosed or committed suicide. Or she could have gotten herself in too deep with the drug and sex scene. You never know what some of those assholes are capable of."

Unfortunately, after many years as a police officer, David knew the truth of her statement all too well. That Roberta was privy to the intimate details of Stella's past was obvious, yet David did not know if that had any bearing on the present situation.

"When was the last time you heard from Stella?"

"Oh, must have been in August. She called me at home, we had a long conversation. She was still in town then, or at least she told me she was. I don't know why she would have lied about that, but anything's possible I guess. She was staying with some guy named Lee, a dealer I think. She told me she really wanted to clean up for good, go back to school. Her dream had always been to open her own dance school."

David thought about the conversation with Gregor, remembering that he'd talked of seeing Stella with Lee a few months earlier. It that were true, the sighting would have been within a few weeks of when Roberta had last spoken with her. What the hell had happened?

"Did she give you any hint that she might be leaving? Maybe she'd met a guy or found somewhere to go to get off the drugs?" Though he didn't feel Roberta was deliberately misleading him, the conversation frustrated him.

"None at all. If anything, I wouldn't have been surprised to see her on my doorstep or back here at the clinic."

"Who do you think can give me the answers I need?"

"I'd track down that Lee character and any of the people he runs with. He was feeding Stella's habit, I have no doubt about that. Maybe her dancing friends, she did stay in contact with some of them. Especially one, an old boyfriend. His name is Sasha Tivol."

David jotted the name down in his notebook. "Anyone else?"

"Yeah, I can't say why, but I think you should take a look at Stella's father."

That surprised David. "George? I haven't heard anything but good stuff about the guy, but all right."

"Everyone has secrets, David."

He had a flash of the attack, bringing the emotional journey he'd gone through in its aftermath to the surface. He thought of Jamie and his inability to fully come to terms with his sexuality.

"True enough. Can I follow up with you if I need to?"

"Sure. Any time." She wrote her contact information in David's book.

A young woman came into the room, and David took that to mean his time was up. He thanked Roberta and excused himself.

The secretary was still at her desk, and two people had taken positions on the reception area's couches. She gave him a brief smile as he passed.

For some irrational reason David felt an enormous sense of relief when the door closed behind him. Delving into Stella's history had brought some of his own past pain to the surface. He'd thought he'd worked through all of his issues, but maybe he hadn't. Just like Jamie was hiding the truth from the people he worked with, maybe David was hiding the truth from himself.

What happened to this girl? And where has she gone?

CHAPTER 4

He met Sean at the gym after an afternoon spent tying up loose ends on another open case. Once satisfied he'd done as much as he could, he'd typed up the final report to send out to the client for payment. The resolution and soon-to-be received funds gave his mood an upturn, much needed after the middling progress of the Barrowman case.

Sean had already begun his workout; David took the treadmill next to him. After thirty minutes he followed him through a series of weight-lifting exercises, content with the mindless yet invigorating process. They finished the session with a sit-down in the sauna.

David tried to relax, letting the heat seep into his body, but the nagging thoughts born from his conversations at the clinic kept interrupting.

"Sean, can I ask you something?" he asked, not certain that voicing his concerns would accomplish anything.

Sean opened his eyes, giving his brother his undivided attention. "Sure, anything."

"Do I seem okay to you? I mean, do you think I've dealt with all the stuff from the attack and leaving the force? Even all the issues with coming out, and Dad's reaction, or what happened with Dana?"

"Well, that was not at all what I was expecting. Where's this coming from? You having some kind of problem?" Sean's posture tightened, brows drawing together.

"I don't know, maybe I am. I have this case I'm working on, and it's made me reflect on my own past. I wonder if I've dealt with everything or if I've just pushed it far enough away that I don't have to acknowledge what happened."

"What do you mean?"

"Like the way I live my life. I work alone, I live alone. This gym is not where I might run into anyone I used to work with. Is that dealing with things?"

"Dave, c'mon. After everything, I think you've done really well. You've patched things up with Dad, you even managed to stay friends with Dana, which I don't think most people would have been able to pull off, considering. As for your job, it's not like you've been shunned, you still talk with people."

"A few," he offered.

"All right, a few. That's better than none. Let's face it, no matter where you live or work, there's going to be some dicks that will have a prejudice against you because you're gay. It's not right, but it is a fact of life. And you were able to use your skills and training from the force to help you set up your own agency, which is pretty amazing. You do well enough, I mean I never hear you complain about money or anything."

He did need to give himself credit. It had been almost a year of physical therapy to get him back on his feet, and he had come through it with flying colours. He'd made himself go to counseling, even though he really didn't want to. He'd attended every meeting with the higher-ups at the police force, participating in the investigation with strength and focus. In the end it had paid off; he'd received a nice settlement from the force plus his pension, which he'd rolled into investments and the set-up of his agency.

The things that stood out; the lack of resolution to the attack and the change in the way others viewed him. No one had ever been charged or reprimanded for the attack, even though there was no doubt in David's mind who the responsible party was. It had been hard enough after coming out; he had lost friends, and working relationships had changed. After filing a complaint against Jeremy Black—one of his own in the eyes of many members of the police force—there had been no going back. He could have taken a desk job, as the hearing loss and knee injury would have kept him from active duty, but the hostility he'd have had to work in wouldn't have been worth it.

Now he had only a few people he kept up any kind of relationship with: a couple of guys with whom he played hockey, and Janelle, a woman who worked in administration. As for getting the inside scoop, there were two active officers that would still feed him information or run a check for him. From the organization that he had given thirteen years of his life to, only five people hadn't turned their back on him.

"Nope, money I'm good for. The settlement gave me a boost, letting me pay off my debt, and the pension gives me a cushion for the times when business is slow. I guess I'm talking less tangible things, not money or injuries, any of that stuff. I mean connections, relations, image, understanding. Does that make any sense?" David cringed as a note of desperation crept into his words.

"Give yourself a break, man. Jesus. You're one of the most honest, together guys I know, and I don't say that just because I'm your brother. I see that. Mom and Dad do. Jamie does." Sean moved up a level to sit next to his brother and gave him a playful punch in the arm.

"Yeah, Jamie."

"What's that supposed to mean? You guys aren't having trouble are you?"

"I don't know how to answer that. I mean, isn't it weird that after being together more than five years, we still don't live together? Is it really healthy to be with someone, be in *love* with someone, who basically denies your relationship?"

"Jamie doesn't deny you. He comes to family stuff, you guys are monogamous."

"Yeah, but it doesn't work the other way around. I have never even met his parents, and certainly nobody at his work knows about me, they don't even know that he's gay! And I just accept it even though I think it blows. Just like I accepted my payout from the force. I let Jeremy Black get away with what he did to me."

"Okay, whoa. First off, if the stuff with Jamie bothers you that much, then you need to let him know. And then you have to decide what you're going to do if he won't change. Do you want to end the relationship? The stuff with Jeremy, well I have to disagree. You didn't let him get away with anything. If anyone did that, it was the Police Department. Even then, I don't know how they could have done anything more than they did. There were no witnesses, at least none that would talk, nothing to tie him to the attack."

David let out a breath. "No, I don't want to end things with Jamie. I love him. I know that he loves me, and that should be enough. It just bothers me that what his job or the legal industry might think of him could mean more than his feelings for me. That's what it feels like to me, like he's ashamed of me, of us."

"Look, you know I'm cool with you guys and with you being gay, but I have to say it's really weird sometimes talking with you about romance stuff with other dudes. Don't you guys talk about stuff like us heteros do?"

David laughed in spite of himself, suddenly so glad to have the type of relationship he did with his brother. He loved his honesty, so refreshing from some of the other areas of his life. "Yes, we talk like other couples do. You're right, I need to tell him this and make him listen. We can't go on like this indefinitely."

"And Black?"

"Jeremy Black is a bigoted, violent piece of shit, and he isn't worth another moment of my time. I know this, but that doesn't stop me from thinking about him and the attack and the effects on my life. I'm only human."

"So, have we settled anything here? You feeling better?"

"Yep, much. I know what I need to do."

"Good, so can we blow this place and go grab a beer?"

"An excellent idea, little brother. You lead, I'll follow."

They ended up at a bar around the corner from the gym, a larger, sports-themed establishment that catered to the working class. The brothers shared an order of nachos and a few beers before heading off to their own homes.

David slept like the dead, and if he dreamed he couldn't recall it when morning arrived.

Sitting at his desk with half a pot of coffee warming his stomach, David worked through the scant information he'd so far collected on the case, hoping that something might jump out at him. No such luck. No one person or incident seemed the direct cause if Stella's disappearance, more likely it was a collection of circumstances and instances culminating in the young woman hitting the ultimate low; in the case of a junkie, that low most likely being an overdose. Of course she may have also experienced a personal epiphany of some kind, making her realize that she needed to remove herself from her current whereabouts and lifestyle for even a chance of recovery and ultimately a new lease on life.

David made a quick sketch to help him visualize how all the people in Stella's life fit together or didn't as the case may be. Family, friends, lovers, teachers, dancers, care providers, and of course her drug connections all played their roles in the series of events leading to the current moment in time. To what extent their presence had affected Stella was yet to be determined.

Certainly the accident that damaged Stella's knee had played a huge part in derailing what could have been a strong, successful dancing career, also the gateway to Stella's drug use and ultimate addiction. Her mental illness couldn't have helped, but would it have led her to an equally dark path, without the pressure of broken dreams and the superficial escape from reality that the drugs offered? The illness might have been managed, or it may have wreaked its own havoc. Did the parents' concern help or hinder the situation? How deeply had the emotional and moral degradation of Stella's dependency and prostitution affected her? Had all of this come about over something as simple, yet nonetheless devastating, as the rejection of a boyfriend?

Too many questions and not enough answers. David decided a good way to proceed would be to run some checks on the names he did have, see if anything interesting surfaced. His hand had just touched the phone when it rang out.

"David Lloyd Investigations," he answered.

The voice on the other end surprised him. "Hey Dave. I only have a minute, but I wondered if you wanted to get together tonight? I should be clear by six." Jamie sounded smooth and a little impatient, as he always did when in work mode.

"Um, sure. Why don't you come by my place? I'll order some

Thai food. I have something I wanted to talk with you about, so this is good timing." A lump appeared in the back of his throat as he thought about the subject matter needing to be discussed, and hopefully settled.

"Okay. Should I be worried?"

"I hope not. Listen, I'm glad you called."

"All right, I guess I'll see you later then. I love you."

"Me too," David responded, the honesty of those two words so intense a surge of adrenaline shot through his body. He said goodbye and hung up.

Without giving himself a moment to worry or second-guess himself, he immediately dialed another number. Before the first ring had completed, a harried-sounding male answered. "Benson."

"Hi Jimmy, it's David."

"Dave, good to hear from you. How's it going?"

"Good, I'm doing well."

"Glad to hear it. Shit, it has to be at least seven or eight months since I've seen you. We should get together for a beer sometime."

"Sure, sounds good. Listen I don't want to keep you, I know how busy you guys are. I just need a couple of names run if you can?" He made it a question, though he would have been highly surprised to be told it couldn't be done.

"Hit me." David rattled off the series of names, which Jimmy dutifully jotted down. In the background, overlapping conversations and ringing phones could be heard, the familiar chaos of life on the force. "I'll call you back later today."

"Thanks Jimmy. Why don't we shoot for Friday night? I owe you a few beers by now."

"Sounds good. Talk to you in a bit." The phone clicked off.

While waiting for a return on his query, David decided to pursue another avenue. No sense wasting time when Stella's safety and well-being might be hanging in the balance. After making a quick call to ensure someone was available to speak with him, he located the destination on a map of the city, then headed out. The wind off the lake had a bite, making his skin feel tight and raw.

The music could be heard as soon as the door opened. A strange energy filled him as he walked the narrow hallway, down towards the back of the building as the contact had instructed him. Along the way, he passed rooms where people worked at desks, on costumes and set pieces, and dancers engaged in training for upcoming performances. In all his life David didn't think he'd seen so many beautiful, powerful bodies in one gathering. The air smelled vaguely of perspiration, a not-unpleasant scent in that particular surrounding.

Straight ahead a door was open, revealing glimpses of what appeared to be the main stage area. A man and two women stood together discussing action that was blocked from David's view. He could hear movement and the piece leading the dancers through their routine. At the door he paused, waiting until his presence caught the group's attention.

One of the women tapped the man on the arm. He turned and, meeting David's gaze, gave a small wave. The man ended his chat and came to meet David at the door. He extended his hand in greeting, "Mr. Lloyd, is it?"

"David, please."

"Hello, David, I'm Marcus James, director of the company. Why don't we go back to my office and we can chat in private?"

With a nod of agreement, the men began winding their way through a series of connecting hallways that seemed to continue on a downward slope. At last they came to a dead-end passage with only one opening. A heavy door had "Director" stenciled on the outside of the frosted glass.

Inside were the mementoes one would expect from a long-standing dance career; awards, photos, old costumes, and shoes. On the desk were piles of music and choreography notes, plus what looked like publicity photos of an upcoming event and some specific dancers. Marcus settled into his well-worn chair, using his hand to indicate that David should do likewise with the one opposite him.

He took a quick perusal of the photos behind the director's desk, noting several he assumed were Marcus in younger years.

"In better days," the man joked.

"You still look like you're in good shape to me. I have a

feeling once a dancer, always a dancer." His statement was flattering but true. The director looked trim and moved with remarkable grace.

"True enough. I try and keep up as best I can. Now, you're not here to talk about my career. This is about Sasha, I believe you said on the phone?"

David smiled, wanting the relaxed atmosphere to continue. When people began to feel scrutinized or threatened, they tended to clam up. "Yes and no. It's more to do with one of Sasha's friends, a young woman you may or may not know."

"I see, go on."

"Her name is Stella Barrowman. She has been missing for a few months now, and her family is understandably concerned that something may have happened to her."

The expression on the director's face hardened. "I know Stella."

"I assume by your tone that it wasn't pleasant circumstances that brought Stella to your attention?"

"It wasn't always that way. I've known Stella since she was about fourteen years old. She auditioned for a spot in one of our summer training camps and was successful, quite an achievement for such a young dancer. She was very talented, but at times difficult to work with. She did finish with top marks, and as such was given a position for the following year without having to audition again. That's how we work when we spot dancers with potential for professional work."

"Difficult how?" David asked, suspecting the answer to his question.

"She was moody at times, which could detract from the quality of her performance."

Her mental health issues, David thought. "And when she came back?"

"She wasn't able to finish the season. She'd had an accident sometime over the school year, damaged her knee. I don't think she was fully recovered physically by the summer, and it showed. Plus her mood swings were even more difficult to deal with. Sometimes she was so full of energy she was almost manic, other times it was difficult to get her out of bed. I suspected drugs, which turned out to be true. She was removed and told if she cleaned up she could audition again the following spring."

"Did she?"

"Yes, and she had cleaned up. We administered random tests over the months she spent with us. She worked very hard, seemed to be very focused on her training and with toeing the line. Never heard of any problems with other students or instructors. After that she seemed to just fall apart."

"Meaning what?"

He squinted his eyes, then began tapping his fingers on the desk. "Well she didn't even show up the next summer session, even though she had a secured spot. And being as that was her final year of high school, she could have parlayed a good season into at least a chorus position for the fall. I found out later she'd spent the better part of the year in rehab and had fallen out with her parents."

Throughout the entire dialogue, Marcus seemed nothing but honest, not even angry per se. If anything, he sounded disappointed.

"How does Sasha fit into all of this?"

"Sasha was Stella's boyfriend for a time, on and off at least. And even when off, I know they remained in contact. Sasha immigrated here when he was sixteen. I signed him on the spot, giving him a job to secure his ability to stay in the country. He met Stella the first summer he was here, and they hit it off right away. They partnered whenever they could, and truth be told they were magical together." Marcus turned his attention away, leaning down to open a lower drawer in his desk. After ruffling about a few files, he withdrew a stack of photos, then passed them in David's direction. Frame after frame captured a young Stella, fresh and lovely like the picture her mother had shown him. A nice-looking young man joined her in many of the pictures, some candids, others in full costume and makeup.

"This is Sasha I take it?"

"Yes, a wonderful dancer and all-around nice guy. He was smitten with Stella."

"I bet that didn't bode well for him in the long run."

"Nope. Her trouble often became his. He was always

running to her rescue, bailing her out, letting her crash at his place. He just couldn't seem to say no to her."

"Was he a drug user?"

"Not that I'm aware of. We have a very strict policy here, which I'm sure you can understand. Dancers have a very short window of opportunity as it is, and drugs are only going to hasten that. Now, he may have experimented, and I know he drank with her before, but it only took one reprimand to nip that in the bud. Sasha takes his career seriously, and that was always a wedge between them. If Stella had been able to get her issues under control, she could have been right there with him."

"Do you think he'd talk with me?"

"I don't see why not. He's here now, practicing. He's one of our first string, not yet a principal, but I hope next year that will change."

"Can I interrupt, or should I come back at another time?"

"No, it's fine. If you don't mind waiting here, I'll go grab him for you."

"Sure, thanks."

Marcus went off to find the dancer, leaving David to an unwatched office and an overactive imagination. After a quick snoop, he found nothing helpful or even out of sorts. There were standard financial records; the lease, payroll, and class fees. All other files contained nothing more sinister than photos, sheet music, and programs. He turned his attention back to the photos while he continued waiting.

The sound of footsteps approaching distracted him. Marcus ushered in the dancer, who from the flush in his cheeks really had been pulled from an ongoing rehearsal. He'd thrown an old pair of sweat pants on over his well-toned body, a damp, form-fitting tank covering his torso. He had dark hair, cut short, a thin nose and pale grey eyes. All around a good-looking guy.

After quick introductions, Marcus excused himself, so the two could speak in private. Sasha leaned against the desk, not quite smiling.

"So, like Marcus said, I'm here on behalf of Stella's family. We're just trying to find out where she's gone, hopefully get her some help."

"She's had help," Sasha said, a slight accent lacing his words.

"Yes, I know about Stella's past, and I understand this has been a long-standing problem with her."

"What do you know?"

Smooth. "Now, why don't we turn that around. I shouldn't be divulging personal information about clients. If you are as close to her as I've been told, then you know exactly what's going on with her."

He paused, debating his options. At last he seemed to relent. "She's an addict, and she has some kind of emotional problem. I mean, I know she was supposed to take medication for something. I could tell when she was off."

"Off her medication?"

Sasha crossed and uncrossed his legs, obviously uncomfortable about discussing his friend. "Yeah, she would get real mean. Do stupid, dangerous stuff."

"Like drugs."

"Yeah, and worse. Some of the stuff she got herself into, man, it makes my skin crawl."

"So you've stayed in touch then? Have you spoken with her recently?"

"Not for about six months. We had big fight in the spring."

"About what?"

"Same thing we always fought about—her. She showed up at my place one night, at like three in the morning. My girlfriend was sleeping over, so that was not a good scene. She's wasted of course. I bring her in, and she proceeds to verbally bash the both of us, fell on my coffee table and broke it, then threw up all over my apartment. My girlfriend stormed off, and I'm left dealing with her like usual. Next morning when she finally wakes up she apologizes and offers to have sex with me to make up for it. That was it. I'd been down that road too many times, always being there for her, just to be dumped and used over and over again. I couldn't do it anymore." He looked astonished at the speech that had tumbled out, closing his eyes and shaking his head.

David waited, letting the guy regain his composure. "So no phone calls, visits, nothing since then?"

"Nothing. I made it real clear, if she wasn't going to lose that scene once and for all we couldn't be friends anymore. I mean she's already screwed up a chance at a dance career, and she's lucky she hadn't already OD'd, or had something else bad happen to her. Her family was pissed at her, she looked awful. It had to stop."

"Hey, look, I'm not arguing with you. I can totally understand where you're coming from."

Sasha paced about the small space for a few moments, tension tight in his shoulders. "Sorry, this just pisses me off so much. She was so good, and she just threw it away."

"Okay, let's backtrack a bit here. Is there anything that you can think of that might help me track Stella down? Any specific people she liked to hang with, or somewhere she might have gone?"

"Have you talked to her family?"

"Just her mother so far. I haven't managed to connect with her father or brother yet. Why, is there something there I should be looking at?"

Sasha hesitated, catching David's internal radar. "I just think if anyone should have answers, it would be family. I know they really tried to help her."

That didn't seem to be the exact truth. "Nothing going on there that might have set her off though?"

"I don't think so."

"What about friends, drug contacts, people from rehab?"

He shrugged. "Well she kept in contact with Elaine Gemmet, a girl we both knew through dance. She runs her own studio now. I know she'd let Stella come and dance there sometimes, you know, after hours. Maybe some of the others, but I'd have to check. As for drug buddies, those seemed to change all the time. Whoever could score was her best friend, right. She hung out with one guy named Lee, a real loser. I met him a couple of times, and he creeped me out. She did talk with this one lady who worked at her rehab, can't remember her name. She taught art. That's about all I can think of right now."

David wrote down all the names, along with the address for the studio. The name Elaine rang a bell, making David think it was one Marjory had given him during their first meeting. He thought of Stella's beautiful face and the potential squandered, and felt a profound sense of loss. So sad, and yet it seemed that everything possible had been done to get the girl the help she needed.

Sasha leaned against the desk again, foot tapping against the tile floor. There was definitely more to the story, but he didn't seem ready to unload yet. It was often hard to break confidences, even when it might be for a good reason. David didn't see how he could get the guy to talk without risking a complete shut down. His posture had turned decidedly defensive, a sign to back off. Maybe if he gave the guy a few days, then took another crack at him he might get somewhere.

"Thanks Sasha. I really appreciate you talking with me." He pulled a card out of his pocket and handed it to the dancer. "My office number and cell phone are both on there. You can leave a message at my office and I pretty much answer my cell twenty-four hours a day. If you think of anything, please call."

Sasha scrutinized the card in his hand. "Sure, will do. Listen, I need to get back. We're close to the opening, and every minute of rehearsal counts."

"Sure, thanks again."

Sasha slipped from the room and didn't look back. *Something he's holding back. Definitely.*

David stopped to say goodbye to Marcus before he left, leaving another card with him. He took a few minutes to watch the performance taking place on stage, finding that Sasha had rejoined the cast. The routine moved into a segment where Sasha was highlighted, matching him with a young woman of equal grace and talent. They moved as one, a breathtaking bit of choreography that showcased the best of both dancers. He imagined Stella in the other woman's place, making the truth of her circumstances that much more depressing.

Outside was even colder than when he'd entered the building less than an hour before. The wind had kicked up, blowing a soft cover of snow across the parking lot. He hoped that Stella had found a place to stay, somewhere warm and safe.

Back at his office, David recorded the information from the interviews and made a few phone calls. He had an interview set up with Elaine, the studio owner, for the following afternoon. He returned the message waiting for him from Mr. Barrowman's secretary, arranging to meet the man later in the week. There had also been a message from his grandmother wondering if he might be available to help her with the set-up for a craft sale the Senior Centre was having on Saturday. He dutifully returned the call, agreeing to help her as he always did to any request she made of him.

After running a few errands he was back home. There were still a few hours before Jamie would arrive, and he decided to put them to good use. He hauled up the boxes of Christmas decorations from the basement, sorting them between the various rooms on the lower level. After taking a ride to the nearest home improvement store, he had a sweet-smelling pine tree to stand in the living room, something he hadn't bothered to do in a number of years. As he decorated it, the thought crossed his mind that he would like to have a small get-together that year. He'd invite his parents, brother, a couple friends and neighbours. Something small, but a way to let people know how much he appreciated them in his life.

He was on the phone ordering dinner when Jamie arrived. His partner was still dressed for work: business suit, tie, highly polished shoes. He went up to David's bedroom, where he kept some clothes and toiletries. David joined him after the order had been placed.

Jamie had changed into jeans and a t-shirt, softening his appearance. David moved in front of him, pulling him tightly against his body, and wrapped his strong arms around his familiar form. He pressed his face into Jamie's hair, suddenly wanting to burst into tears. He took a few moments to get himself under control.

Jamie responded in kind before pulling out slightly from the embrace to cup David's face with his warm hands. He guided his lips to David's, a kiss both tender and urgent. Something came to life within David, like the flick of a switch. He backed Jamie up to the bed, ordering, "Take off your clothes."

Jamie didn't argue. In less than a minute both men were naked on the bed. David was more aggressive than usual, pushed on by the irrational thought that Jamie might leave him after he brought forward what he wanted to discuss. Jamie played along, giving as much to the encounter as he received. Their sex life had never been anything to complain about, but that night was especially exciting. When they'd both been satisfied, he pulled David against him, letting his head lie on his chest.

"What's going on with you?" he asked, stroking David's hair. His breath was warm and pleasing against his ear.

The doorbell sounded, a welcome interruption.

"Shit, the food. Come downstairs." He pulled on his pants, grabbing a shirt as he left to answer the door.

He was filling two plates when Jamie joined him in the kitchen. Without words he led him to the family room, lit only by the multi-coloured lights on the Christmas tree. They sat on the floor, across from one another, eating and enjoying a comfortable silence.

Jamie finished and pushed aside his empty plate. "Well, that was delicious. The food and upstairs, but there is obviously something you want to talk to me about. I have to admit the suspense is killing me, so can we get to it?"

David swallowed and laid his plate on top of the other. "Yep. I've been trying to figure out the best way to go about it, and I guess I just need to come out with it. Pull the band-aid off."

"Not getting any clearer." The lights were casting a strange hue over Jamie's fair complexion, distracting David's thought process.

"I was wondering why we don't live together."

"What? That's what this is about?" Jamie seemed relieved, as though he'd been expecting David to announce he had cancer or something equally awful.

"Well that's part of it. In a way a big part of it."

"A big part of what? You have to be more specific here if you want me to participate in this discussion in any meaningful way."

David felt a cramp in his stomach. "Look, we've been

together for five years now. That's a long time. I feel like all the essential things are in place—we love each other, we are committed to one another, but then there's this huge disconnect from all of that. I guess I need to know if you are ever going to finally come to some kind of peace with who you are, enough to not have to separate the different aspects of your life?"

A flicker of emotion passed over Jamie's face, but David was not able to read it clearly. "You mean am I ever going to be completely out at work, and with my family, right? That's the disconnect you're talking about?" His voice was quiet, scaring David even more than if he started to yell.

"Yes, that's exactly what I mean."

"Is that what all this is about?" He waved his hand in the direction of the plates, then the Christmas tree. "The food, the decorations, upstairs? What do you want me to say?"

David went to Jamie, taking his hand. Thankfully Jamie allowed it, though his tension couldn't have been more obvious. "I want you to put our relationship on an equal status with your job. I want you to let go of your fear. Yes, some things will change, but not all for the worst, like I know you think they will. Sure, some people may be different towards you, but who cares? You're an excellent lawyer, and that's the only thing that matters."

"It's not the only thing David. Jesus, this is my reputation, my relationship with my family."

"Your reputation is based on your job performance and your work ethic, not who you sleep with. And what kind of relationship is it with your family if you can't be honest with them?"

"Have you forgotten what happened to you?"

"Of course not." David lived with the scars of that truth every day, his hearing loss and knee issues a lifelong consequence. "Nothing that bad will happen to you, Jamie."

Jamie was silent for a long time. "I need a drink." He got up, moving toward the kitchen, and David had no choice but to follow him.

He opened a beer and took a long swallow before looking in David's direction. "So is this an ultimatum? If I don't come clean with my work and family, are you going to end things?"

"That's not what I'm saying." *Was it?*

"So do you expect, me to walk into work tomorrow and announce to everyone I talk to that I'm gay? You want me to get on the phone right now and call my parents and tell them I like men, and that you and I have been fucking for the last five years?"

"Jamie, don't. That's not fair."

"And this is?"

David's anger was rising in tempo with Jamie's defensiveness, but he forced himself not to yell. "Yes Jamie it is. I am your boyfriend, partner, whatever label you want to put on it, and I don't deserve to be treated as some dirty little secret. I want to meet your parents, have family dinners that include both sides. I want to go to social functions with you—as your date. I want to be able to meet you for lunch at work, you know, be in the crowd to cheer you on when you give speeches and win awards. I want to be important to you."

Jamie started to cry, his neck and cheeks flushed with colour. "You are important to me. I love you more than anyone else in the world."

"Then you need to start acting that way."

David went to him, and though Jamie resisted, David pulled him into his arms and hugged him like the world was ending. In a way it was for Jamie. He'd been so ensconced in his self-imposed lie for so long, it had become a safe place for him. Breaking free of his fear would not be easy, David knew that, but he couldn't live the lie himself anymore. His well-being depended on being free of shame and uncertainty.

Jamie was crying like David had never known, with deep, heaving sobs that left his shoulder drenched. He felt Jamie's pain as his own, a shadow of guilt layered over his feelings of relief.

Jamie pulled away. "Just give me a minute. Please."

David waited as he went upstairs, remorse thick and choking when he returned to the kitchen, his suit draped over one arm. He came to David and kissed him, for the first time a sensation he did not relish. "You're leaving then?"

"I need some time to think. I'm not saying no, David, please understand that. I know this is the right thing to do, I just need to figure out how to do it. You're right, I'm scared." A tear slipped down one cheek, which he quickly wiped away.

"Okay. I can respect that. Don't shut me out though, promise me. I'm here for you."

Jamie kissed him again, this time lingering. "I know. I'll call you tomorrow."

As the door closed behind Jamie, pain filled David's chest. Worry and righteousness took up a boxing match under his ribcage, a horrible, burning sensation he hoped never to feel again as long as he lived. The tires along the driveway could have been driving over his heart for all the agony the sound instilled.

It was a long time before he was able to fall asleep.

CHAPTER 5

He couldn't have been asleep for more than an hour when the sound of his cell phone woke him. A glace at the clock radio showed it was 3:14 a.m., a time when phone calls only brought bad news. His immediate thought was that Jamie had been in an accident.

He snatched the phone off the bedside table and pressed it to his ear. "Hello?"

"David Lloyd?" The voice was male, breathy and not familiar.

"Yes."

"I hear you been asking questions about Stella."

The statement caught him off guard. He'd been expecting a police officer, or maybe a hospital clerk. He sat up. "Yes, I have."

"Then stop."

His heart gave a funny, off-tempo thump. "Why is that?"

"'Cause if you don't I'm gonna cut your balls off and stuff 'em down your throat." Click. The phone went dead.

David was a strong man, had faced and been involved in physical violence many times over his years of police service, but still the threat elicited the reaction it was intended to. A cold sweat broke out over his body, and the surge of adrenaline knocked aside any clinging vestiges of sleep. Whatever Stella had gotten herself mixed up with had to be pretty bad to have thugs calling in threats in the middle of the night. He didn't like the thought, but David knew the smart thing to do would be to keep himself armed at all times as he proceeded with the investigation.

When five thirty rolled around and he still hadn't managed

to fall back to sleep, he gave up. He took his handgun from the bottom drawer of his dresser, along with cleaning necessities and a box of ammunition, and went downstairs. Once the coffee had brewed, he took a steaming mug to the table and started on the weapon. The ticking of the wall clock seemed unnaturally loud, grating at his already agitated state of mind.

While moving through the procedure he ran over the events of the last week, trying to figure out who the caller might have been. He'd spoken with several men, including Gregor and Ritchie from the bar, Dr. Garfield, Marcus, and Sasha. He was reasonably sure that the voice had not belonged to Sasha or Dr. Garfield, neither of whom seemed a likely candidate for threats or physical violence, though he couldn't completely write them off. People were often capable of actions that could surprise in both good and bad ways. What Marcus's angle would be, he couldn't wrap his head around either.

He would have bet money that the caller had been Ritchie, who undoubtedly had things to hide, or someone close to the man, like the as-yet-unseen Lee. Maybe they had put one of their cronies up to the task, and that was why the voice had not sounded familiar? A strange sound made him realize he had the box of ammunition gripped in one hand, shaking it about like an explosive maraca. After dumping a few bullets onto the palm of his hand, he loaded the now-pristine weapon.

He made a mental note to follow up with Ritchie, and to take another swing by Joe's Bar to try and catch Lee in residence. Failing that, he'd have to see if he could get the guy's address. The thought cycle made David realize that he hadn't reconnected with Jimmy, and there was sure to be some leads to pursue from whatever he had managed to unearth.

A long, hot shower made him feel almost human. He dressed in jeans and a dark red shirt. As he combed his hair, he took a long hard look at himself, the lack of sleep manifesting as a tightness around his cool blue eyes. His jaw line was holding, and only a wash of fine lines had appeared on his face. A strict adherence to both cardio and strength training exercises kept his body trim and defined. He could still easily pass for being in his thirties. None of that made him feel particularly good at the moment; only smoothing things out with Jamie would bring a lift to his current mood. That understood, he still had a job to do.

The still dark morning greeted him with a slap of bitter air. It had snowed overnight, and the barren lawns and empty street lay under a heavy blanket of white. He was halfway to his office before the heater began to make any difference in the temperature inside his car. One of the few perks to being up that early was he found a parking spot in front of his building, where he could basically step right from his car into the front foyer.

After hanging up his coat, he immediately put on a pot of coffee, ignoring the nagging voice inside his head that warned him he'd be a jittery bundle of nerves by lunchtime if he consumed any more caffeine. His message light was merrily blinking away, and a pile of paper waited for him at the fax machine. Good times.

When he realized the swirling cream in his coffee had become hypnotizing, he gave his head a good shake. Jumpiness or no, even a sour stomach wouldn't be a deterrent to a few more cups of coffee. He needed it after only about an hour of sleep. He heaped in some sugar, taking the cup with him to his desk to review the phone messages.

His mother had called, sorry she missed him. Mrs. Barrowman called to check in, asking David to call her back. There were three hang-ups, then Jimmy's voice came on letting him know that he was faxing over some reports for him to review. That explained the pile of paper. The last message was a surprise. Christian Barrowman, Stella's brother, had called to set up a time to meet. David had yet to speak with the guy, had not even left a message with him. Maybe Mrs. Barrowman had prompted him?

On to the faxes. He'd run backgrounds on both Ritchie and Lee, throwing in Gregor for good measure. Not surprisingly all three turned up records. Gregor had been charged for a number of assaults, the most recent offense taking place almost a decade previously. Since then he'd kept his nose clean. Not so for Ritchie and Lee. Both had records all the way back to their young offender days. Ritchie, age thirty-two, was currently on probation for an arrest ten months ago. He'd been stopped on suspicion of a DUI, which turned out to be true as he'd blown almost twice the legal limit. A search of his car had turned up marijuana and cocaine, as well as an unlicensed handgun. He'd pleaded guilty, spent three months in jail, and was under the watch of the probation office for the next two years. He'd been arrested at other times over the years for various offenses; burglary, drugs, assault, driving offenses, and passing bad checks. Obviously not the sharpest tool in the shed.

Lee seemed a bit more savvy in the ways of a career criminal. He'd had a few bumps in his early twenties; one DUI, a minor pot bust, and a couple of fights. Since then he'd had nothing more than some parking tickets. Jimmy had passed along some notes, letting David in on the thoughts of the police force. Lee ran with a crowd known to have ties to drug smuggling and organized crime. The feeling was that Lee had secured himself a cushy role as a "middleman." He didn't have access to the higher-ups, and he also didn't do direct selling either. He received larger shipments, which were divvied up to a number of dealers. He collected the profits, minus his pay, and returned it to the suppliers, thus completing the circle of crime. There was some risk, but not as much as others took on, and by staying quiet and keeping his dealers in line, Lee secured the protection of the bigger fish, namely those who kept him off the radar of the police.

Christian and Arthur Barrowman did not have records of any kind, even their driving records were squeaky clean. Not unexpected. Sasha was also a criminal virgin. The next record he read surprised him so much, it seemed to jump up and slap him in the face. Marcus Edwin James, age forty-eight, divorced, father of two, had been arrested on suspicion of rape of a sixteen-year-old girl, after the girl's mother had brought the complaint to the police. He was arrested and questioned, but never formally charged when the girl refused to give the police a statement. There was no other evidence, and the man had never been in trouble before, so the police had no choice but to set the man free.

The girl was Stella Barrowman.

A heart-to-heart with Jimmy hadn't shed any new light on the accusation against Marcus James. Jimmy hadn't worked the case, but had a close buddy who did. He told David that his friend never liked Marcus for it, but had wondered after interviewing Stella if she hadn't been assaulted by someone. With the girl's past trouble with drugs, and admission of a mental health problem, the case would have been a hard sell, but with her refusal to make a formal statement it went dead in the water.

He did have to wonder why Marcus hadn't mentioned it when he'd interviewed him. Embarrassment was sure to be a key factor. Being accused of rape wouldn't be high on anyone's list of topics for conversation, but given Stella's problems and the subsequent dismissal of the case, David felt the man should have been honest about it.

He was a few blocks from Best Foot Forward, the dance studio owned by Stella's friend Elaine, when his cell phone sounded. Before the first ring had even completed, he had it to his ear, hope like a vise around his chest that the caller was Jamie.

"Hello," he said.

"David? It's your grandmother." At eighty-five years old, Rhea Lloyd's voice was still clear and strong, sounding like that of a much younger woman. David couldn't help but smile.

"Hey Nana, what's up?"

"I forgot to ask you what you wanted for dinner tonight?"

Right, Wednesday. "Um, how about your famous roast chicken with all the fixings?"

"Can do, handsome. See you around six."

"Bye."

He pulled the car into a small lot beside a building David suspected had been a church in a former incarnation. The stairs had been cleared of snow and covered with salt to prevent slipping. Inside the door was an area to hang coats and put outside shoes. David faltered for a moment, wondering whether he should remove his shoes and enter the space in his sock feet. He decided to wipe them thoroughly on the mat instead.

"Hello," he called out, not wanting to startle anyone who might be inside.

Music answered him, coming from ahead and to the right. It was a modern song, heavy in bass. The closer he got to the source, the stronger the vibration through the floor. The main studio loomed, the doors open to allow a glimpse of the bright interior.

He stopped at the door, taking in the caramel- colour flooring, the brightly painted walls emblazed with the studio's name, and the multitude of dance photography art. One wall contained floor-to-ceiling shelves overflowing with trophies of every size and configuration. A young woman was dancing to the music, a routine that would have required as much stamina as talent. As the performance progressed, she caught sight of him, motioning in his direction that she would be right with him. She walked toward an impressive sound system at the far end of the room and turned the music down to a conversational level.

"Sorry about that. My competition team has started up again, and I was just trying to get in some more work on one of the routines." She was hardly out of breath as she spoke, impressive after the intensity she'd put in to her dancing.

"No problem. Have to say, it looked fantastic."

She smiled, giving David a quick once over. She angled her body towards him, giving him a clear view down the sports-bra-like top she wore. "Thanks. I'm Elaine."

David offered his hand, giving a slightly flirtatious smile in return. "David. Thanks again for agreeing to meet with me on such short notice."

Her hand lingered a few moments longer than necessary. "Of course. No problem. Why don't we go back to the team's lounge. There's some place to sit down at least." She pointed to another door near the sound system and started walking. Across the rear of her very short shorts was a bedazzled "dance." Her legs were long and well-defined. Hair that was pulled back into a ponytail hung halfway to her waist in a flow of chocolate brown waves.

The team lounge was a long room with shelves for bags, a

table and microwave, and two couches lining the back wall. Elaine took a spot on one of the couches, and since she seemed inclined to flirt with David, he took advantage by sitting next to her. She gave him another appraisal, smiling like a wolf who'd spotted prey.

"You dance at all, David?"

"Not if I can help it. No sense inflicting that type of visual abuse unnecessarily."

"Oh, I don't believe you're that bad. I watched how you walked in here, you have some style going on."

"Ah, thanks."

She leaned forward, showing off ample cleavage and a hard, flat tummy. The woman was giving all the signals that she was interested and available, so David became very conscious of walking the fine line between simple flirting and giving her the okay to go to the next level.

"So I understand that you and Stella were friends?" A nice, open-ended statement that an interviewee could run with.

"Yep, for about ten years now. We met at a summer dance training camp. She was fourteen and I was fifteen. We became friends right away and kept in touch after school started again, even though we didn't go to the same place. Stella was upper crust, right, me, I come from a more middle-class home. I did used to love visiting her house when I was a teenager, that girl had everything. The best clothes, a car, money, tickets to anything she wanted. And God, she was a good dancer."

"You know Sasha then?"

"Of course I know Sasha. Stella and I both had a crush on him, but she won. Too bad, I loved the accent."

"So you know they've remained close?"

"Yes, I know about their relationship. That poor boy could never seem to get her out of his system. No matter what crap she got herself into, he always stood by her." Her tone could have been annoyance or jealousy.

"He said as much to me yesterday. But he did manage to finally stand up to her last spring and hasn't heard from her since."

Elaine frowned. "Really? She didn't say anything to me about it."

"So you've seen her since last spring?"

"Yeah, a few times. I let her practice here. Even where she was, Stella still liked to be the best."

"Where she was? I don't understand."

Elaine's eyes widened, before she gave a small bark of laughter. "Oh, you don't know. Sorry, yeah, Stella danced over at The Scarlet Letter, when she could keep it together that is. The clients loved her. I mean, why not. Right? She's gorgeous and the girl can move."

"So she was working as a stripper?" The fact shouldn't have come as a surprise, but somehow it did.

"Yep, on and off for the last three years. She made good coin too. Too bad she always ended up blowing it on drugs."

"Did anyone else know about this?"

"Um, Sasha did. He came and helped her with routines sometimes. He loved the girl and missed dancing with her. Don't know that he ever went and saw her perform though. The parents were in the dark, I'm pretty sure. I can't answer for her drug buddies. Not my crowd."

David let the information sink in. So both Marcus and Sasha had been holding back? Interesting. Drugs, prostitution, stripping, false accusations, mental illness. What else had this woman been through in such a short lifetime?

"Is there anyone you can think of that might help me find her? Friends from school or dance? Any names or places she might have mentioned?"

Elaine gave the question some thought before answering. "She did stay in touch with a couple of girls from her school. One named Janice and the other was Sinclair. She was close to a few people from rehab, some girl I never met and one of the people that worked there. I think she was friendly with one of the dancers at the Letter named Raven True. Stage name obviously, but I do remember her talking about the woman."

David jotted down the information. "By school, you mean Bartholomew Academy?" This was the school listed in the background information Marjory had supplied him with.

"Yes. I think she even managed to graduate. Might have something to do with the money her parents donated."

"So her parents were known to buy Stella out of trouble?" That didn't surprise David.

"Yeah, you know, I think out of concern at first, then as the trouble went on it was more to save face. Stella's dad is some big-wig business guy, and having an out-of-control daughter wouldn't have been good for his rep."

"Right. And how would you describe your relationship with Stella?"

"What do you mean our relationship? We never had sex or anything like that," she snapped.

Her reaction took David by surprise. "That's not what I meant. I just wondered if Stella had ever pulled anything on you, like getting violent or stealing?"

"Nope, nothing like that. Sometimes she came in too wasted to practice, and I either sent her on her way or tried to get some food into her. I did give her money, but she never asked for it, and she never took anything. She was a messed-up girl. Mostly I felt sorry for her, you know? Not angry."

"Well to go back to the other, did Stella have romantic or sexual relationships with women?" Something about her answer struck David as off.

"Why, that turn you on? What is it with men and lesbians?" When David didn't comment, and he really didn't have anything to offer on the subject, she continued. "She never told me as much, but I wouldn't have been surprised. She wanted love, and to not be alone. I think she felt like she couldn't count on anyone, like everyone had screwed her over. Maybe that doesn't make sense, it's just what I always felt was going on with her. If some woman had been good to her, I think she could have responded to that. And not to be blunt or disrespectful, but when she was down and needed to score I think she'd have slept with just about anyone."

She continued on, talking about their past, sharing some personal memories of happier times. Throughout the discussion she offered the names of a few of Stella's haunts, including Joe's Bar and a cheap motel that David knew to be a magnet for lowlifes of all kinds.

"Does she have a key for the studio?"

"No, why?"

"Just crossed my mind that she might sneak in to have a place to sleep when money was tight."

"She could have knocked on my door if she was that bad off. I don't have kids, so she wouldn't have been bothering anyone but me."

David let the implication of Elaine's single status hang in the air. "What are your thoughts about the family?"

"Her mom was all right. She tried really hard anyway. Her dad was gone a lot with work. I didn't see him very often, and Stella didn't talk about him too much. Her brother was sweet but such a goody two-shoes. Stella doesn't know this, but I ran into him at a party once when we were in high school. He was in first year of university. I totally threw myself at him, and he turned me down cold. Told me it wasn't appropriate or some shit like that. Seriously, what guy would turn down getting laid with no strings attached?"

"Not many. Especially with a girl like you." He gave her an appreciative look, though it made him feel like a total ass. He was glad he did because she picked up on the compliment right away.

"I'm sure a guy like you wouldn't have turned me down."

Wow, she was laying it on thick. "Of course not. If I wasn't taken, I wouldn't say no now either."

"Too bad."

"Okay, other than the fact that Christian has no taste in women, anything else you can tell me about him?"

She smiled appreciatively. "Like I said, he's a straight ace. Always top of the class in school, never got in trouble. Only dated girls his parents liked. I think the only disappointing thing he ever did was to not go into business like his father. But Stella told me he works with troubled kids or something, so it couldn't have been that much of a disappointment."

"So no affairs, drinking, or drug problems?"

"Not that I ever heard about."

"No money problems?" He didn't think so from what he'd researched about the family so far, but it didn't hurt to ask.

"Hardly. To me it seemed they had more money than they knew what to do with. I mean they even helped my mom out with some of the costs with my dance training. My dad took off when my sister and I were little, so money was always tight. They were good that way. I mean they certainly spent money on themselves, but they were also generous with those close to them. They give to lots of charities and stuff."

"I was vaguely familiar with the name before Marjory came to me, I guess from articles in the paper and such. It's sad to know that Stella's gone down this road, since it seemed she had every opportunity to get help and have the support of people who love her."

A pained looked passed over Elaine's face, and she made a small noise in her throat. David waited for her to add to her already generous interview, but no further information was forthcoming. It seemed they'd come to the point where his questions seemed intrusive rather than helpful.

He stood. She gave a forced smile, rising to her feet to escort him to the door.

His hand was on the handle when she spoke again. "Do you have a card? In case I hear from her or something."

"Of course." He fished one from his pocket and handed it over.

She let her fingers brush over his as the card exchanged hands. "What's your girlfriend's name?"

"Jamie," he answered. The truth, sort of.

"You tell Jamie to keep an eye on you. Good men are hard to find."

"Will do. Thanks again for the help."

She watched him walk down the steps to the sidewalk. There had been a definite change in her attitude toward the end of the conversation, and the way she was staring as he made his way to his car unsettled him. What had triggered the reaction? He couldn't put his finger on it, but he wouldn't have been surprised to find that he'd only scratched the surface of the truth as she knew it.

The house was warm and filled with the mouth-watering aromas of a home-cooked meal. Nana Lloyd bustled about the kitchen, putting the finishing touches on David's requested dinner. Fresh baked rolls sat in a basket, a plate of butter waiting to be slathered over their flaky surface. Gravy bubbled on the stovetop as the rest of the meal was brought to the small table. David sat, a glass of wine in hand, letting his grandmother dote on him as he knew she liked to.

The kitchen was dated, yet functional. It had looked the same for as long as David could remember, a familiar comfort that he wouldn't have traded for modern appliances or granite countertops. A small radio sat on the counter, turned to a soft rock station that his Nana liked to hum along to as she cooked. A sigh escaped his lips. Outside of his own home, there was nowhere else he felt more at peace.

"So you have a new case you're working on, hon?" David's Nana was quite fond of pet names.

"I do actually. A missing persons case. Only been at it a few days, so I'm not sure where it's headed yet."

"Hopefully not to the morgue." Nana was also blunt.

"Agreed."

She joined him at the table, heaping his plate with chicken, mashed potatoes, veggies, and a generous layer of gravy. He ate every last bite, mopping up the remains with several of the rolls. Her cooking prowess never failed to amaze or satisfy.

While letting the giant meal settle, David sipped at the wine and took a good look at his grandmother. She smiled as she went through the motions of heating the pie and making the whipped cream. She had aged for sure, but still hung onto a vibrancy and stamina that seemed lacking in too many elderly people. She gave the impression of being able to last forever, and though that couldn't possibly be true, he relished the closeness they shared. In many ways she was his closest friend, one of the first to be immediately on his side when he decided to let his secret out of the bag.

"How's Jamie? I haven't seen that handsome man of yours in a while now. You need to bring him by, so I can get a decent meal into him."

He should have known he couldn't have passed a visit with Nana without an inquiry about Jamie. She was genuinely very fond of him, partly because he was a great guy, but also because David had kept the worst of their issues from his grandmother's notice. He didn't like to worry her.

"He's good, I guess."

She turned, wooden spoon in hand, and gave David a look that could still make him squirm. "Don't you fib to your grandmother. Tell me what's going on."

She pulled her chair up alongside his, invoking the feeling of being a young boy sitting with her on the old sofa, a picture book open on her lap. A force to be reckoned with at times, his grandmother was also one of the most loving, compassionate people he had ever been lucky enough to know.

"Oh, where to start Nana?"

"Just spit it out, I'll make sense of it. Don't worry, I'm not so old that I've lost my marbles yet."

"Okay, here it is in a nutshell. Jamie has not told his family or his work about being gay, or obviously about our relationship. I don't want to live my life like that, where I'm treated like something to be ashamed of. I told him as much last night, and he didn't take it well. I can't say for sure what's going to happen now."

"Wow, when you have a predicament, it's a doozy. You know I love you, and I have always been proud of you. I will always support you, and I can tell you I am one hundred percent on your side with this. I don't care if it's a man and a woman, or two men, no one should be treated with anything but the utmost respect and pride. If he can't give you that, then no matter how much it may pain you now, in the long run, it's best to move on. If your grandfather had tried anything like that on me, I would have left him quicker than the blink of an eye, and you know how I felt about him." David did know that his grandparents had loved each other very much, and that her husband's passing had all but done his Nana in.

"I love him though, Nana. I really do. Other than this, he's perfect. He's not abusive or jealous. He doesn't try and control me. I can talk with him, we have fun together, and we're compatible in the..."

"In the bedroom. Yes, I get it. I'm old, not stupid. So I guess this is why Jamie's parents have never joined us for Christmas or birthdays."

"Yep. He celebrates with my family, then goes to his alone and pretends he's single."

"That sucks, my boy. If I thought it would help, I'd go put him over my knee and give him a good spanking."

The image brought forth a burst of laughter from both of them. "I wish that was all it would take."

His Nana grabbed his hand, all the merriment faded from her face. "You have to know this is all on him, David. You are totally justified in refusing to accept this."

"I do know, but I appreciate the reassurance. I've been lying to myself about this being okay, as long as he's been lying to everyone else. I can own my part in things, but I can't go on like this anymore. Not after all I've been through."

"You've always been strong, which can sometimes be as much a curse as being weak is. People expect more of you, they take more from you."

"I think it runs in the family."

"Smooth, very smooth. Now are we going to have some pie?"

"Of course. I expect when I come here for a meal that I will have to waddle my way out to my car afterwards."

His Nana rose and pulled the warm pie from the oven. She brought him over a generous piece smothered with whipped cream. His mouth watered as the aroma touched him. For the few minutes he sat, enjoying the taste and the comfort of being with his grandmother, everything else seemed very far away. Like the snow outside, which would melt away in the spring, he hoped the pain and worry of the present would vanish as though it had never existed at all.

CHAPTER 6

A few restless hours at home spent pretending he wasn't waiting for the phone to ring was almost more than he could bear. There was no way he would be falling asleep anytime soon, even with the enormous meal moving through his digestive system. He decided a visit to Joe's might be the distraction he needed.

The sand-coated snow crunched like popcorn under the wheels of the car. Traffic was light, the sidewalks all but deserted. David found a place to park less than a block away from the bar. As he walked to his destination he could see a few people loitering in proximity to the bar's front door, just like the last time he'd come. The cold didn't seem to be a deterrent to the smokers, puffing away while hunched under the limited protection of their winter coats.

Inside the space held more patrons than had been there in the daytime. A large group congregated at the rear, sitting at the tables and playing pool at all three tables. David made his way to the bar. Music pumped through the sound system, a rock song that David recognized but couldn't name. Gregor nodded when he caught sight of him, this time accompanied by another person behind the counter. A young woman in an obscenely short denim skirt was loading drinks onto a tray, which she then deftly lifted and carried out onto the floor.

As he took a seat, he realized the same man who had been there the last time was there again. He sat, hands wrapped around his mug of beer, staring at the countertop as though it would somehow communicate with him. His drunkenness was quiet and unobtrusive, so no one paid him any mind. After serving a few customers standing at the bar, Gregor came to stand before David.

"What can I getcha, David?" His giant hands rested on the edge of the bar, fingers the size of sausages.

"You remembered my name. A beer would be great, whatever you have on tap."

With a nod, Gregor pulled a mug from the shelf behind him and filled it with practiced hands. When David offered him money, he waved away the payment and was on to his next customer.

He turned, beer in hand, to survey the crowd. The majority of those gathered were men in their twenties or thirties with a sprinkling of young women. Of those, most were dressed provocatively and wore too much makeup. Blonde hair of the over-processed variety seemed to be the popular choice among the female customers, making it difficult to distinguish one from the other. One man in particular had several women flocking about him as he played a game of pool. Off to one side of the table sat a familiar figure.

Ritchie looked up at about the same time that David made the connection. After seeing the detective, he immediately flicked a look in the direction of the pool table. The man took a shot before coming to the table where Ritchie sat to have a sip of his beer. Ritchie said something to him, and both looked in David's direction.

With mug in hand, he waded through the crowd. The man had not returned to his game, instead continuing to stand at the table, a gentle smirk on his lips. He was dressed in expensive jeans and a dress shirt which he had rolled up to the elbow. His dark hair was long but stylish, and he wore no jewellery except for a gold watch. His eyes were such a dark blue they were almost black, regarding him with cautious interest. When David was within conversation distance, he held out his hand.

The move surprised David, but he took the hand as though all the thugs he dealt with participated in such niceties. "You must be David," he said in a pleasant voice.

"I am. Lee is it?"

"That's right. Ritchie tells me you've been asking about

Stella." Again, the voice was smooth, not a hint of hostility or nervousness.

"Her family has asked me to look for her. She's been out of touch for several months, and they're understandably worried." David carried on with the same tone, letting Lee lead the conversation.

"You know she's a junkie?"

David nodded.

"Then you probably also know she's been known to disappear before. Sometimes she goes on a bender, other times she tries to dry out. The girl is unpredictable."

"That's what I've been told. Her family thinks this time is different, because they haven't heard a peep from her, and her standard MO is to call the mother looking for money. Or they get called in when she's picked up or ends up in emergency. None of those things have happened."

Lee took a sip of his beer, looking thoughtful. "So what's your take? You think she's OD'd or something?"

"Could be. Could also be that's she's just fine and just doesn't want anyone to know where she is. There're lots of possibilities."

"With Stella there always are." He and Ritchie had a good chuckle over the innuendo.

"You have any thoughts on where she might be? Has she been in contact with you recently?"

"Nope, just like you said, I haven't heard from her in a few months. I guess it has been a long time. She usually turns up here sooner or later. But if her folks don't have any answers and no one around here has seen her, then I don't know what to tell you." He remained even and agreeable throughout the conversation, but something about him set off David's warning bells.

He tried a different approach. "What about Raven True? You know her?"

"The dancer? Sure, I met her. I liked to watch Stella dance sometimes, and I had a drink with the two of them a couple of times. I don't know anything about them being friends outside the club, but I guess they could have been."

"She maybe someone Stella would go to if she were looking

for a place to crash?"

"I guess. Can't say for sure." He gave a sideways glance to Ritchie, who responded with a non-committal shrug.

"Any other friends come to mind?"

"No."

"What about any of the people Stella came into contact with while working for you?"

"I don't know what you're talking about," he responded a little too quickly.

"Look, I'm not a narc. I'm not here to bust your chops. What you do is not my concern. I just want to find out what's happened to this girl."

"Sorry, buddy. I have nothing else to tell you."

Ritchie nodded his agreement.

"So you don't mind if I ask around the bar then?"

"Go ahead."

David perused the patrons, finding that few would meet his gaze. Lee must have carried weight with the crowd, meaning David would not be told anything useful, but he had to try. As suspected, no one would give more than an admission of having seen the girl in the bar. There were no claims of friendship or guesses as to possible whereabouts.

One young woman, who couldn't have been a day over twenty, seemed especially nervous when questioned. Her heart-shaped face was framed by a mass of sandy curls, and her cheeks still held a subtle amount of what his grandmother would call "baby fat." As soon as David moved on to the next person, she made a beeline for the door.

With no new information gathered, David decided to head home. He gave Gregor a wave as he passed the bar. Outside the cold air pounced on him, making him realize how warm and fragrant the interior of the bar had been. A few people still huddled near the door, different faces but the same intent. He pulled the collar of his coat up around his face, cursing himself for having left his scarf at home.

As he crossed the street to the block where he'd parked, a figure stepped out of a darkened storefront. The movement gave him pause, slowing his progress until he realized it was the young woman from the bar. She fell into step alongside him, an aroma of smoke clinging to her clothes.

"Can I talk to you? Privately."

"Sure."

"Can we go to your car? It's cold out here."

David pointed to his car, parked about ten feet from where they stood. He unlocked the doors and they both sat, the uncomfortable silence that settled between them was like another presence in the vehicle. He turned the key and hit the heater.

"So you wanted to talk."

"Can we go somewhere away from here? I don't want anyone to see me."

David pulled away from the curb without another word, moving past the bar. He drove for several minutes before pulling off again at a road that was decently lit.

"Thanks. Sorry, I don't mean to be a pain."

"No problem. If you have some information about Stella, then I'm happy to do whatever makes you comfortable. What's your name?"

She turned, and when she smiled she looked even younger than she had in the bar. A small scar ran across her upper lip. "Jenny. You're cute."

"Thanks. That's not what you brought me here for is it, 'cause I'm not interested in any transactions."

"No, sorry. It's just the guys I usually hang with are nothing much to look at. Anyway, yeah, I wanted to talk with you about Stella. I couldn't say anything back there, 'cause Lee was keeping an eye on everyone."

"So he's told people to keep quiet?"

"Yep. If anyone talks, he said he'd have someone break their legs. When Lee talks, people listen."

Nice. "Okay, so what do you want to tell me?"

"I don't know what he said, but he and Stella are tight. He's been real pissed that she's missing. They had a big fight back in September 'cause Stella was looking pretty rough and he wanted her to clean up. He didn't think she could sell the way she was."

David remembered that Gregor had said something similar. "You saw this fight?"

"Yeah, it happened in front of me and a few of Lee's other girls. He likes us to keep ourselves looking good, 'cause we can make more money and get guys to buy more product. Stella looked like crap, real skinny, bags under her eyes, dirty hair."

"Was she still dancing then?"

"I don't think so. She was so shaky she could hardly stand up straight. Anyway they got into it. Lee smacked her around a bit and told her she wasn't getting any more drugs from him until she cleaned up. Stella started to cry, begging him not to cut her off, but he wasn't having it. He literally tossed her butt out the door."

"Did you see her after that?'

"Once. About two weeks later. I saw her getting into a car with a guy in an area where the working girls hang out." She gave him an address, an area notorious for all sorts of criminal behaviour. "It was a nice car, like expensive. I didn't see the person real good, but I'm pretty sure it was a man."

"You know if anyone else has seen her or heard from her?"

"Nope."

"Anything else you want to tell me?"

Jenny seemed to debate her options. "Well I already screwed myself, so I might as well tell you everything. I seen her with this woman a lot. Like this woman hung out with her and Lee, I'd see them talking, getting into a car together sometimes. She never partied, and she wasn't on the streets or anything."

"Can you describe her?"

"Dark hair, maybe Stella's age. Always dressed real nice."

"Ok, that it?"

"There was this guy too. I only saw him once, but I remember 'cause he didn't look like someone Lee would hang out with. Real clean-cut, vanilla looking. He came and picked Stella up, and he and Lee had a real intense conversation. When I asked Lee who he was, he smacked me. He did not want to talk about him at all."

Perhaps a lead at last? "Would you know the guy again if I showed you a picture?"

"I think so. Any of this help?"

"I don't know yet, but it sounds promising. Is there any way I can get a hold of you?"

"It's best if I call you. If anyone tells Lee I been talking to you, he's gonna kick the shit out of me."

David pulled out a card and handed it to the girl. As an afterthought he passed along a few twenties. "My office and cell number are on there. Call my cell any time. You know you can get out of this any time you want?"

"And do what? Work at McDonald's or go on welfare?"

"There are other options."

"Not right now." She opened the door and stepped out. "Thanks for the bucks."

The door closed and the girl walked away. David watched in his rear-view mirror until she turned a corner and disappeared from sight. With a sigh of defeat he pulled the car back onto the road. Instead of driving home, which would have been a good idea, he doubled back to Joe's. This time he didn't go in but waited in his car. A few hours passed before Lee and Ritchie left, heading to a car up the block.

Ritchie took the driver's seat, with Lee his passenger. They pulled out, and it was all too easy for David to slip in behind them. A few times he almost lost them as they traveled an odd series of roadways, until ending up in an industrial area near the lake, where many businesses kept storage and shipping facilities. They pulled into a lot that straddled three large warehouses, entering the closest one. David waited for about thirty minutes, even venturing out in the cold to look for a way to peer inside, but had no such luck. The ground level did not have windows, and all the doors were shut with heavy padlocks to keep unwelcome company out. He jotted down the address and added the incident to his list of things that needed further explanation.

When he got home, a message waited for him on his answering machine. Jamie had called about an hour earlier. "Hi Dave. I told you I'd call, so I am. I'm meeting my mother for lunch tomorrow, and I'm going to tell her. I'm not feeling very good right now, so please be patient with me. I'll call you soon."

He sounded sad and worried.

Great, another thing to keep me from sleep, he thought.

The house was very quiet and empty. David lay in bed, staring at the shifting shadows on the ceiling until sleep finally took him.

For the second time, David was awakened in the wee hours of the morning. It was not the ringing of his phone that disturbed his sleep this time, but a loud crash and then the insistent wailing of his car alarm. He jumped from bed, almost to the door before he doubled back and grabbed his gun from his bedside table. His upper torso was bare, so he threw on a coat and slipped his feet into a pair of runners sitting by the front door.

He took a deep breath before throwing the door open, only to be met with nothing more sinister than a gust of blowing snow. Before he even reached the bottom step, he could see that several windows of his car had been smashed. Upon closer inspection, he also found that tires were slashed, the vehicle now resting on its rims on the ice-encrusted driveway.

"Mother fucker!" he said, kicking one hubcap so hard he had to bite his tongue to keep from crying out.

Movement in his peripheral vision grabbed his attention. He whirled about, gun drawn. It wasn't the vandal coming back for another round, but Mr. Albert from across the street, obviously awakened by the commotion. He stopped dead in his tracks, one hand clutched to his chest.

"Oh my God, Mr. Albert. I'm sorry." He lowered the gun. "I thought you were the person responsible for this."

"It's all right, son. Everyone has the right to protect their home and property. And it's people, not person." The hand had moved from his chest to clutch at the two sides of his unzipped jacket. His blue-stripped pajama bottoms were bunched up at the top of a mean pair of galoshes.

"Sorry?"

"It was two guys who did this to your car. I don't sleep much, and I was up watching a movie on the television. I heard something and looked out my window. Saw two guys on your driveway. One was bent down taking a whack at the tires, the other had a bat or stick of some kind, smashing the windows in. I called the police."

"Did you see what they looked like?"

"Not really. It's dark, and they both had coats and hats on, and gloves. One was bigger than the other, taller. That's about all I could tell from where I was."

"Of course. Come inside. The police will want to talk to you since you called it in."

Mr. Albert nodded and followed David into the house. He flicked on the lights, which he'd neglected in his haste to get outside. As the man stood uncomfortably in his foyer, he realized they'd never been in such a position before. David had been inside the other man's house a few times, when he helped him move some furniture, or had done a minor repair. Most of their interaction with one another over the past ten years had been simple greetings across the street, or sidewalk to front porch conversations.

"Please come in, Mr. Albert. Have a seat in the living room. Can I make you some coffee or something?" David indicated the room just ahead of where they were standing with a sweep of his hand.

"Well, maybe it's time you started calling me John. I think we've known each other long enough to be on a first name basis."

They moved to the living room, where they each took a seat on a separate piece of the matching furniture set. A few minutes passed in silence.

"Sure do take long enough."

"Yeah," David answered. "Must have been more important things to attend to than a case of vandalism."

"So where's that fella of yours?"

The question came out of the blue, surprising David. "Jamie's at his place."

"You're ah, partners, right? Whatever you guys call it."

"Yes." Hesitation.

"So how come you still have separate places? Wouldn't it be cheaper to share a place, not to mention more convenient, to, you know, do stuff together."

He could have laughed at how careful the man was trying to be in wording his inquiry if it weren't for the fact that the same thing had been weighing so heavily on his mind in recent weeks. "You know, it would make a lot of sense. I'll have to bring it up with Jamie."

"You know, I don't mean no disrespect. I got nothing against you guys or any gay people for that matter. What people do in their own bedrooms is no one's business but their own." A slight flush had begun to creep into the man's face.

"Agreed." Any further awkward conversation was interrupted by the patrol car pulling up in front of the house.

Less than thirty minutes later the car was towed to a nearby garage. The police had collected information to file in a report that would most likely never be resolved. He bid farewell to his neighbour and re-entered the house.

After the events of the night and the distance between him and Jamie, the house felt particularly gloomy. He returned to his bedroom and crawled under the mess of covers. He fell asleep quickly, too exhausted for worry.

CHAPTER 7

When he finally opened his eyes, the clock told him it was nearly ten thirty, hours past when he normally started his day. He felt hungover, his tongue heavy and dry. The thought of sleeping the daylight hours away appealed to him, but there was work to be done, namely a meeting with George Barrowman. Stella's father had been able to squeeze in a half-hour with him at three.

He took his time with a shower and breakfast. As he pulled on his coat he realized he didn't have transportation, thus a stop at the car rental agency delayed his arrival to the office even further. Once again the answering machine was blinking, which he forced himself to ignore until a pot of coffee had brewed and a steaming mug sat before him on the desk.

His mother had called again. Dammit, he'd have to get back to her soon. Christian Barrowman had also called a second time. After hearing out the messages he'd have to call the man back. Several hang-ups occurred, then a man's voice played back to him.

"Next time it won't be your car taking a beating, it'll be your face." Click.

Lovely. David must have touched on something important to be stirring up the trouble he was, but nothing clear-cut had made itself known to him yet. Best to keep moving forward and let the pieces fall into place.

He dialed the number Christian had left, letting it ring several times. Just as he was about to hang up, someone snatched the receiver at the other end of the call. "Hello."

"Hello, can I speak with Christian Barrowman?"

"This is Christian." The voice was soft, young sounding.

"Great, I caught you. This is David Lloyd returning your call. I apologize for taking so long to get back to you."

"That's fine. I'm sure you've been hard at work looking for Stella."

"I have. Is there any chance I might be able to speak with you today?"

"I have clients booked for the rest of the day and a therapy group tonight. Unless you want to meet me after the group, say around eight thirty?"

"Sure that's fine. Where will you be?"

He gave an address on the east side of downtown, a large building that housed various social service agencies and government offices which David was familiar with.

After ending the call, he pulled the hand-written notes he'd made of his conversation with Jenny from his coat, transcribing them to the computer where he kept all his current cases. He printed a hard copy to place in the files and saved the data to his portable device, as was his habit. He'd been burned once when a terrible virus had crashed his hard drive, corrupting most of several years of cases. It had been nightmare re-creating everything.

The piece about the man Jenny had seen with Stella irked David. Could be nothing more than a horny guy looking for some quick action, but he could also be someone known to Stella on a more personal level, a friend or family member. The unknown man's connection, if any, to Lee also begged for a closer inspection. He'd need to put the guy under surveillance for a while, see what turned up.

Who else? Flipping back from his notes on Jenny, he came across his interview with Elaine, another source that needed to be documented. He also needed to make a time to follow up with both Sasha and Marcus to see what else they'd left out when he'd questioned them.

He spent the remainder of the time before his appointment with Mr. Barrowman on paying bills, filing, and generally catching up on paperwork that had been left for too long. Times were set to meet with Philip Halladay, the principal of Stella's former high school, and with Janice Collins and Sinclair Brown, the two friends Stella had stayed in touch with since her school career came to an end. Janice arranged for both her and Sinclair to meet him for lunch on Saturday. She offered the use of her home, where they would have privacy.

All too soon the time had come to get on the road to meet Mr. Barrowman. His office was located on Commerce Court, an aptly named street that housed many of the city's largest financial companies, bank head offices, brokers, and other business types. Through his research he'd learned that Mr. Barrowman's specialty was overseas investments, the reason for his frequent and sometimes extended traveling. His many successful endeavors had moved him to the top of the company, along the way snagging him several impressive awards and speaking engagements at important economic conferences.

Mr. Barrowman's assistant had left word with the parking attendant to let David enter without cost. He was given a pass, allowing him to park close to the elevator that would take him to the part of the building he needed to be in. He traveled to the fifteenth floor, which held the offices of the CEO, the Chief Financial Officer, and others of the upper echelon of the company. His shoes clacked along the marble floor as he moved through the enormous central hallway. Sunlight streamed in through the large panes of tinted glass lining the corridor, adding a touch of warmth to the sterile feeling of the space. He passed several offices before finding the right one, doors marked with plaques announcing the home of various vice presidents and other important positions.

The door marking George Barrowman's office opened into a large space which held a sitting area comprised of soft brown leather couches, a table full of financial literature, and a water cooler. Here the marble had turned to a plush carpet the colour of dark chocolate. Opposite this area was the secretary's space, a gigantic L-shaped desk, angled so as to provide a definition between her area and the rest of the room, as well as to offer privacy to whatever data might be displayed on her computer monitor. Behind her the wall was lined with manuals, binders of reports, and various awards for the Foreign Investments branch of the company for which she worked.

The secretary was an older woman, very attractive but stern. She was dressed in a crisp white blouse and dark suit. A small gold brooch had been pinned to one lapel, and plain gold studs adorned her ears. Her makeup had been applied with a subtle hand, her hair cut in a short, almost masculine style that only powerful, older women managed to make appealing. She caught his gaze with sharp, grey eyes.

As he approached, he smiled, and her prim manner wavered. At last she gave a small smile in return, a reaction David took as a triumph.

"Hello, I'm David Lloyd. I have a three o'clock appointment with Mr. Barrowman."

"Yes, of course. Please take a seat."

She rose from her desk, and after a quick knock on the door that David assumed led to Mr. Barrowman's private office, she disappeared inside. A few minutes later she reappeared and advised David that Mr. Barrowman was ready for him. He thanked her and entered.

Mr. Barrowman sat at a desk that occupied at least one-third of the office, the surface gleaming beneath the clutter of paperwork. Behind him the wall held floor-to-ceiling windows, offering a panoramic view of Toronto's financial district. Curtains had been partially drawn, dimming the amazing display somewhat but still keeping the room full of natural light.

Mr. Barrowman stood, offering his hand over the wide expanse of his desk. His suit jacket had been removed, now hanging over the back of his leather chair. His appearance was just what one would expect from someone in his position; conservative, expensive clothing, neatly trimmed grey hair. The only accessories he wore were his wedding ring and a watch. He reminded David of Martin Sheen, similar features and stature, a handsome man who wore his age well.

David shook the man's hand before settling into the chair on his side of the desk. Mr. Barrowman sat, a neutral expression on his face. David took a moment to peruse the space; the ten-foot ceilings, the original artwork on the walls, the row of gleaming plaques and framed certificates. Definitely the space belonging to someone who had experienced a long and successful career.

"Well, first of all, thank you for seeing me Mr. Barrowman. I know you are a very busy man."

"This is my daughter we're talking about. I am happy to do whatever I can to help find her, though I must be frank, I am not as concerned about this situation as Marjory is." His fingers were laced together, resting on a small pile of folders.

"Yes, your wife said as much in our initial meeting. I take this to mean, you think she's simply gone on a bender or has run off with someone."

"Well, it wouldn't be the first time. The girl can be very thoughtless. She knows we worry when we don't hear from her, especially after the couple of close calls she's had with overdoses. She was once hospitalized with a severe case of pneumonia because of her poor nutrition and the conditions where she was living at the time." A distinct tone of disgust had crept into the man's voice.

"What are your thoughts about Stella's problems? Is there any specific incidents or people you can think of who might have brought about this situation with your daughter?"

"Well the accident, of course, where she damaged her knee. That seemed to be the catalyst to Stella's downturn."

"But I understand that Stella had issues even before that. Your wife says she was difficult as a child, had a hard time keeping friends."

George Barrowman took a moment to think about the question. "I suppose so. Marjory would certainly know better than I. I'm afraid my work keeps me away from home a great deal. My wife has been much more of a hands-on parent than I have."

"Did you have a good relationship with your daughter?"

"I think so. As a young girl she did like to spend time with me when I was home. Of course as she got older she began to drift, like most kids do. Once all this business with drugs and the criminal behaviour started there was little in the way of communication between us."

"Did you feel that Stella's diagnosis made the problems with her more understandable?"

He gave a humourless smile. "That's where my wife and I have very different opinions. Don't get me wrong, I'm not one of these people who don't think mental illness is a serious issue, many people need and benefit from psychiatric care. In Stella's case it was just another way to manipulate, a way to defend behaviour she knew was wrong. I was never one hundred percent comfortable with the label. I think aspects of the care she received at the Davenport Clinic helped, at least for some time, but I often wondered if she wasn't giving Dr. Garfield the answers he wanted just to make the process go faster and easier for her."

That was an interesting take on things. "What aspects?"

"Well, she really enjoyed the art therapy, and the private sessions she had with Dr. Garfield seemed to unburden her, if that makes any sense. Stella is a very bright girl. I think on some level she knew there was a way out and that she was deliberately not taking it."

David switched gears. "What about her relationship with her brother?"

He frowned, a crack in his controlled persona. "What do you mean by that?"

"I mean were they close, do they fight?" Silently, David wondered about the suspicious reaction to an innocent question.

"They were close as young children. They fought like most siblings do, but nothing out of the ordinary. Christian has always been very involved with his education and extracurricular activities. After the problems with Stella started, he distanced himself. It's not that he didn't love his sister, he just didn't want her troubles to hinder his dreams."

"I can understand that."

"Honestly I think he was very understanding. So much of our time was taken up dealing with Stella. All the counselling and the meetings with teachers, the police involvement. And there was Christian getting straight As, keeping his nose clean, and he never complained."

"Right. What about school friends, or people from the dance community. Anyone come to mind who I should talk with?"

"I'm not sure. I think Stella stayed in touch with Janice from school, maybe a couple other girls. You'd really have to ask Marjory about that. Now she was very close to a boy named Sasha, someone from dance. I often hoped that he would be able to straighten her out. He is a lovely young man, clean-cut, dedicated to his profession. And he must have the heart of a saint to have put up with Stella's nonsense for so long."

"Yes, I've talked with Sasha. You're right, he seems like a very together guy. Anyone else? I know she's been hanging around a rough crowd these past few years. Can you remember any names?"

"One time when Stella was in the hospital, a man came to see her. He looked all right on the outside, but there was something very unseemly about him. I think his name was Lee."

Lee, right. "Okay. I'll look into that. Anything else you want to add."

"Not that I can think of. All I can say is I hope this is just another episode of Stella being Stella. It's been a terrible burden watching her go down this path."

"Any guesses as to where she might have gone?'

"No, I'm sorry."

"If I find her, what's the plan?"

"A new rehab. Long term and far away from here. Maybe somewhere in Europe."

"All right then, thanks for your time." David stood, handing over a card to the other man. "I may be in touch again."

"Of course."

As he left the office, he felt George Barrowman's eyes boring into his back. He made sure to close the door behind him. Passing by the secretary's desk, she looked up and made direct eye contact with David. He paused as she looked as though she wanted to speak with him, instead handing him a folded piece of paper.

"Good afternoon, Mr. Lloyd." Her words were clearly a dismissal.

"Yes, and to you." He palmed the paper and slipped it into his coat pocket.

Once in his car he pulled the note from his pocket, curious.

It was brief and the point clear:

I'd like the opportunity to speak with you privately.

She'd left a number to reach her at and a name: Sheila Cooke. Things were obviously not as proper as Mr. Barrowman would like David to believe.

As he was thinking about when to try to squeeze a conversation in with her in the already busy next few days, his cell phone rang. He didn't recognize the number on his call display.

"Hello."

"David?"

"Yes."

"It's Jenny. The, um, girl from last night."

"Right. Hi Jenny, what can I do for you?" He was surprised to hear from her again so soon.

"Well, it's more like what I can do for you."

"I don't understand."

"Listen, I can't talk long. I just want to tell you that Lee is not happy about you asking questions."

"How do you know this?" Back to Lee again.

"'Cause he came to my room this morning. Someone saw me getting in your car last night, and he wanted to know what we talked about."

"Okay, what did you tell him?"

"Nothing. Just that you offered me a ride and I said yes 'cause it was so cold. I said you asked about Stella again, and I said I hadn't seen her for a few months. That's it."

"Did he believe you?"

"Dunno. He smacked me around a bit, and I didn't say nothing. He probably thought I'd spill it if he hurt me."

"Are you all right?"

"Yep. I'm good. You just watch your back, okay?"

"Yeah, and Jenny, please be careful."

"I do my best," she answered.

"Don't be afraid to call if you need anything."

"I'll keep that in mind." She hung up.

Well that was interesting. The fact that his car had been damaged and Jenny was given the third degree within the same time period had to be more than coincidence. Someone definitely had their back up. Now, was it Lee himself or was someone else putting the pressure on him?

He couldn't explain it, but David felt a sense of protectiveness toward Jenny. He'd met many young women in similar circumstances during his years on the force, and those cases always seemed to stick with him. It was the idea of someone forcing or manipulating a weaker person into a life that would most certainly be their demise that stuck in his craw. It brought his mind back to the fact he'd essentially been forced from the police department, and how what had happened to him had been wrong in so many ways. *What is it about this case that keeps making me revisit my own past?*

A workout seemed like a good way to release some tension. He pulled away from the parking garage and headed in the direction of the gym.

Who knew what would turn up at his meeting with Christian?

After a satisfying workout, David returned to the office with some take-out Chinese food. He ate while listening to the most recent batch of messages. The garage had called to let him know it would be a couple of days before his car would be ready. There were a few more hang-ups, an offer to have his carpets cleaned, and his brother wanted to borrow his ladder. Nothing earth-shattering.

As he transcribed his notes from the meeting with George Barrowman, it struck him as odd that the man had not mentioned Elaine when asked about his daughter's friends. If the two women had been as close as Elaine described, then certainly George would have known about her. *A deliberate omission or a moment of forgetfulness?* He jotted down a note to make sure he asked Christian about the friendship.

There were many things that seemed as though they could lead somewhere, or offer some insight into what may have driven Stella to either embrace or attempt to escape the bitterness of the life she was so deeply embroiled in, yet nothing concrete. Sure, it seemed likely that Lee, or even Ritchie, might know where Stella was or why she had left, if that's what had happened. Maybe Sasha had lied about the circumstances of their fallout. Had Marcus actually assaulted her as a teenager, leading to a lifetime of shame and anger which she smothered with drugs? Had her addictions, instigated by the necessary medication from her knee injury, simply gotten the better of her again? There were still many unanswered questions.

The evening passed quickly. David had just enough time to get to his destination and park before eight thirty. He locked up, taking a last look about the space, itching with indecision. Had he forgotten something? Whatever it was would have to wait.

Traffic was light, making his arrival quicker than expected. Once parked, he took the time to put on his gun holster, sliding the loaded weapon into place. It wasn't his habit to walk about armed, though he had the proper paperwork to do so, but considering the recent threats and the damage to his car, it seemed to be a good idea. His coat hid the bulk well, but it would be available if needed.

A security guard sat at a desk in the lobby of the building where the organization that Christian worked for was located. David signed in, noticing that few offices were in use at that time of night. The display board outside of Second Chances announced its schedule of programs and drop-in therapy groups, as well as confidential private counselling for any number of issues. When he stepped through the door, a few people were lingering, a mismatched group if he'd ever seen one. Truth be told, hard times and crises crossed many boundaries, including sex, race, and social status.

A young man exited a doorway to the right of the main entrance, accompanied by a young woman who must have spent the better part of the session in tears. Her face was mottled, eyes bloodshot. He gave her a comforting pat on the back, and the woman made her departure. The two remaining men shook hands with the younger man, whom David took to be Christian, then also left.

The man came over, smiling. "Are you David?"

"Yes." He offered his hand.

They shook. "I'm Christian. Give me a sec to lock the door. Sometimes we get someone trying to get back in after the session is over."

David watched as he closed the door and turned the deadbolt. He was a pleasant looking guy, somewhat bland but approachable. His outfit consisted of a nice pair of jeans, a button-down shirt that he'd rolled to the elbows and Nike runners. Sandy hair, the same colour as his sister's, was cut short and neatly combed. His easy smile showed teeth too white and straight to have come from nature alone.

"Why don't we go in my office?"

The room they left was a reception area and computer access station. A row of computers lined one wall, with instructions such as: "No porn!" and "Not for social networking!" A battered desk sat in one corner along with stands for pamphlets about every type of service one could ever possibly need.

David followed Christian into his office, a cramped space overflowing with files and books. A table, which served as Christian's workspace, sagged under the burden of the computer, printer, and phone that rested on its surface. He squeezed through the narrow opening between the table's end and the wall to take his seat. Behind him were inspirational posters meant to uplift, but for some reason they seemed gimmicky.

A flimsy folding chair like one found in a discount-store card table set was the only other place to sit. It creaked when David sat, and he could have sworn he felt the frame give.

"Sorry, but we run on a shoestring budget here."

"So I guess you're not in the profession for the money."

Christian laughed. "No one gets into social services to get rich, but you're right, I make peanuts here. I supplement with some part-time work for one of the city's school boards."

"And your discipline is?"

"I'm a registered social worker."

"I see. Anyway, if you want to get to it, I don't mean to hold you up any longer than necessary."

"No problem."

David's phone rang. He automatically pulled it from his pocket to check the caller ID. When he saw the number, he gave

Christian a gesture to say he needed to answer it and returned to the larger room.

"Hi Jamie. What's up?"

"I just got back from dinner with my mother." He sounded strange, and David couldn't tell if the emotion in his voice was concern or relief.

"How did it go?"

"Okay. Not great, but not terrible either."

"What does that mean?"

"Well I told her I was gay. Flat out, no playing around. She dropped her fork, and for a second I thought she might faint, but she recovered herself. We went through the usual stuff. Was I sure? How did I know?"

"Did you tell her about us?"

"Yes, and that's when she got angry."

"How so?"

"Well after the initial shock, she seemed to accept things. But when I told her I had a boyfriend and that we'd been together for a number of years, then the shit hit the fan. She was really pissed off that I'd been hiding you from her and my dad. She also told me that it wasn't very respectful of me to treat you that way either."

"I like this woman already."

"Well, good because she wants me to arrange something for you guys to meet as soon as possible."

"Wait, what about your dad and your sisters, and other family? Don't you want to drop the proverbial bomb on everyone, get things out in the open once and for all?"

"My mom thinks dad and my grandparents are going to be a tough sell. They're very conservative, and I hate to admit it, but pretty close-minded."

"Your sisters?"

"More like my mom. Her parents were great people. Her mother was a public-school teacher, and her dad owned a travel agency. They both met lots of different people over the years. My dad's family is very white-collar, totally by the rules."

"Sounds like a mismatched couple."

"Some people would say the same about us."

A noise caught David's attention. He turned to find Christian standing in the doorway, smiling. *"Touché.* Listen I'm meeting with a client right now, can we talk later?"

"This late? Yeah sure, call me when you get home."

"I will. We still have lots to talk about."

Jamie sighed. "I know. Bye."

"Bye."

His slipped the phone into his pocket and gave Christian his attention. "Sorry about that."

"It's fine. Lady problems?"

"Something like that."

A look passed over the younger man's face. For some unknown reason the expression unsettled David, he would swear the hair on the back of his neck had stood up.

"It happens. So should we continue?"

"Sure." He followed Christian back into the office.

"So, how are things going?"

"Well, everyone seems to think that Stella's simply gone on a bender somewhere. Well, everyone except your mother anyway."

"I can see why people would think that. She has done it in the past. I understand where my mother is coming from too. It has been a while now with no word from her."

"So when was the last time you saw or spoke with your sister?" David opened his notebook.

Christian thought about the question for a few moments. "I think it was in the summer. Maybe August? She called me wanting money."

"Called you at home or at work?"

"At home. It was in the evening."

"Did you give her money?"

"No, I told her I would come and get her and take her to the hospital or a clinic or something. She sounded really messed up. I knew if I gave her money, she was just going to go and buy more drugs."

"She refused I take it?"

"Yep. She called me a bunch of names and hung up on me. I haven't heard from her since."

"Okay. What's your take on the situation? What do you think has happened?"

"Honestly, I'm going to have to agree with the majority here. I think she's gone off with someone, and either the drugs haven't run out yet or she's in the hospital somewhere. Or worse."

"Any thoughts as to who she might have gone off with?"

"Nope. I don't know any of her drug buddies. I tried to stay clear of that. I mean I visited her in the hospital, I tried to support her when she made efforts to get clean, but when she was using she was pretty much out of my life. I hope you don't take that the wrong way. She's my sister, and of course I love her, but I wasn't going to help her kill herself."

"So the names Lee and Ritchie don't mean anything to you."

"No, sorry."

"Can you think of any friends from school or dance that might help?"

"She's still friends with a woman named Elaine. I think she owns her own dance studio now? And a guy named Sasha. He was Stella's boyfriend for years. I think she'd stayed in touch with some girls from school, but my mom would know better about that."

So Christian remembered Elaine. "What do you think about Elaine? I understand she spent a lot of time at your place."

"She's an all right girl. Very pretty, but a little wild for me. I think she had a crush on me, so I used to keep my distance. She was one of the few people that Stella stayed friends with for a long period of time."

"What do you know about Stella's accident?"

The colour slipped from Christian's face. He shifted in his seat. "That was a very bad time for her. She'd already started having trouble in school, her behaviour had become erratic. That accident put her over the edge. She was never the same."

Something about his words did not ring true. "How so?"

"I think dancing was the one place where Stella was free. She was so talented, and when that was taken from her, she seemed to give in to her problems."

"But she recovered, right? Her knee, I mean."

"Yes and no. I think the injury healed fine, if that would have caused her problems later on, I don't know. But the drugs had taken over by then, and she could never shake them. Nothing seemed to matter except for getting high."

"Right." Time to switch gears. "Did you know your sister was working as a stripper?"

He blinked several times, the fingers on one hand twitching. "No, but I guess I shouldn't be surprised. She needed to get money for her drugs somehow."

"So you don't know anyone by the name of Raven True?"

"No. I would definitely remember a name like that."

"How would you describe your family? Was there anything going on at home that might have contributed to Stella's problems?"

Another episode of blinking. "Not that I can think of. My parents are good people, we had more than enough money growing up. Stella and my mom were very close, and she always stuck by her through everything. She came every time she called, spent thousands of dollars on her therapy. There was nothing she wouldn't have done for Stella."

"And your dad?"

"My dad's all right, he just wasn't around a lot. He was always away on business."

"You and Stella got along all right? Until her drug problems started anyway."

"Yeah, we played together when we were little, stuff like that. I'm four years older, so once I hit high school we didn't have much in common anymore. Then like I said, her problems started, and I was busy working my way to university."

"Is there anything you can think of that might help me find your sister?"

"I'm sorry, but no. I feel like I've just wasted your time here, but there is really nothing I can think of."

"Well, here's my card." David handed one across the desk, which Christian briefly looked at. "If anything comes to mind, please call."

"I will."

"Well then, I won't take up any more of your evening."

"I hope you find her soon. It's killing my mother not knowing."

"I'm doing my best."

As he walked back to his car, David had a sudden urge to follow the man. Something about Christian rubbed him the wrong way. No one could be that vanilla.

He pulled his car up to the block where the building was, waiting with the lights off. Christian came out and walked to the lot across the street. He drove a newish Volvo, a nice, sensible car. As he pulled out, he turned left. David waited a moment then followed at a comfortable distance.

They ended up in a seedy part of the city, mere blocks from where Stella had been seen getting into a car with an unknown man. *Interesting*. Christian slowed his driving, crawling along until he found a place to park. David passed him, parking the next block up. He could see the man in his rear-view mirror as he got out of his car and approached a group of prostitutes loitering in front of a small bar.

As Christian chatted with some questionable company, a sudden tap at his window startled him. His heart slammed about in his chest. When he saw a familiar face peering in at him, he felt sheepish. He lowered the window, and Jenny clasped her hands over the frame.

"Hey handsome. Seems like we keep running into each other." She smiled, showing a cut on her lip. The makeup she wore did not completely mask the bruise about her left eye.

"Yes, we do."

"Stella's not around, if that's who you're looking for."

"That's not why I'm here. Listen, you see the guy down the next block talking with some of the girls?"

Jenny took a quick glace, then nodded.

"You know him? He a regular?"

"I can't see his face clear enough to tell."

She stood away from the car to get a better look, and as she did David saw the girl was dressed in nothing more than fishnet stockings, a short leather skirt, and a thin jacket, despite the bitter cold. She came back, shaking her head.

"Sorry, some other people came out of the bar. I can't see."

A group crossed the street, blocking David's view. He turned back to Jenny.

"You want a lift?"

"Nope. Need to bring in some money tonight."

"I can't convince you to come even if I buy you a nice dinner?"

She smiled, breaking David's heart. "Another time, handsome."

"Remember, I'm just a phone call away."

She gave him a mock salute and sauntered away. With disgust he saw an older, greasy-haired man approach the girl. They had a quick exchange and started to walk toward the area of some nearby, cheap hotels.

When David looked back Christian's car was gone. *Shit.*

CHAPTER 8

After a long and heartfelt talk with Jamie, which hopefully started the process of being able to move on with their relationship, David fell into a heavy sleep. He awoke the next morning more refreshed than he'd felt in days. Even the small amount of snow that had fallen overnight didn't deter his positive mood. Mr. Albert had been out also, shovelling off his steps, and they shared a thoughtful exchange of hellos.

Philip Halladay met David at the front door of Bartholomew's Academy, in part because the school required a security card to enter and also because of the enormousness of the campus. He felt it would be simpler to meet, and he could lead David to his office. It proved to be a good plan; the hallways had zigzagged to the point that David wasn't sure he could find his way out without a map.

Mr. Halladay was a small man with thick dark hair and a neatly trimmed beard, reminding David of a human-sized rodent, a ferret perhaps. He wore round, wire-framed glasses and a conservative grey suit. He would have guessed the man's age to be in the late-fifties range, but he seemed fit and walked at a brisk pace through the winding hallways.

At last they reached their destination after passing several facilities that one would not normally see in a public high school. The building that housed Mr. Halladay's office contained an indoor pool, a dance studio, and through one set of windows David was sure he'd seen tennis courts. Inside the office it was a tad too warm for David's liking, making the room stuffy and claustrophobic despite its generous proportions.

"Can I offer you coffee or tea?"

"No thank you. I don't want to be any trouble."

"All right then." He walked around the side of his desk to take a seat, making David muse about the number of times he'd been in a similar circumstance in the past few weeks. "I am sorry to hear about this business with Stella, though I have to admit it doesn't come as a surprise."

"Yes. I understand that Stella's behaviour was quite trying during her high school years."

Mr. Halladay smiled, nodding. "Yes, a troubled girl most definitely. I've been in the education business for more than three decades, and I've seen a lot in my day. Stella was one of my more difficult students."

"I know that Mrs. Barrowman has contacted you, giving permission to speak with me, so you can give me some insight into her behaviour during this time. Any specific teachers or classmates she might have been close to. I have to tell you I'm really grasping at straws here. It's like the woman has simply disappeared."

"Well, I can tell you I was looking forward to having Stella here at Bartholomew's. Her brother Christian had been one of our top students, and I guess I assumed that Stella would follow his example. I went back and reviewed her file after I got your call." He opened a substantial folder, sitting in the middle of his neatly arranged desktop. "Now she started off all right in grade nine. Her grades were fine, minimal absences. There was one note from the school counsellor saying that her mother had been in to speak with her about Stella's lack of friends, but no other input from teachers. Then in the fall of grade ten she had her accident. After that she bounced back and forth between being a complete hellion and seeming as though she were trying to play by the rules."

The accident. "A lot of people have commented about the change in Stella after the accident. Can you comment in more detail about that?"

"She was off for a couple of weeks. When she came back, she was a different person. She skipped class, refused to participate when she was there. She barely completed enough work to pass her courses. Several times I caught her in compromising positions with male students. Her behaviour was erratic, sometimes she was docile, other times the slightest thing would send into a rage. If it weren't for her parents, I probably would have expelled her."

"So you spoke with the parents about all this?"

"Many times. We tried to work with them to get Stella the help she obviously needed. We set up weekly session with our counsellor, checked in with teachers. It wasn't enough. When the drug problems came to light, the parents sent her to a rehab clinic. When she came back, she seemed better and finished the second semester with the help of a tutor and private therapy."

"Did she ever give any reason for her behaviour to the school counselor? I mean was she having problems with any of the students? Did she talk about troubles at home or with a boyfriend?"

"No, it was mostly about her dancing. She was in considerable pain as she healed, and then went through some physiotherapy. I gather you know that's when the drug dependency started?"

"Yes, I understand she was trying to self-medicate to be able to get back to dancing, and that led to her addiction."

"Yes. Nasty business. You know it did always bother me that the circumstances of the accident were not entirely explained."

That got David's attention. "How so?"

"Well, why in the world was a fourteen-year-old girl running barefoot into the middle of oncoming traffic?"

David played along as though he'd heard this before. "Yes, I wondered the same thing myself."

"I know that Stella had some issues before that, as her mother had explained to me, but even so that kind of behaviour seemed extreme."

"Of course. Did Stella ever tell you herself what happened?"

"No. She talked with Ms. Stacey, our counselor, but she's always maintained that she can't remember why she was out. Apparently it's not uncommon to have some short-term memory loss after such an experience. Funny though, witnesses say she was running down the sidewalk, then just cut out into traffic, right in front of the car that hit her. When she came to at the hospital, she said the last thing she remembered was being at home. Her parents were still at work, and I believe Christian had been away at university."

"And after grade ten, how was her behaviour?"

Again he referred to the file. "Grade eleven seemed pretty quiet, grades mediocre. She had a boyfriend then, I remember him coming to pick her up at school on a number of occasions. A dancer." He snapped his fingers, squinting as though trying to force something from his brain. "I can't recall the name."

"Sasha," David supplied.

"Yes, that's right. I hoped she'd put the whole mess behind her and was moving on to greener pastures, but no such luck."

"So her final year was not a success?"

"Not at all. There were many outbursts, two suspensions. She came to school once so high she passed out in one of the girls' washrooms. Her parents put her in another rehab, this one for several months. She was back for a short while, didn't manage to complete all her requirements. Then she was gone."

"Okay. Did she have any friends during this time?"

"Not many at this school. Two girls she had known since elementary school, Janice and Sinclair. She was in and out with them. I think they put up with her mostly because their parents were friends."

"Does the name Elaine sound familiar?"

"I don't think so. A student here?"

"No, a friend from dance."

He shook his head.

"Is there anything else you'd like to share with me?"

The stern confidence faltered. "Well, now this is just speculation, but I really think something bad happened to the girl. More than the accident, I mean. She was beautiful, smart, a talented dancer, and then she seemed to just implode. In my experience, there's usually a reason for things to happen that way."

"She did have mental health issues."

"I realize that. I don't think the problems escalated because of a lack of concern or effort to get her help. I think Stella refused to deal with whatever it was, but it was too much to handle emotionally. The drugs and the boys, all of that, was to cope I think."

"And you don't think this would have come out in therapy?"

"Maybe, maybe not. She was a smart girl. If she wanted it to remain a secret, she may have done just that."

"Why? To protect someone? Do you think she was afraid of retaliation?"

"Maybe. There's no sense guessing though, without knowing the root of the issue."

"Did you ask her parents about this?"

"I did speak with her mother. She told me that she wondered the same thing, but Stella never told her anything. After she entered into psychiatric care, I think it all got swept by the wayside, just an unfortunate accident."

"Do you think her time at the rehabs helped her at all?"

"Yes. The Davenport Clinic stay did help, but once back to her own devices she crumbled again. You know Dr. Garfield is on our Board of Directors?" His beaming smile indicated how proud he was to have such a distinguished member of society associated with the school.

"I didn't know that. Is this how the Barrowmans heard about the clinic?"

"I think Dr. Garfield and Mr. Barrowman belong to the same golf club, something like that."

"Isn't that a conflict of interest or something to have him treat their daughter?"

"Dr. Garfield is a highly respected psychiatrist. The Barrowmans wanted the best for Stella. This was private care after all, they were free to choose whom they wished."

"Of course." The explanation didn't sit well with David, and Mr. Halladay sounded the tinniest bit defensive. He'd have to explore that avenue in more detail.

"Have you had any contact with Stella since she graduated?'
"Not at all."

"Any teachers or other staff who might have kept in contact?"
"Not that I'm aware of."

The conversation seemed headed in the same direction as all the previous ones he'd had on the case thus far; concluding that Stella had gone off voluntarily. Whether she was still riding high somewhere or if she'd crashed and burned, maybe permanently, was anybody's guess. Mrs. Barrowman had told David she'd called all the hospitals in the area, and no Jane Does matching Stella's description had been brought in during the time period in question. She'd also checked with the police a number of times to see if her daughter had been arrested, but no luck in that direction either. He didn't suppose it would hurt to ask again.

"I think that's all for now Mr. Halladay. Please call me if anything comes to mind."

The only new bit of information he'd managed to turn up was the questionable circumstances of Stella's accident. He would need to speak with Mrs. Barrowman about that, maybe check in with Dr. Garfield to see if Stella had remembered any more details. Or perhaps it was like Mr. Halladay had suggested, and it wasn't a question of remembering but more a case of admission. But of what?

David sighed, frustration making his skin tight and itchy. The case was going nowhere. He was simply spinning his wheels, revisiting the same ground without any new insight. Yet someone was annoyed, or worried enough to be sending threats. So where were the cracks in the cover-up starting? Obviously, George and Christian had issues they wished to keep secret, ones that would tarnish their images, but did that relate in any way to Stella's disappearance, or even the events leading up to it?

As he pulled out of the parking lot, he realized how close he was to the dance company's rehearsal site and impulsively decided to swing by. Like the last time, the place was swarming with activity. He wandered in, only to be stopped by a dishevelled young woman who wanted to know what his business at the studio was. After a little flirtation, he learned her name was Sara and that she was the company's secretary. By the time he had her blushing, she was all but offering him the keys to the place. Marcus, she helpfully supplied, was in his office.

He only took one wrong turn, accidentally ending up in a hallway that contained the changing rooms of several of the company's principal female dancers. He retraced his steps, realizing he should have taken a left instead of a right, and finally ended up outside Marcus's door. It stood open a few inches, soft music playing.

David knocked.

"Come in," Marcus called, and the music came to an abrupt end.

He stepped inside, expecting the expression of surprise he found on Marcus's face.

"Well, you're not who I was expecting."

"Sorry, I hope you don't mind me stopping by. I was in the area, and something had come up that I'd like to speak you about."

"Sure. I can use a break from these financial reports anyway." The top of the desk was littered with papers and empty coffee cups, a sign of a long and engrossing process. His hair was mussed, as though he'd been rubbing his hands through it.

"Well, I'm sorry to say that this might not be a better topic for you, but it's important that I clear the air."

Marcus leaned back in his chair, shoulders slumping. "This is about Stella's accusation isn't it?"

"I have to wonder why you didn't tell me about it yourself? It begs my attention when I pull information like this from a police report." He let that comment sit between them.

"I didn't mention it because it was a horrible mistake and one of the worst times in my life. Stella retracted her statement, and the charges were dropped. I told you the girl was messed up, and I knew this was just part of her sickness. Now don't think I wasn't totally pissed, because I was. Jesus, can you imagine being accused of such a thing? By some kid? It's disgusting to even think about."

"Look, I can understand being embarrassed, but you still should have told me. It makes the whole scenario look much worse than it is. I understand that the charges were dropped, but don't you wonder why she did this? I mean why would she accuse an innocent person of raping her? I know the girl has problems, but that doesn't make any kind of sense." He watched the man closely for his reaction.

"Honestly I don't know why she did it. Like I told you last time, she had a good summer, had an offer to come back after school ended, and instead she did this, and she never danced for us again. Believe me, I racked my brain over and over about it, you know, wondering if I'd done something to make her think I was hitting on her or that I wanted to. The accusation just came out of left field. At the time, I chalked it up to the drugs." As the old pain came back, his speech picked up tempo.

"Did you not think it possible that someone had raped the girl? Maybe someone she was afraid of pointing a finger at?"

"I guess it's possible. I was only thinking of myself while it was going on. It would have ruined me. I mean, can you imagine an accusation like that against a director in the business I'm in? No female dancer would want to come anywhere near me."

Looking out for one's best interests was a natural reaction to a situation such as a false accusation, so it didn't come as a shock that Marcus hadn't bothered to ponder the reason for such a desperate action. "No, I get where you're coming from. You can understand why I'd have to question you about this?"

Marcus sighed, rubbing at his temples as though a headache had settled in. "Sure, I understand. But you understand me, I don't want this getting out. Nothing happened, and I don't want to rehash all that crap again. I'm sorry the girl's in trouble, I really am. I would have loved to be able to guide her career, and on a personal level I wouldn't wish her problems on anyone. I really hope you find her and that she's okay."

He sounded sincere, bitter, but sincere. The itch had come back, persistent and demanding that he find out the truth behind the whole sad, twisted mess. *What had happened to this girl?*

"Did the police ever mention to you that they were looking at anyone else?"

"No. They never said as much, but I got the impression they were writing her off as unstable."

"The parents ever talk to you after the charges were dropped?"

"The mother called and apologized to me. She was horrified. I don't think she wanted it getting out any more than I did. It would have been a big embarrassment for the family, what with her husband in the position he is and everything. In fact, she remains one of our biggest personal financial donors every year. We don't even have to call during our funding drive, she mails in a check every fall."

Wonder why she didn't mention the incident? "Thanks for your time Marcus. I appreciate the candour."

"Sure. Listen can you shut the door on your way out? I really need to finish up these reports, or our board is going to be calling for my head." His smile was tired, pained.

As David started up the hallway, a figure stepped out from a nearby doorway. The movement startled him, giving him a small surge of adrenalin.

"I'm sorry. I didn't mean to startle you," Sasha said. He was dressed in yoga-type pants and a dark hoodie, his eyes hard and angry.

"No worries. I'm glad I ran into you. Can we talk?"

"Yeah, sure. I'll walk you out." He started toward the main entrance.

"Are you all right Sasha? You seemed a bit pissed off."

"No, I'm good. Just tired. What did you want to ask me?" His tense posture remained.

"Ah, I was wondering if you knew any details of Stella's accident?"

"What do you mean?"

"Well, like why she was running down the road at that time of day? Any idea about what might have set her off or where she might have been going?"

"No, I really don't. Stella couldn't remember after the accident. At least that's what she told me. We didn't get close until more than a year after it happened."

"Okay. What do you know about Stella's father? Any issues there?"

"Just that he wasn't around a lot. I know Stella thought he loved her brother more, that she was a disappointment compared to him. Why are you asking? Has something turned up?"

"Unfortunately, no. I've got a few more avenues to pursue yet."

They reached the front door. Outside a light snow was falling.

"Please let me know if anything turns up. I feel terrible about the fight I had with her. I keep thinking that if I hadn't gotten mad at her, she might have come to me, maybe she wouldn't be missing now."

"Don't beat yourself up. We don't know what's happened yet." He started to turn away, when he remembered something he hadn't yet asked about. "Did you know Stella was working as a stripper."

His eyes narrowed. "Yes."

"Did she ever talk to you about a dancer named Raven True?"

"No, why?"

"Nothing. Just someone else I need to talk with."

They looked at each other, Sasha seeming even more tense then just minutes before.

"Thank you for doing this."

"You can thank me when I find her."

As he walked to his car, a defeated Sasha watched through the glass doors. He understood the man's frustration; he'd spent two weeks on the case already and had turned up next to nothing. After his interview with the Stella's school friends, and a visit to the club where she worked, there were not too many other places to look. Someone had to know something, but whoever they were, they weren't talking. At least not to him.

His car door had barely shut when his cell rang. He didn't recognize the number, but answered in case it was someone with information. "Hello."

"Dave, Jimmy here. We still on for a drink tonight?"

Shit. He'd forgotten all about it. "Yeah, sure. When and where?"

"The Diamond. Say around eight. A couple of other guys are coming, so we can maybe get in a few rounds of pool."

"Sounds good. See you then. Oh, Jimmy wait. Can you run another address for me?"

"Sure."

David gave him the warehouse information.

"I'll let you know what I find when I see you later."

As soon as he clicked off, the phone rang again, startling him so much he dropped it. After retrieving it from the floor of the car he answered. "Yes."

"Is this David Lloyd?"

"It is."

"Hello David, it's Sheila Cooke calling. I was hoping you might be free to speak this evening."

Suddenly everyone wanted to talk with him. "Of course. What time?"

"I get off at four thirty, so could we meet shortly after that? How about I come to your office?"

"I'll be waiting."

She said a quick goodbye and hung up.

The rest of the day was spent at the office. David re-read the notes from all of the interviews he'd conducted, plus the original information from Marjory. Again and again the comments came back to Stella's accident. David could see the clear connection between her recovery and the beginning of her drug addiction, but the unanswered questions grabbed David's attention more than the known facts. This was a young woman with talent and good looks who came from a family with money. Even more than that, Stella had people who cared for her, who wanted to help, and yet she had still ended up in a sad and dangerous lifestyle.

What am I missing? With no other ideas springing to mind, David began calling every hospital and rehab facility in the city, with no success. Calls to the morgue and police stations were also dead ends.

A knock at the door pulled David back to reality. His computer monitor showed a time of four fifty, so he assumed the visitor to be Sheila. A quick glace about the office showed everything to be in order, the only clutter the mess of notes on his desk top.

Sheila had a glistening dampness clinging to her coat and hair, the remnants of melting snow from her walk from her car to the building. David had been so engrossed in his work he hadn't noticed the snow had started again.

"Hello Sheila. Please come in."

"Thank you. Dreadful parking down here."

"Yes, I know."

She removed her coat and sat down. David resumed his spot, feeling slightly empowered to be the one behind the desk for a change. Sheila was looking about the space, lips in a tight line.

"So, I suppose you're curious about my wanting to speak with you?"

"Of course. You don't seem to be a woman to play games or waste people's time."

A ghost of a smile touched her lips at the compliment. "Right on both counts. I should also tell you, I am not one to talk out of turn. I have been with the same company for twenty-four years, and have been Mr. Barrowman's secretary for almost ten. I work hard, and always use discretion and tact, but I'm afraid with this business of Stella being missing, I can no longer hold my tongue."

"All right. I'm here to listen."

"Mr. Barrowman is a wonderful businessman, highly respected, but he is also a voracious womanizer. I'd heard the rumours long before I even came to work for the man. I simply kept my mouth shut and turned a blind eye, but a few instances over the years have caught my attention."

Interesting. "Such as?"

"Well, a short while after Stella had her accident there was a story going around that he was involved with one of Stella's friend's mothers. It was a messy affair, apparently broke up a marriage, sent the woman to the bottle. Stella found out somehow. She came to the office one day in a complete rage. I could hear her and her father arguing through the door. From some of the comments Stella made, I gathered this wasn't the first time something like that had happened. The poor girl was so worked up when she came out that I had to drive her home. She was still in her brace, and I didn't want her walking about and hurting herself any further."

"Stella would have been about fifteen?"

"Yes, that's right."

So that would have been the terrible grade-ten school year that Mr. Halladay had spoken of. Perhaps Stella's father had been the one to set her off?

"Do you know who the woman was?"

"No, I'm sorry, I didn't catch a name."

"Anything else?"

"Well there was always talk about the escapades that he and some of the other higher-ups got into when on trips overseas. You know, massage parlours, strip clubs, and red-light districts. I can't say for sure how much is true, but the talk was persistent. Someone even mentioned that Christian had accompanied him on one such trip, though I don't know how much stock I'd put into that. The boy is about as straight as they come."

David didn't comment about the fact that he'd seen the young man talking with a group of prostitutes just the night before. "But he must have been aware that something was going on with his father."

"I suppose so. Like I said, there was talk, but any actual goings-on were discreet. I never saw him with another woman, or overheard any inappropriate calls. "

"Did Marjory know about any of this?"

"Not that I'm aware of, but you'd think she must have been at least suspicious."

"So do you think this has some bearing on Stella's disappearance?"

"I think this behaviour on the part of her father did a lot of damage to that poor girl. I didn't have a lot of direct interaction with her, but she seemed so lost and angry."

"If she already had some emotional issues, and then drug problems, a betrayal by her dad could have sent her over the edge."

"I agree. And I think she confronted him with that a few years ago."

David perked up. "When was this?"

"Oh, maybe four years ago. She came to the office unexpectedly. She looked awful, so skinny and pale. She barged in her father's office, and they got into it. She called him all kinds of awful names, saying how he cared more about sex than his own children. Then she told him to back off of Bobby. She told him he wasn't going to hurt anyone else close to her."

"Do you have any idea who Bobby is?"

"No, sorry."

"You're sure she said Bobby?"

"Absolutely. She threatened her father that if he didn't back off, she'd expose him for the pervert he was."

"Was that it?"

"No, they actually quieted down for a bit. I couldn't hear any more of the conversation, but when Stella finally left she was much calmer."

"So after this confrontation you ever overhear any other conversations of a similar nature?"

"No, after that I don't think I saw Stella again, at least not until this past September."

"What happened then?"

"She came in, asked to speak with her father. He let her in his office and they had a conversation. It was very quiet, I have no idea what was said. When Stella came out, she was crying."

"So you think this is directly related to Stella disappearing?"

"It does seem suspicious. I don't know that I think her father has hurt her or anything gruesome like that, but something happened between them. Maybe she needed money?"

"Could be."

They sat for a moment in silence. Wow, talk about a bombshell.

"Well Sheila, I really appreciate you coming to me. This is definitely something to look into."

"You understand I need my name kept out of it? I have a few more years before retirement, and I'd like to end my career on a positive note."

"I understand."

She stood. David walked her to the door, shaking her hand and thanking her once more. He had to wonder who else knew about Mr. Barrowman's extracurricular activities. Surely if Stella shared the truth with Dr. Garfield, he would have told David about it. Another question for the fine doctor, along with an inquiry about the circumstances of Stella's accident.

David really hoped Stella was off somewhere with Bobby, living off her father's guilt money. He hoped she was safe and clean, far away from the people who continued to hurt her.

The Diamond implied far too much class for such a dive. The place was several steps up the social ladder from Joe's, but was certainly nothing to write home about. David drove carefully into the bar's pothole-riddled parking lot, easily finding an empty spot. The night was early, and most of the regulars had yet to arrive. Closer to the door was a small, dark-coloured car with a figure sitting inside. He thought it was a man, the face turned away and a cell phone pressed to his ear.

David stepped inside, catching sight of many familiar faces despite the grimy lighting. The bar was a favourite for police officers, EMTs, and other community service employees. He received a few waves and hellos as he made his way through the haphazard grouping of tables, heading toward the bar at the far side of the room. Jimmy, along with a couple of his fellow officers, was there already. The beer was flowing.

An odd sensation crept over his skin, pulling his attention away from his destination. As he looked to the right, his gaze locked with another man's, the last person on earth that he wanted to see. Jeremy Black tipped his beer in David's direction and smirked. With effort, David kept himself going, not letting any visible reaction to the man's presence escape him.

"Hey Dave. Good to see you," Jimmy said, giving him a good-natured slap on the back. The man was about a decade older than David, short and soft around the middle.

"You too."

"You remember John and Marco?"

"Sure." He shook hands with both the men before ordering himself a beer. "Can I get everyone another round?"

"Never turn down a free beer," Marco said.

The bartender hurried off to get their order. David kept his back to the direction of Jeremy's table, refusing to give the man the satisfaction of seeing his discomfort.

"So how's things going for you these days?" John asked.

"Good. No complaints really."

"And you're fine, you know, after the incident?" He seemed to be treading lightly, trying not to be insensitive, but still curious.

"Yep. I mean, I won't ever get my hearing fully back in my left ear, and my knee acts up sometimes, but other than that I'm good as new."

Marco flicked a look behind David. "Any leads on who jumped you?"

"Not anything that will stick, but I think we all know who's responsible."

The beers were placed on the bar. David slid some money at the bartender and grabbed a bottle.

"Black's an asshole. I never did like him much, but if he could do that to a fellow officer, then he's shit as far as I'm concerned." Marco looked genuinely pissed at the idea. His dark complexion had taken on a yellowish hue under the harsh lights of the bar. He had enough gel in his hair to keep every strand smooth and unmovable.

"He'll get what's coming to him." Jimmy gave David a half-smile then took a long swig of his beer.

The men chatted for a bit, talking about who'd retired, the new recruits, and some big cases recently closed. When one of the pool tables opened up, they grabbed their drinks and set up a game. David stood to one side with Jimmy, watching the other two men have their turn. During one perusal of the bar he caught Jeremy staring at him, and if looks could kill David would have been done for. He turned away, still feeling the bastards eyes boring into the back of his head.

"Listen," Jimmy began, "I almost forgot. That warehouse you asked about. It came back as being owned by a numbered entity that owns a few shipping/importing type businesses. Nothing funny came up for the business, so I ran the address for incidents, and it came back clean too. I guess you can try and run the number, see if you can shake any more info that way."

"Okay, thanks."

Jimmy put a hand on his arm, instantly getting his attention. "You okay Dave? With Jeremy being here, I mean?"

"Fine."

Jeremy Black was drunk, being loud and obnoxious and calling lots of attention in his direction. His fellow drinkers took his lead, slamming their bottles about and calling out "friendly" insults to other patrons of the bar. The poor waitress serving their table had been ogled and groped at every stop. David wanted nothing more than to go over and punch the man in the face, but he knew the satisfaction of such an action would be short-lived.

As Marco and John's game came to an end, David felt a tap on his shoulder. He turned—half-expecting Jeremy or one of his cronies—surprised to find Lee and Ritchie instead. Lee smiled with a smooth cockiness, but Ritchie seemed jittery, his gaze darting all about him. One hand was curled into a fist at his side.

"Hello, David. You have a minute to chat?"

Jimmy had started to set up the table, and the other two had gone to the bar for another drink. David gave Jimmy a sharp look before walking off with the men. They moved to a space along the wall, near the corridor to the washrooms. Once again, Lee was dressed in an outfit that looked casual, yet David knew had cost him a buck or two. Ritchie was unshaven, his mouth curled in a grimace, which revealed his rotten teeth.

"What's up, Lee?"

"I hear you're still asking around about Stella."

"That's right."

"Well, I'm here to advise you that it would be in your best interests to let the matter go. You're stepping on some toes here."

"That so?" He smiled, not backing down an inch. "So I guess you're the one behind all the fun phone calls I've been getting lately?"

Ritchie smirked.

"And the damage to my car?"

"I don't know what you're talking about," Lee answered, the model of sincerity.

"Well you can tell whoever that I'm not going to stop looking until I find the girl. And if anyone's hurt her, there's going to be consequences."

"Really? A cream puff like you thinks he's going hurt anyone? That's a joke."

A shuffle of footsteps distracted the men.

"Well hello there, David. So nice to see you again. This your boyfriend?" Jeremy asked, indicating Lee. The two men with him chuckled.

The smile left Lee's face like the flick of a switch. "Fuck you. I'm no faggot."

Jeremy's eyes turned black, his rage instantaneous. "You better watch who you're telling to fuck off, buddy." His breath reeked of alcohol.

"That so?"

One of the men with Jeremy stepped in closer. Ritchie took the movement as a threat, throwing a punch in the man's direction. He connected, but awkwardly. The man returned the hit, knocking Ritchie backward into the wall. Suddenly fists were flying, one taking David in the cheek. He pushed back, realizing the hitter had been the other man with Jeremy. Jimmy came rushing at the group, grabbing Ritchie by the back of his coat. He'd managed to get Jeremy to the floor, where the man lay bleeding from his mouth and nose.

"What the hell are you guys doing? You're police officers, not thugs," Jimmy bellowed.

"He started it," Lee said, jerking a thumb at Jeremy.

One of Jeremy's buddies helped him to his feet. "We're fine, Jimmy. Just back off."

Jimmy ignored him, turning his attention to David. "You okay, David?"

"Yep. Good."

"Then I suggest everyone goes about their own business."

Jeremy shrugged, then with a smirk wiped the blood from his mouth onto the sleeve of his shirt. He walked off, the other two men following. Lee and Ritchie remained, waiting.

"You too. Get out of here, before I decide to run you in." Jimmy stared the younger men down.

"Sure, pops. Listen David, this conversation isn't over."

"Lovely to see you again Lee."

He and Jimmy watched as the men walked through the

crowd. Jeremy had returned to his table, also watching the men leave. As the door closed behind them, he moved his gaze back to David.

"That asshole has a lot of nerve," Jimmy said, disgust lacing his words.

"He always did. Listen I refuse to let that guy get the better of me. Let's go play our game of pool and pretend he doesn't exist."

"Sounds good to me."

A few hours later David came out to his car. No one waited for him, and the rental car was still in one piece. In any event he was armed and now royally pissed.

He'd be damned if Jeremy Black or a couple of criminals like Lee and Ritchie were going to push him around. He was going to find Stella, and make whoever'd hurt her pay.

CHAPTER 9

Saturday morning began with a long workout with Sean, followed by an enormous breakfast at a buffet restaurant within walking distance from the gym. Over eggs, pancakes, and a scandalous amount of bacon, David caught his brother up on the case, including the reason for the bruise on his face from the fight the night before, and the issues in t r6telationship with Jamie. Sean, by comparison, had no drama going on in either his professional or personal life. He worked as the manager of a medical testing lab, where he pushed more papers than test tubes. He and his girlfriend had been together for several years, enjoying one of the most stable relationships that David had ever come across.

"So he finally told his family, eh?" Sean said, a forkful of eggs waiting to be consumed.

"Not family. Just his mom."

"Well, that's a start, right? He's making an effort, so that must make you feel better. He doesn't want things to end between you two."

"How do you know?"

"Because I've seen you guys together. I can tell how he feels about you."

"Well, I just hope I haven't started something that's going to come back and bite me in the ass. If his dad freaks or rejects him, he's going to take it really hard."

"Then you'll be there for him."

David pushed back from the table, grinning. "When did you get so wise, little brother?'

"You got the looks, so I guess it was only fair that I get the brains."

"Funny. Listen you want to have a little holiday get-together at my place this year?"

"Yeah, sure. Who's coming?"

"I haven't asked anyone yet, but just family and a few friends."

"Sure. Just let me know when."

David paid the bill and the brothers went their separate ways. Back at home, David put in some time on household chores and got his laundry up to date. Then with the bathroom gleaming and the floors vacuumed, he dressed in a presentable outfit and headed off to Janice Collins's house, where he would meet with her and Sinclair Brown.

Janice lived just outside of the city, in an area where people owned estates and enough land to house stables. The Collins home boasted an impressive holding area for what must have been a multitude of horses, several of which were being exercised as David followed the long, winding drive to the house. An older woman with a fine line of hair along her upper lip answered the door and ushered David into the dining room where the women waited.

Two attractive but overly manicured women looked up as David entered. "Your guest," the older woman said before disappearing.

"Please come join us, Mr. Lloyd," one of the women said. As he reached where they sat, she offered her hand. "I'm Janice, this is Sinclair. Please sit."

Janice was very small boned, almost childlike, with thick ebony hair. A pointy chin kept her from being classically pretty, but she was certainly attractive. Sinclair was almost as pretty, but the excessive makeup she wore detracted from, rather than added to, her appeal. Her cover-up was too dark for her natural colouring, which, by the bright, orange-red shade of her hair, David assumed was a milky white. Her eyes were crystal blue, so light they verged on having no colour at all. Her lips and chest had been enhanced with something, giving her a top-heavy appearance.

"Thanks for taking the time to meet with me, ladies."

"Oh, Janice loves any excuse to entertain." Sinclair smirked, her words sounding chiding and unfriendly.

"Don't mind her. She's still grumpy because her husband's cut off her plastic surgery allowance."

They both giggled, but Sinclair's eyes remained hard. David had no idea what the proper response to such a statement was, so he simply nodded his head. The woman who'd answered the door returned with a food-laden cart. She placed plates in front of everyone and left the cart to the side. Janice dismissed her with a wave of her hand.

"What looks good, David?"

He was still quite full from breakfast, but he took a turkey sandwich and some Caesar salad to be polite. Janice poured some wine, which he refused, taking a glass of water instead.

"So Stella has disappeared again, has she?" Sinclair asked between bites.

David wiped his mouth. "Yes. She's been gone for a few months now. No one's heard from her at all. Her mother is very worried."

"Yes, Marjory would be all in a twitter wouldn't she." Sinclair gave a sour look.

"How can we help?" Janice asked.

"I understand that Stella keeps in contact with the two of you? Is that correct?"

"Yes. Well me more than Sinclair. She calls me at least once a month."

"So have you heard from her recently?"

"No, I haven't. Not since the summer probably. She called me one evening, sounding totally trashed. She was crying, something about her dad, but I couldn't really understand her. Then she hung up."

"Was this usual behaviour for her?"

"What wasn't? You never knew how that girl was going to act."

"Okay, let's backtrack. How do you know Stella?"

"Our parents know Stella's parents, they run in the same circles. We all went to the same elementary and high school."

"So you know her family well?"

Sinclair giggled. "Yep, and all the dirty laundry."

"Don't be such a bitch, Sinclair. Your mom's a drunk, so you don't need to be pointing fingers."

Sinclair made a face, but with the size of her lips, David couldn't tell if she was pouting or not.

"Well, if there's something to tell, I'd love to hear it."

"Well Stella's always been an odd one, even when we were little. Sometimes she's nice, seems to want to socialize, and other times she's just plain weird. Like holing up in her room, doesn't want to talk with anyone. We just got used to it. When things were good, she'd hang out with us, when they weren't we did our own thing."

"What was her family's reaction to this kind of behaviour?"

"Well, her mom just doted on her. Her dad was sort of indifferent, when he was there any way."

"And Christian?"

"Christian was a goody two-shoes. We never bothered with him."

"So did this behaviour change as you got older? Did she ever give any explanation for her actions."

"She got even crazier once we hit high school. The only thing she seemed to care about was dancing, then when she got hurt she just went off the rails."

"Like really wild. She'd fuck anyone who gave her the time of day, she did whatever drugs she could get her hands on. And she could be mean. Lordy, some of the stuff that came out of that girl's mouth," Sinclair added.

"What do you know about the accident?"

"Well she got hit by a car and hurt her knee."

"I know that part of it, but any idea why she was running down the street without shoes on?"

The women looked at each other, sharing a dark look.

"What?"

"Well, Stella came to Sinclair's house that day. We were both there, she lived just around the corner form Stella's parents. She started pounding on the door, screaming. We came down, and she was just hysterical, screaming about needing help. She actually scratched me when I tried to touch her. We thought she was high, and we told her to leave. I guess after that she had her accident."

"What do you think she needed help from?" David made a note to check if Stella had been doing drugs before the accident.

"I don't know. Like I said, we thought she was just being an idiot. We didn't think she actually needed help." Janice looked guilty and began to push her salad around on her plate with a fork.

"Was Stella on drugs back then? I thought her problems with that stuff started after the accident."

"She was on antidepressants, I think. And I know she drank sometimes."

"Okay, so after the accident, she was out of control?"

"Sometimes. Other times she was like a hermit, just staying home. We were kids, you know, we got tired of her shit and just stopped calling her."

"But you stayed in touch?"

"Yeah, I mean we still hung out sometimes, then when she moved away from her parents, we really only saw her a few times a year, usually when she needed money or a place to crash. I went out with her and her druggie friends once, and it was too scary for me."

Sinclair nodded in agreement with her friend.

"Do you know a girl named Elaine?"

Both of the women burst out laughing.

"What's so funny?"

"Of course we know Elaine. She was one of Stella's dancing friends. She so wanted to fit in with the rich girls, but didn't quite cut it. Then when all the shit happened with her mother, she sort of disappeared. Well, from our social scene anyway."

"Sorry, what shit with her mother?"

"She was fucking Stella's dad. Big scandal. Broke up her marriage, the dad left, and she tried to kill herself or something."

David remembered Elaine saying her dad had died when she was a small girl and that Mr. Barrowman had helped her family out. Why had she lied about that?

"So this was common knowledge?"

"Well Stella had a major flip-out when she found out. I mean, we all knew about her dad, right. He liked the ladies, but I guess it was too close with it being a friend's mother." Sinclair looked down at her nails, as though the conversation was boring her.

"Right. So Marjory and Christian would have known about this too?"

"I assume so."

"Did Stella ever tell you guys anything about why she was doing the stuff she was? Obviously she had money to get help. And despite the crap with her dad, her mother seems to care and would help her any way she could."

"It was the drugs." Another bored look from Sinclair.

"But why was she doing the drugs? Like you said, she loved dancing, she could have made her escape that way, if there was something she was trying to get away from."

"We really don't know."

David took a moment to think about the conversation. There was something, he could feel it. "Did you to know Sasha?"

"Mr. Dreamy Ballerina? Of course."

David ignored the nickname. "What did you think about him?"

"He was a nice guy, way too good for the way Stella treated him," Janice said.

"Yeah, even when he knew she was using, or sleeping with other guys, he always came when she called."

"Ever heard of anyone named Raven True?"

"You mean Stella's lesbian lover?" Giggling again from the two. The childish and haughty antics were starting to wear on David's nerves.

"You know that for a fact?" he asked.

"We went and saw her dance a couple of times, well strip. One time the two of them did this number together, and let's just say it was very suggestive. There wasn't a guy in the place without a boner after they finished."

An interesting twist. Now what did that have to do with Sasha?

"So the women were close then?"

"Yes."

"Do you think Stella would have gone to her for help?"

"Maybe. It's hard to say with Stella."

"Do you know a guy named Lee?"

"Oh yeah, an asshole."

"He gets good pot though," Sinclair said.

"Jesus, Sinclair!" Janice admonished, a blush creeping into her cheeks.

"Look ladies, I'm not here to pass judgment. If you like to smoke up a little, it's none of my business. Do you two ever contact the guy directly?"

Janice shook her head, but Sinclair smirked. "Occasionally, when I run out of other options."

"I see, and do you have to go to him?"

"Yep, I usually meet him in a bar called Joe's. I don't want him knowing where I live."

That was smart of the girl at least. "Ever see anyone with him that you recognized?"

"I saw Elaine once. I don't know if she saw me, but they were talking at a car parked in front. Looked like they were having an argument of some kind. Anyway he went into the bar and she walked up the street."

"Could you hear them?"

"No, I was in my car."

David was at a loss as to anything else he could ask of the women. Though they didn't seem to be the most thoughtful of people, they had been forthcoming, shedding new light on people that would need further scrutiny.

"Well, that about does it then. I'll get out of your way now."

"Oh, don't rush off. Finish your lunch," Janice said.

He didn't see any way out of it, so he spent the better part of the next hour listening to gossip about people he didn't know and forcing blueberry cheesecake and coffee down his throat. Finally he excused himself with a small fib about needing to meet another appointment. Janice walked him out, and she seemed sincere when she said she'd be willing to help in any way she could. David thanked her and left.

The truth was, the only thing on his agenda was a plan to watch a movie. As soon as he walked in the door, he made a beeline for the family room and plopped down on the couch. His brain was swimming, and he needed to have a few moments to unwind. He hadn't had a break in weeks.

Five minutes into the movie the phone rang. When he saw Jamie's number on the display, his stomach gave a little flutter. He smiled, almost as giddy as a schoolboy getting a call from his secret crush. "Hello gorgeous."

"Back at ya. You have a minute?"

"I do actually. I'm taking a bit of a break this afternoon."

"How about tonight?"

"I haven't thought that far yet. What's up?"

There was a small pause. "Can you come to dinner with me and my mother?"

His stomach gave another flutter. "Sure."

"Great. I'll come pick you up around six, and we can meet my mom at the restaurant."

"Okay, should I dress up?"

"I reserved a table at Carmilla's."

"So I should dress up." Carmilla's was an expensive Italian restaurant in Toronto's entertainment district.

"You know I love you in a suit and tie."

"I'll be presentable. See you later."

"Sure." Another pause. "And David, I've really missed you the last few days."

"Me too."

The call made David realize he still hadn't called his own mother back. He did so, picking a date for the holiday get-together. He asked her to invite her sister and family, and anyone else she thought might like to come, and get back to him with the numbers. She seemed really excited to be invited over, something he had not done very often over the years. He told her he loved her and promised to call more often.

When four o'clock rolled around, David jumped in the shower, taking a long time in washing his hair and body, even using some exfoliating cleanser that his mother had given him. Once out, he shaved and brushed his teeth and, after pulling out his best suit, lay down on the bed. He felt decidedly nervous, more so than he ever thought he would be. He had envisioned the moment many times, meeting Jamie's family, but now that the time had come, he realized the difference it would make for both of them.

At quarter to six, he slipped on the suit and his dress shoes, splashing on a cologne that Jamie was fond of. Self-consciously he smoothed his hair over his left ear, though the hearing aid was so small he need not have bothered. No one ever noticed it but him.

Keys rattled in the front door as Jamie let himself in. David came down the stairs. When Jamie caught sight of him and an ear-to-ear grin spread across his face, David laughed.

"Wow, you look amazing."

"You too," David answered.

Jamie always looked good, possessing a striking "pretty-boy" look, more model than machismo. David sometimes felt brutish by comparison.

There was an awkward moment where neither was sure what the next move should be. David stepped closer and hugged his partner. They kissed, softly, silently, letting each other know that everything was all right.

Jamie noticed the bruise. "What happened to you?"

"Just a scuffle with someone involved in the case I'm working on."

"You okay?"

"Perfect."

He let the matter drop. "Ready?" Jamie asked.

"Let's do it."

Mrs. Brennan was already seated at the table when the men arrived. She was small and thin, and David could see where Jamie had gotten his looks from. She smiled when she saw her son, the action lighting up her whole face. She wore a red pantsuit with a black silk blouse and a nice set of heels. Up close, there were fine lines about her eyes, but the rest of her face was milky smooth with a youthful glow.

The men stopped at the edge of the table, waiting until the hostess left. Jamie leaned down and kissed his mother on the cheek. She smiled and offered her hand to David.

"You must be David."

"Yes. A pleasure to meet you Mrs. Brennen."

"Oh, please call me Susan. Sit down."

They sat opposite her at the table. Jamie placed his hand on top of David's, the skin warm and clammy. He was nervous, a condition that rarely affected him. His mother looked down at their hands. She smiled, but tension in her jaw belied her own anxiety.

"Well thank you for agreeing to dinner. I know that all of this must have come as a shock."

"I'd be a liar if I said I wasn't surprised." Her fingers tapped at the base of her throat. When she realized what she was doing her hand dropped abruptly to the table. "Now I don't want you to think I'm upset about this, or...disapproving. It's just a change."

"I understand," David answered. "My parents were the same way."

Susan relaxed at his words. "Really. I have to confess, I've been feeling terrible about how I reacted the other night when Jamie told me. I know it must have been hard for him, and I wasn't very receptive." Her fingers were now tapping on the table.

"You were fine, Mom. You could have freaked or stormed out. You stayed and talked with me."

Small dots of colour had appeared in her cheeks. "So how did the two of you meet? How long have you been together?"

"We met in court," Jamie started, looking to David. "Almost five years ago now."

"And I asked your son out, and we've been together ever since."

"How did you know, that he was gay, I mean?" She bit her lip, as though regretting the words once they'd left her mouth.

David desperately wanted to make a joke, but he didn't know how well it would go over so early into the conversation. He played it safe instead. "I didn't, not for sure, but I thought I picked up on something from the way he looked at me. So I took my chances."

"Oh. Are you a lawyer too?"

"No, I'm a private detective."

"But you met in court?"

"Yes. David was a police officer then. He testified in a case I was prosecuting."

"I see. So you didn't like being a police officer?"

The question hung there, both men looking at each other. Susan picked up on the discomfort, blushing even more.

"I had an accident. I hurt my knee and lost some of my hearing, so I wasn't fit to be an officer any longer."

"I'm sorry, I didn't mean to bring up a painful subject."

"It's fine. Everything's worked out now, and I enjoy my job."

The waitress came to inform them of the specials and take an order for hor d'oeuvres. They all asked for the shrimp cocktail, and Jamie ordered a bottle of wine.

"So you two have been dating for five years? How could I not know anything about this?" Her incredulousness was genuine.

"I don't let anyone know. Not really. No one at my work knows anything about my personal life. The only people who know anything are David's family."

"And they're okay with you two, with your relationship?" She was trying so hard to be non-offensive it made David's heart ache.

"Yes, they've welcomed me with open arms." Jamie clutched even harder onto David's hand.

The waitress arrived, a welcome distraction. They all took a few moments to enjoy the shrimp and wine, Susan letting her gaze wander over the restaurant's other patrons. Nearby a young couple sat together, laughing and touching each other like those who've reached a certain level of comfort in their relationship do.

"So tell me about your family, David."

"Ah, my mom's a secretary at a doctor's clinic, my dad's an accountant. I have a younger brother, Sean. He manages a medical testing lab. I'm quite close with my grandmother, my dad's mother. They all live in the city. I don't know what else to say, we're just a regular family."

"That sounds nice."

The table slipped into silence, which after several minutes became uncomfortable. All around them were happy sounds and warm, savoury aromas.

"So Jamie tells me you're occupational therapist?" David said.

"Yes, that's right. I work with children."

"Well that must be a very rewarding job."

"It is. It's nice to know that when I go to work every day, I'm making a real difference in someone's life." For the first time in the conversation her words were relaxed, expressing a warmth and joy that matched the easiness of her smile.

"And my dad's a lawyer, though corporate, not a prosecutor like me."

"Yes, your dad was very proud that you'd chose to follow him into law. One of Jamie's sisters is also a lawyer. I don't know if he's told you that."

"Yes, Samantha. She practices family law, right?"

Jamie nodded, Susan drinking in their easiness with one another.

"So all those times you've gone away, saying you're going with friends or people from work, you've actually been going with David?"

"Ah, yes. We took a trip down east last year, and out to The Calgary Stampede the year before that."

"And my cousin's wedding in Victoria."

"Right. We haven't managed to make it anywhere warm yet, but it's in our plans."

"You must have enough vacation time to go for a couple of months by now." He turned to Susan. "Your son works so hard, never takes time off."

Her expression softened. "Yes, he does. Always has. I never had to nag him about homework or check up on him." She was staring at them openly. "Wow, I'm sorry. It's just, you two, you seem so close, like a real couple."

"We are a real couple Mom."

"I didn't mean it like that. This is just so real. I mean, I believed you the other night, but seeing you two together is a totally different thing. You know I used to worry about you working so hard, that you were closing doors for yourself. I used to think you'd be an old bachelor, but now..."

"Now you know I have someone who loves me, and that I'm happy."

A tear slipped down her cheek. "Yes."

Jamie pulled his hand away from David and reached for his mother. A phone rang, but Jamie and Susan were oblivious. David pulled the cell from his pocket.

"Hello."

"Yes, can I speak with David Lloyd please?" a female voice asked.

"This is David." Jamie looked back at him and he shrugged.

"Mr. Lloyd, I'm calling from Toronto General Hospital. We've had a young woman brought in, she's been beaten very badly. She has no ID, but your card was in the pocket of her coat. Do you think you could come down and identify her?"

"Is she dead?"

"No, but her injuries are severe. She's unconscious, and she may be for some time."

"All right. I'll be there in a few minutes."

"Thank you."

He returned the phone to his pocket. Jamie and his mother were both looking at him with worried expressions.

"What's going on?"

"I need to leave, I'm sorry. There's been an incident, and I need to get to the hospital."

"I'll come with you," Jamie said, starting to rise.

"No, please finish your dinner." He stood and pulled on his coat.

"Dave, please. This sounds serious. I'm coming with you."

"I apologize, Susan. I hope I can make it up to you another time?"

"Of course. I hope everything's all right."

She watched until David and Jamie were out of sight. In the car, Jamie let out a big sigh.

"Relieved?"

"Sort of? I mean I'm glad you two met, but I can see what an adjustment this is going to be, and she's the understanding one. I'm not looking forward to the talk with my dad."

"Don't worry until there's something to worry about."

Jamie switched gears. "Okay, so what's going on? Who's in the hospital?"

"I don't know for sure, but I have an idea."

Like all hospitals, parking was at a premium. It took almost fifteen minutes to find a spot remotely close to the emergency entrance. David and Jamie entered, heading to the triage nurse. After explaining the call he'd received, she called another employee to take them to the area where the girl was being treated.

A handful of people scurried about the bed, treating numerous injuries and monitoring various machines the girl's body had been hooked up to. One of the staff saw them approaching.

"Are you David?" the woman asked.

David looked at her, reading the nametag: Dr. Oosterman. "Yes, I am."

"Do you know this girl?"

David walked closer to the bed, and as soon as he saw the long sandy hair he knew it was Jenny. Yet the body before him was completely unrecognizable as the pretty young girl he'd met. It didn't seem as though one inch of her body had been spared from injury. Her face was swollen and mottled with bruises. Her arms and legs were held in blocks, obviously broken and waiting to be set. Dried blood coated her from head to toe.

"What happened to her?"

"Not sure. Looks like she'd been beaten with a bat or a pipe of some kind. Someone called 911 anonymously, saying they found her lying in an alleyway. She's lucky to be alive frankly. She has multiple fractures, internal bleeding. I think someone wanted this girl dead."

"How could anyone do something like this?" He couldn't pull his eyes away from the girl. He felt hot, his heart beating too fast.

"David, are you okay?" Jamie's voice was far away. He flashed back to the night of his own attack, remembering the pain and the sound of fists against his body and breaking bones.

"David." Jamie tugged at his arm.

"I'm fine."

"So do you know who she is?" the doctor asked again.

"Her name's Jenny, I don't know the last name. She's a prostitute."

The doctor jotted down her name. "Okay. There's a couple of officers waiting. Can you tell them what you know?"

"Sure. And can you put me down as a contact. I'd like to be kept informed of how she's doing."

"Sure." The doctor returned to her patient.

"David, what is going on here?"

"Something bad obviously." He started walking in the direction of the waiting room, frowning. They'd passed the officers on the way in.

"Is this the same something that got you punched in the face?"

"Yep."

"Then maybe it's time to turn this over to the police."

He stopped, grabbing both of Jamie's arms. "Not a chance. I need to find out what is going on, and I need to make sure Stella's okay."

"You have to consider that she might be dead. Look what happened to someone who simply might know something." His hand flicked in the direction of Jenny.

"I have considered it. If she is dead, I need to find her body, and I need to know why." He was shaking, his veins feeling as though they'd shrunk too small to allow his blood to flow normally.

"You're taking this much too personally."

"Someone has just beaten the shit out of that girl. That does not sit well with me."

"Me either. Whoever is responsible deserves to be behind bars. I just want you to calm down before you fly off the handle here and do something stupid."

Jamie was looking at him, concern bright in his eyes. David suddenly grabbed him and pulled him into a crushing embrace. He felt a sob in his throat threatening to escape. This incident was too close to his own experience. The sounds and smells of the hospital taunted him. When Jamie hugged him back, he relaxed.

"Sorry. You're right. I don't know what it is, but this case is stirring up a lot of stuff with me. I am taking it very personally."

"Let's go talk with the police and then get out of here."

David gave the officers what scant information he had about the girl, including her connections to Lee and the area where he suspected she kept a room. When there was nothing else to be done, he and Jamie headed back to the car.

They drove without talking, the falling snow and the car's wipers the only disturbance to the night's silence. Jamie touched his shoulder.

Without looking at him David said, "I saw Jeremy Black."

"What? When did this happen?"

"Last night."

"Is that where you got the bruise from?" He could feel Jamie's agitation like another presence in the vehicle, chaffing and heated.

"Not from Jeremy, but one of his buddies."

"Jesus, David. What the hell happened?"

"It's this case. He just happened to be there and got mixed up in an altercation with one of the people that I think knows what happened to Stella."

"I don't understand."

"Listen, I have an interview that I haven't gotten around to yet. You want to come with me?"

"Right now?"

"Yeah, this is one that I was only going to catch in the evening anyway, and a Saturday night is the perfect time."

"Where are we going?"

"To the Scarlet Letter."

Jamie smiled, then started laughing. "A strip club?" David nodded. "Well, you sure know how to show a guy a good time. First a beaten prostitute and now we're going to see the peelers. Whew-eee."

David also burst out laughing, breaking a tension that had silently wrapped itself about his chest. The throbbing, acing flow of adrenalin slowed, making him feel as though he could finally catch his breath. It was good to have Jamie at his side.

Now if Raven True was on stage that night they might actually get some answers.

The Scarlet Letter announced itself in giant, neon red script, alongside flashing images of well-endowed women in various stages of undress. Two bouncers of frightening proportions watched the door, letting in only those they deemed worthy. Cover was a shocking twenty dollars.

They entered the place, momentarily blinded by the sudden plunge into near-total darkness. A young woman in a top cut so low David was surprised they couldn't see her belly-button checked their coats for another five dollars each. She gave them a practiced but pleasant smile before handing them their tickets.

Through another set of doors they passed into a large, two-story room. On the main floor, an impressive stage took up a majority of the space, with a series of tables encircling the front half. All of these tables were occupied, the men's eyes glued to the action on the stage. A gorgeous young black woman with breasts that seemed to defy gravity was strutting her stuff to the captive audience.

Two bars flanked the stage where men and women were sitting or waiting for their drink orders. A small area was cleared in front of the stage for dancing, with more tables filling the back of the room along with access to washrooms. Several people were looking over the upstairs railing to the stage, and from what he could make out, there was at least one other bar on the second floor. The bass was so heavy it made David's hearing aid whine.

"So what's the plan?"

"Find the entrance to backstage and try and get back there."

"Right."

"I'm serious."

"Did you see those guys at the front door? I'm sure there will be several more of them guarding the dancers' changing area. How do you think you're going to get back there?"

He gave his partner a wink. "Charm."

"Lord help us."

"C'mon. Let's get a drink and find out if she's even working." David had filled Jamie in on Stella's connection to Raven True on the drive over.

They made their way to the closest bar and ordered a couple of beers. The bartender was wearing a black vest with nothing under it and a pair of hot pants. *Scarlet Letter* was stenciled across the rear of the shorts. She sauntered off on a pair of four-inch heels to get their drinks.

"Twelve dollars," she said after placing two bottles on the bar.

David handed her fifteen. "Is Raven dancing tonight?"

She leaned down, displaying her cleavage to maximum effect. "Yep. She always dances on Saturdays. Just so you know, she doesn't hook up with customers, but I do." She ran a finger along his arm and gave him a hungry look.

Jamie moved closer to David's side. "Sorry, I don't swing that way." He tossed his head in Jamie's direction.

She looked Jamie over, understanding coming across in her expression. "Well now. You're both a couple of cuties. I wouldn't mind doing you both."

"We appreciate the offer," David said, looking her right in the eye.

Jamie gave him a funny look, then smiled at the girl. "Yeah, we'll definitely keep you in mind."

"Well. I'm here all night if you change your mind, boys."

She left to take another order, giving Jamie a cheeky wink as she talked with the other customer. David took a swig of his beer.

"Like I said earlier, you have certainly shown me an interesting night tonight."

"And it's not over yet."

The bartender stopped in front of the men. "Raven should be on in about ten minutes."

David smiled, and she made a fanning motion with her hand.

"Jesus, you are such a flirt sometimes." Jamie was still smiling, but sounded annoyed.

"A good detective must use all the tools in his arsenal. Sometimes a little flirting gets me information."

"So you do this often?"

"Only when I need to."

"Maybe I need to come out on business with you more often."

"You're cute when you're jealous."

The bartender and an equally scantily-clad waitress were standing by the cash register, watching the men talking. Jamie leaned in and gave David a forceful, open-mouthed kiss, to which the bartender gave an enthusiastic thumbs up. The waitress giggled as she loaded up her tray then disappeared into the crowd.

They sipped at their drinks, commenting about the odd collection of customers moving about the club, everyone from just-of-legal-drinking-age boys to men and women who must have been collecting their old-age pension for many years. Like they said, sex sells, and with the price the club charged for drinks, it was selling well.

The music changed, and a round of applause worked its way through the crowd. Flashing red lights began crisscrossing the empty stage. The curtains opened, revealing a shadowy form crouched down. With a series of elaborate moves, the figure moved out onto the tongue of the stage, revealing a tall, well-proportioned woman, waist-length hair as black as night swaying behind her. The crowd knew her well, many chanting her name with drunken enthusiasm, "Raven! Raven!"

The woman put on an impressive show, David had to give her that. She was supremely flexible, bending and twisting in ways that, if he hadn't seen it with his own eyes, he would never have thought possible. The woman's moves, in addition to a strong, yet very feminine body, were a hard combination to beat. The stage, covered in bills, proved the dancer's popularity.

The music ended, and the spotlight moved to her now naked form. Her body glistened with some type of body spray, catching a rainbow of colour. She strutted off to thunderous applause and demands for more.

"That was hot," Jamie said.

"You sure you don't like girls?"

"You do not have to be straight to appreciate a gorgeous woman."

"True enough. Now for our part. We need to have a little chat with Miss True."

The two men started toward the door they'd determined was the access to backstage. A hulk of a man rested on a stool before the door. Raven's performance had stirred up the crowd, making the move to the entrance a slow and laborious process. The thunderous music returned, the pressure it put on David's ear so intense he thought about removing his hearing aid. A group of middle-aged men cut in front of them.

"Holy shit, you see the ass on that girl! Makes my wife look like a heifer."

"You wife is a heifer," one of the other men quipped.

"Oink, oink." They dispersed in a gale of drunken laughter.

The bouncer was now speaking with a much smaller man, his back turned to David and Jamie. The bouncer smiled then leaned back with a security card to open the door. As the other man passed through, he gave a quick look back into the bar. When David recognized him, he stopped short. Jamie bumped into him, the toe of his dress shoe gouging into David's heel.

"What?"

David turned back to Jamie. "I know that guy."

"The one who went in?"

"Yeah."

"So, who is he?"

"His name's Sasha. He's a ballet dancer and Stella's former boyfriend."

"So why is he here?"

"Good question." His appearance made David wonder about the truthfulness of their conversation. Maybe the fight between him and Stella had been worse than he'd let on, or had occurred more recently. And he'd denied knowing Raven.

The bouncer sat with his meaty arms crossed, scanning the crowd with wary eyes. David stopped before him, Jamie just behind, and gave him his best easy-going smile. He offered his hand, which the bouncer simply stared at.

"Okay. My name is David Lloyd. I'm a private investigator, and I really need to speak with one of your dancers. She may have some information about a missing girl."

"Who?" the man asked, face neutral.

"This missing girl?"

"No, the dancer."

"Raven True."

The bouncer gave a snort of laughter. "Nice try buddy. You know how many guys I get trying to access Raven. She don't socialize with customers."

David fished a card from his pocket and handed it over. The bouncer stared at it for a long time, then back to David's face. "What's his story?" the bouncer asked, indicating Jamie.

"He's my partner."

"Right. Give me a minute." He got up, entering the door behind him. There was a flash of light as it opened, then the firm click of a lock falling into place.

"That's what you call charm?" Jamie asked.

A few minutes later the bouncer returned. He did not look impressed with the news he'd been asked to deliver. "She said give her ten minutes and she'll meet you out back. There's a private parking lot behind the bar. Go out the front door, around the corner on Bryce. Another guy will be watching the lot. I'll give him the heads up you're coming."

"Thanks." They were starting back when the man grabbed David's arm.

"Don't try no shit with my girl. Got it?"

"Loud and clear."

Like salmon fighting their way upstream, they moved through the horde of people, passing by the bar where the flirty bartender gave them a wave goodbye. She blew David a kiss, which he pretended to catch. Jamie just shook his head. Near the door to the coat check hallway was a small grouping of tables. At one a young man sat alone, sipping a mixed drink of some kind. Christian.

"Oh shit," David said, turning his head.

"What?" Jamie looked around.

"Someone else I know. Stand beside me, so he doesn't see me."

Jamie did his best to block the taller man as the passed by the tables. David kept his eyes straight ahead, hoping for the best. When the doors swooshed closed behind them, he gave a sigh of relief.

"What is going on?" Jamie demanded as they waited for the girl to retrieve their coats.

"Jesus, that was Stella's brother in there." He looked back as though the man were right behind him.

"Why the hell would he be here?"

"I don't know. Something fucked up is definitely going on here, I just need to figure out what it is."

They ducked outside as soon as their coats were in hand. The wind snapped at their exposed skin, a bitter cold even more pronounced after the uncomfortable humidity inside the club. They turned the corner, seeing the booth at the mouth of the parking lot. A man watched as they approached. He stuck his head out of the small box of warmth where he sat.

"You David?"

"Yeah."

"Go ahead." He slammed the small window shut again, returning his attention to the monitor on the shelf before him.

The men walked past the mechanical arm in place to prevent unwarranted access into the lot. The spots were numbered, almost full with a series of well-kept vehicles. The back wall of the club and two other large buildings boxed in the space. The backdoor of the club opened, and a woman with long dark hair stepped out. She was dressed in tight jeans and a puffy, waist-length jacket. A large purse hung over one shoulder. She raised her hand, waving in their direction, and started walking over. Then all hell broke loose.

A shot rang out, impossibly loud in the near-silent lot. It came from behind, so close that David's left ear felt as though it had imploded. He grabbed at the side of his head, simultaneously turning to make sure Jamie was all right. The woman screamed, and a car engine roared to life. In the distance he could hear a man's voice yelling.

Another shot sounded, this one connecting with one of the parked cars to the men's right. A car alarm started wailing, shattered glass hitting the icy concrete. He and Jamie crouched by the end of another car. David looked out, trying to spot the shooter, but the bright lights in the parking lot made it difficult to see to the road. A car raced by, splashing wet snow in his direction. He looked up to see two figures inside, but no clear features of either person. The car hit the barrier at the street entrance and kept going.

Footsteps pounded against the ground, coming in David and Jamie's direction. The runner skidded to a stop, the man from the booth they could now see. He had a gun in one hand, and he was breathing hard. "You two okay?"

They both stood. "Yeah, we're good," David answered. "You get a look at the shooter?"

The man shook his head. "Not really. It was two guys. They came up the street just after you two, walked past the lot. Then I heard a shot. I came out as they fired the second time, and then they ran off. Musta had a car parked somewhere close by."

"Was that Raven who drove out of here?"

"Didn't see her face, but that was her car. Some dude was driving."

The night was so cold their collective breathing made a halo of smoky residue about their grouping. Jamie slipped his hand into David's.

"Fuck! I hit the alarm, so the cops should be here soon. C'mon inside, they going to want to talk to all of us."

They followed the man inside the back door while he moaned about the incident having to happen on his night. David wasn't too impressed either, considering he was most likely the intended target, but he kept his mouth shut. The bouncer from the stage door met them in a short hallway. If he'd seemed annoyed earlier, now he was furious. His face was so red, David worried he might be on the verge of a stroke.

"I knew there was something funny about you," he accused, stabbing a finger in David's direction.

"Hey now, I wasn't the one shooting." It was the only defense he had, since his presence had surely instigated the situation.

"Ian, calm down. Just go and keep an eye on the door. Act like nothing's going on."

The man hesitated, glaring in David's direction before doing what he was told. The man from the booth turned to them.

"Sorry, he's a hothead sometimes, but he really looks out for the girls. My name's Michael by the way."

"You know my name, and this is Jamie."

"C'mon back to Raven's room. No sense standing out here in the hall. We'll just be in the girls' way." As if on cue, a woman stepped out of one of the closed doors, dressed as a very naughty elf. She gave them a once over before heading on her way.

Michael led them to another closed door, using his pass card to access it. He pushed the door open and ushered them inside. "I'll wait at the booth. Don't touch nothing." He shut the door without an answer.

The room was small, one wall a dressing table lined with a frightening amount of cosmetics. Opposite this was an open closet stuffed with an array of exotic outfits. A series of wigs lined a shelf above the clothing. Leopard print carpeting covered the floor. A red velvet chaise had been pushed into one corner, the only other seat besides the chair before the dressing table.

A giant mirror filled the wall above the table, lined with lights bright enough to show every pore on one's face. Tucked into one corner of the mirror's frame was a small photo. It was the only personal item in the room, catching David's attention.

He pulled the photo out, remembering the face though he had never met the girl. He came to sit beside Jamie on the chaise, handing him the photo. "Meet Stella."

Jamie's gaze briefly flicked to David's face, then back down to the photo. It was a more recent photo than the one Stella's mother had shown David. Her face was thinner, but still as lovely. Something about her expression haunted David, pain and bitterness lingering in her eyes.

"She's a pretty girl," Jamie said.

"Yep, a shame to have gone through all she has."

Jamie passed the photo back. David couldn't look at her face without feeling like a failure.

"What do you think has happened?"

David shook his head. "I really don't know, but there is something fishy going on with the brother and the father. Then there's this stuff with Lee." Jamie made a face that indicated he didn't understand. "Sorry, that's Stella's dealer. He's who I was talking with last night when the fight broke out. He knows something, or he's involved somehow. I think he's the one responsible for Jenny's beating, even though what little she told me hasn't really been of any help."

A chorus of women's voices sounded outside the door.

"This is messed up, David. Someone took a shot at you tonight. You have to hand this over to the police." Jamie's voice had a pleading, anxious tone to it David had never heard before. It unsettled him, making him feel defensive and guilty.

"No way. I'm happy to share what I know, but I'm not ending my own investigation."

"Dave, please. I couldn't handle it if you were hurt, or worse. The last time, with the attack, God, it just about killed me."

The statement hung in the air, part admission, part warning.

"You can't ask this of me, Jamie."

"Oh, but you can demand that I have to come out to my family and colleagues, right? Are your feelings the only ones that matter in this relationship?" Jamie was shouting now, having risen from the chaise.

David's voice rose in kind. "Oh, that's nice. There's no comparison with the two. Fuck!" He desperately wanted to punch something.

A knock at the door startled them, cutting the argument short. Michael entered with two police officers. He seemed to pick up on the hostility. "These are the guys. I'm going to be back out at the booth if you need me again."

He closed the door behind him. The officers, both male, were now almost nose-to-nose with Jamie and David because of the confines of the space. David introduced them to the officers.

The taller one, an older man with a military-short haircut began. "So you were coming to meet with one of the dancers, is that correct?"

"Yes, a woman named Raven True."

The police officer made a note, a smirk tugging at his lips. "Have you met Miss True before?"

"No."

"What was the nature of your business with her tonight?"

"I'm a private detective, and Miss True is a friend of a young lady I am trying to locate. I simply wanted to ask her if she knew where the missing woman is."

The officers exchanged a look. "Why is this matter not being handled by the police?"

"The woman I'm looking for is a known drug addict with a history of running away and other questionable behaviour. The parents have filed a missing persons report, but they felt it wasn't being taken seriously. They're worried about their daughter and they want to find her."

"Do you have any idea who might have shot at you tonight?"

He gave Jamie a look, who shrugged. "I have no proof, but I have a feeling it's connected to a man named Leland Makowski. Either he did it or one of his associates."

"And by associates, you mean?"

"Drug dealers, criminals."

"He fits in with this investigation also?"

"Yes, he's been known to supply the woman in question with drugs and also shop her out as a prostitute."

"Anything else you want to add."

"Nope, that's it in a nutshell."

"We need your contact information and that should be about it." Jamie rattled off his number, and David handed over a business card.

"You know, your name sounds familiar," the smaller officer said, looking at the card.

"I used to be on the force." David felt his shoulders draw together, muscles tensing.

"I guess that's where I came across it."

The officers left, running into a small group of dancers eavesdropping at the door.

"Let's get out of here," David grumbled.

They walked to the car without talking. The wind blew the snow around, a heavy, wet precipitation that clung to their hair and clothing. The street in front of the club's parking lot had been cordoned off, the flashing lights of the police car catching in the falling whiteness. They drove by without comment.

"Your car's back at my place," David said, after ten minutes of torturous silence.

"Yeah, so I guess that's where we're headed then?"

David knew he'd been a jerk. Jamie was only worried about him, and there had already been distance between them. "I'm sorry I snapped at you."

"I'm just concerned."

"I know, and I appreciate it."

"Why don't I stay at your place tonight?"

"Is that what you want?" Jamie gave him an exasperated look. "Sorry. I'd love for you to stay."

They managed to get back to David's house without another argument, accident, or being shot at again. It was nice to have Jamie stay, even though David was restless and unable to fall asleep for many hours. Hearing his partner's even breathing and feeling his warmth beside him was a comfort beyond measure.

The loaded gun in the bedside table also gave David peace of mind.

At last, he curled alongside Jamie, gently resting his arm over him, and closed his eyes.

CHAPTER 10

David's eyes refused to open for several minutes after he woke the following morning. When they finally did, he rolled over to look at the time. It was early yet, the room draped in fading darkness. Jamie was still fast asleep. He slipped out of bed as quietly as he could, pulling on some pajama bottoms and an old sweatshirt. He went straight for the coffeemaker when he reached the first floor.

As it began to perk, the teasing aroma filling the kitchen, David sat at the table. He had pulled a pad and pen from one of the drawers and set about writing down all the details of the night that he could remember. Then with a cup of coffee in hand, he retrieved his notes from the meeting with Janice and Sinclair. With everything fresh in his mind, he knew he had to touch base with Marjory Barrowman to try and sort out fact from embellishment. Too many conflicting stories had been told at this point, muddying the waters and possibly prolonging access to the truth about Stella's disappearance.

It was only eight thirty, not exactly a polite time to be calling anyone on a Sunday morning, but David needed answers. He dialed the Barrowman's home number, hoping for the best.

After several rings the phone was answered. "Hello?" The female who answered didn't sound as though her sleep had been disturbed.

"Hello. May I speak with Marjory?"

"This is."

"Hello. This is David Lloyd calling. Please excuse the early hour, but it's the first spare moment I've had in weeks."

"It's no bother, David. To be honest I haven't been sleeping all that well, and I've been up for a few hours already."

"Is it possible for us to get together some time today?"

"Of course. Your office?"

"That sounds good. Let's say one o'clock?"

"I assume you haven't found her yet?"

"Not yet, but I'm definitely ruffling some feathers. I think something will come to light soon."

"Well, that's good news. See you soon."

"Bye."

He'd picked up a few presents for his family during an afternoon of errands, so he set about getting them wrapped and under the tree. Christmas was fast approaching. It would be nice to have Stella's case resolved before then, for the ease of mind of all the affected parties. If she were alive still, David imagined that Christmas with her loved ones would be a welcome experience. He wondered, while tidying up the mess of paper, if Jamie would like to invite his family over for the get-together he'd planned. Maybe it was still too soon.

A quick scan of the fridge let David know he didn't have much in the way of groceries. He ran out to one of the twenty-four-hour stores and stocked up. He'd surprise Jamie with a big breakfast, something he couldn't remember doing in recent months. The shower was running when he returned.

David quickly emptied the bags, then set about making a veggie omelette with cheese, Jamie's favourite. He also cooked up a mess of bacon, whole-wheat toast, and brewed some fresh coffee. A bowl of washed, cut strawberries was on the table when Jamie entered the kitchen. David turned from the stove, smiling when he found Jamie dressed in a pair of his sweatpants and a t-shirt from a concert he'd attended as a teenager.

"Nice," he commented, and kissed him on the cheek.

"It was this or the suit."

"Seriously, I like it. Take a seat and I'll get you a coffee."

Jamie did he was told, an amused expression on his face. He took a few sips of his coffee before asking, "What's all this for?"

"I just wanted to do something nice for you. Is that a crime?"

"Nope. It's just a surprise after the tension between us."

"We're working on that right? No need to make things harder than they need to be."

"Okay."

David brought the plates over to the table. They ate and sipped coffee, talking about nothing serious. The morning slipped closer to lunch, and David knew he'd better start getting ready for his meeting with Marjory.

"Listen, I was wondering if you wanted to ask your family to come over for a Christmas get-together? I've planned something with my family, and I thought I'd ask a couple of friends, maybe Dana and her boyfriend."

He could see Jamie bristle, and it wasn't at the mention of David's ex-wife. "I don't know about that. Let's see how it goes with my dad first, okay?"

"Sure. So what's the plan there?"

"I'm not sure. We bailed out so fast last night, I didn't get a chance to ask my mom. I'll give her a call this afternoon."

"If you need support, just let me know."

"Yep. I guess the next obstacle is work." He sighed.

"Just take it at the pace you need to. I'm not expecting you to go in there waving a pride flag or anything."

Jamie smirked. "Yeah, that would go over well with all the uptight, old-school lawyers at the Ministry. But I'm not going to outright lie anymore, I promise you that. If a situation comes up where I can mention you, or say something to let on the truth about me, I will."

"Maybe someday soon, I can come take you out for lunch?"

"Sure. Soon."

"'Kay, well I'd better clean up. I need to get down to the office. I'm going to meet with Marjory Barrowman and try and clear the air. I think she hasn't been entirely honest with me."

"Sure. I have some work to prepare for court this week anyway. I'll help you clean up and then head home."

They bustled about in comfort, like many long-term couples do, and had the kitchen cleaned up in a matter of minutes. Jamie retrieved his clothes from the night before. He promised to call later in the evening, after he'd had the chance to speak with his mother.

The streets had been cleared by the time David left for his office. He managed to find a spot on the next block and was only mildly wet by the time he reached the front door of his building. The snowfall was sparse but heavy, more water than ice. It dropped to the slushy sidewalks with audible plops.

On the weekends his building was all but deserted. Most offices were occupied by accountants, lawyers, and therapists, or other professionals who didn't work outside of a Monday-Friday time frame. He barely had his coat off when the front door buzzer sounded, another indicator that the meeting was occurring at an off time.

The knock sounded a few moments later. He started to the door, then was struck by a sudden panic that it might not be Marjory waiting on the other side. He had his gun with him, under the black zip-up hoodie he wore. His heart gave a painful slam as the knock sounded again.

"Marjory?" he called out.

"Yes," she answered, making David feel foolish.

He opened the door, locking it behind her. She looked at him strangely as she handed over her coat.

"Everything all right, David?"

"Please take a seat." He went to his own, suddenly unsure how to begin.

"You seem a bit jumpy."

"I am actually. Someone took a couple of shots at me last night."

The startled look that came over Marjory's face couldn't have been faked, her eyes about leapt from their sockets. "What are you talking about?"

"Well, I was out last night, interviewing some of your daughter's associates, and two shots were fired at me. Whether someone actually wanted me dead or was just trying to scare me I can't be certain, but like I said on the phone, someone is obviously worried that I'm going to expose them."

"What does this have to do with Stella? I mean, I understood she ran with a rough crowd, what with the drugs and everything, but shooting at people?"

"I have to say, Mrs. Barrowman, that this case has become much more complicated and involved than I initially thought. I think that you might have been holding back on me."

"What do you mean?" Her shock turned defensive.

"Well, things about your husband and son for one, also this business with accusing Marcus James of raping her."

"What things about George and Christian are you referring to?" Her lip trembled.

"I've heard from numerous sources that your husband has had some interactions that have hurt and embarrassed your family, and others for that matter."

"I don't know what you mean."

"I think you do. There was this affair with Elaine's mother for one, which apparently wasn't the first time something like that had happened."

"Those are lies. People with money and authority are always targets for gossip and blackmail. That woman was a nut, the daughter too for that matter."

David played along. "Why do you say that?"

"She came to me and tried to tell me that she and George were having an affair. I didn't believe her. I confronted George with her, and he denied it. She had no proof at all. Nothing. And this was after we had already paid for Elaine to attend a summer training session with the Ballet Carlisle. Can you imagine the nerve of that woman?" Her face had become an alarming shade of red, though her words were eerily soft, as though she had no force of belief to put behind them.

"What about Elaine? You say she had issues also?"

"Well, if what her mother had done wasn't bad enough, she tried to say she'd slept with George too. A sixteen-year-old girl. It was disgusting."

"Yet, didn't Stella do something similar? I mean she accused Marcus of raping her."

"Stella is sick! She couldn't be blamed for that."

"You honestly believe that your husband is entirely innocent? Hasn't there been talk of other affairs and all kinds of wild behaviour when he's off on business trips?"

"Is this what you brought me here to discuss? I thought I was paying you to find my daughter, not to try and smear my family's name."

"I am looking for your daughter, but I have to wonder if this family drama is at least a part of what's keeping Stella away. And you haven't even asked me about Christian yet."

"What about Christian?"

"I met with him the other night, had a nice chat. Then I followed him, and do you know where he went?"

"Where?" She didn't meet his gaze.

"He went to a rather nasty part of town and got out of his car to talk with a group of prostitutes. I believe he picked one of them up to use their services."

"That's awful. My son would never do anything like that. He's a good man. He helps people."

Maybe she was right. He hadn't actually seen him leave with one of the prostitutes after all. "Did you know your daughter worked as a stripper?"

Her eyes welled up with tears. It took a few moments before she could speak. "No, I didn't know that, but it doesn't surprise me."

"So you don't know anyone named Raven True?"

"No, I don't. Is this one of Stella's friends?"

"She's also a stripper. That's who I was going to see last night when someone shot at me."

Marjory broke down. All traces of the dignified, controlled woman vanished, and she became a mother terrified for her daughter's well-being. "I just want to bring Stella home. I don't care what she's done."

"What about what's been done to her? Are you prepared to deal with that?"

"Of course I am. I have always tried to help her."

"What if that means opening your eyes to things that might be happening in your own home? Can you put Stella's safety and health above everything else?"

She opened her purse, rummaging through the contents. David pushed a box of tissue across the desk. She grabbed several and wiped her face. "I love my daughter."

"I don't doubt that. But that's not what I'm asking."

"Just find her, and whatever the truth turns out to be I'll deal with it."

She pulled a check from her bag and handed it to David

with a shaky hand. "I'm sure I owe you more in fees by now."

"Thanks."

They arranged for another meeting the following Friday, if nothing turned up in the meantime. David knew that she'd been aware of her husband's antics all along but had turned a blind eye. Whether she understood the depth to which his behaviour had affected Stella was another matter. It could very well be that this one aspect of the case had nothing to do with Stella's disappearance. Elaine, Christian, and Sasha had all lied or kept information from him also.

David noticed then that his message light was blinking. He played back the calls, finding a message from Dr. Garfield, who had finally secured permission to pass along the contact information of Stella's runaway buddy from rehab, and an even more surprising message from Raven.

"David, it's…Raven. I'm sorry about what happened tonight. There's so much you don't understand. I want to talk with you."

She left a number and asked for David to call her as soon as possible. David hung up and dialed the number, only to get voicemail. He left a message to call him on his cell phone.

Now what? Dr. Garfield would not be available on a Sunday; he'd have to call the clinic in the morning. Feeling antsy and frustrated he locked up the office and returned to his car. He ended up at the gym, where he ran ten kilometres on the treadmill, burning off as much tension as calories. After a relaxing session in the sauna, he headed to the hospital.

He'd decided while in the midst of his run to check in on Jenny and see what the status of her condition was. Last night had been such a shock that he'd forgotten he had a couple of people he was friendly with there who might slip him more information about the girl than the attending staff would be willing to give. It wouldn't hurt to check and see if Stella had been treated there after her accident.

After several minutes of difficulty in trying to locate the girl, it was established that Jenny (no last name) had been moved to the intensive care unit. Once there David learned that she was in a medically induced coma in hopes of relieving swelling of the brain. Her multiple injuries required her to be in an almost complete body cast. He was allowed to look in on her briefly. Her face was still swollen, the bruising so pronounced her skin had taken on the colour of a ripe plum. The sight of her still body made David's stomach turn. Anger rattled through him, a surge so powerful his bones ached.

He couldn't stop the image of Stella in a similar condition from appearing in his mind. The depths of depravity that humans would sink to never failed to amaze him. What in the world could be worth hurting another human being so badly?

He wandered through a series of hallways in search of a familiar face. One of the nurses he knew was off on vacation to Florida, and another was home with the flu. He took his chances that a secretary he'd befriended when she'd been an emergency room clerk was in her office. She now assisted the director of patient records in the hospital, and was known to put in more than her regular hours. The sight of her open door made him smile.

"Knock, knock," he said, looking in from the doorway.

Jean Aronsen sat at her desk, typing faster than anyone should be able to. She looked up and grinned.

"Well, what a nice surprise. Come in."

"Thanks. Hope I'm not bothering you?"

"Nope, just catching up on some minutes. Boring as hell, so I appreciate the distraction. I'll guess this isn't a social visit?"

"It never is with me."

"You work too hard."

"That's the pot calling the kettle back."

"All right, agreed. We both have no life but work. So what can I do for you?"

"I'm wondering if you might be able to see if there's been any info about a woman that was brought in last night. She's in ICU, the only name they have is Jenny."

"Funny, I just pulled a fax off the machine, haven't even updated the system yet. The police ran her prints and came back with a name." She looked through some papers on her desk before finding the one she needed. "Jennifer Whitestone. Twenty years old. Born in Halifax. I guess they're trying to track down her mother."

"Anything else?"

"No, that's it on short notice."

"Can you check someone else for me?"

"Don't give me the puppy dog eyes, boy. You know I'd do it anyway."

Jean was old enough to be his mother, but she loved to be flirted with. "Stella Barrowman. She had an accident about nine years ago. Just wondering if she was brought here?"

"I suppose you have permission to request this information," she asked as her fingers flew across the keyboard.

"I have been hired by the mother to find the girl."

She shushed him, looking over the information on the screen. "I can't pull the file for you right now, it's down in archives. I will share with you what I see here. She was brought in by ambulance after being hit by a car. She had a broken knee and three ribs, and a concussion. She stayed in the hospital for two days and then was released to her parents. She had a surgery about four months later, and physiotherapy. Hmm, that's odd."

"What?"

"Well there's a note that social work was called in to speak with the girl, but no report. Can't tell if she was actually seen or not."

"So that's not standard I take it?"

"No, and with a child I could only see social work being called if there was suspicion of some kind of abuse."

"Think you can find out more about it for me?"

"I'll do what I can."

"Sweet. I owe you lunch."

"You owe me several lunches by now, darling. Some day I may actually collect."

He fished a card out and handed it to her. "Please call me as soon as you know anything. You can get me on my cell anytime."

"This a serious one?"

"About as serious as they come, you know, before you end on a steel table."

"Got it." She gave him a little once over. "You look good. Things going all right?"

"Yep. Can't complain."

"You and Jamie still an item?"

"We are. Almost five years now."

"Good to hear. I'll be in touch soon."

David left, the sound of furious typing following him out into the hall. His stomach grumbled, reminding him he'd missed lunch.

He hit a fast-food drive-through on the way home and ate while watching reruns of *Paranormal State*. Jamie called, letting him know that his mother had decided to talk with his father on her own. He promised to give an update when he had one.

He went to bed early, asleep almost as soon as his head touched the pillow.

CHAPTER 11

As soon as nine o'clock rolled around the next morning, David called the Davenport Clinic. He'd been at the office for an hour already, his brain more in need of answers than sleep. To his surprise, he was put right through.

"Dr. Garfield."

"Hello, Dr. Garfield, it's David Lloyd returning your call."

"Oh yes, David, right. One moment, I have the information written down." He could hear papers being shuffled about. "Yes, here we go. The patient's name is Marcy Anderson. She's married now, her maiden name was Miller. Anyway, she'd agreed to speak with you. Here's her information." He rattled off the number and an address in a nicer, suburban area of the city.

"Do you have a moment to answer a few more questions?"

"I have about fifteen minutes. Then I have a patient coming in."

"I wonder if Stella ever spoke to you about issues with her father. I know we covered this when I came in to see you, but I've learned quite a bit about the family since then, and it doesn't quite jibe with the information you provided me with."

"Can you be more specific?"

"I can be blunt if you'd prefer. Mr. Barrowman has had numerous extramarital affairs, of which Stella was aware. On at least one occasion, the affair was with the mother of one of her friends. Did she ever speak to you about this?"

Dr. Garfield cleared his throat. "No, she did not speak to me about this, but it would explain her attitude toward her father and perhaps her feelings toward men in general."

"And you weren't aware of any of this independently?"

"No one ever made such statements to me directly, as in not Mr. Barrowman himself, or Stella's mother or brother. I have heard rumors."

"Rumors? And you didn't think such things should be shared with me?"

"This is information that I can't verify, David. If it was untrue then I would be no better than the people spreading the stories in the first place."

David's frustration was so high, he wouldn't have been surprised to find steam shooting from his ears. "What about Christian? Do you think this attitude toward women has been passed down to him?"

"Well, I really can't say. I only spoke with the young man on a few occasions, and as I said, nothing of the sort was ever brought up."

"All right, in your medical opinion, would it be likely that acceptance of such behaviour could be passed from father to son, if the son had knowledge of these activities?"

"A parent's behaviour, attitude, and morality would always have a significant impact on a child. Many take on the same beliefs as their parents, though sometimes a child can go in the complete opposite direction."

"And would a mother turning a blind eye to such behaviour feel like permission to a child? Could it be perceived in such a way?"

"It could, and depending on how young an age such feelings were ingrained, it could have a long-standing impact on the person."

"Did you know about the accusation of rape Stella made against her dance instructor?"

"Yes, of course. An unfortunate circumstance of course, but these things sometimes happen with people with Stella's kind of emotional issues. She retracted her statement and seemed remorseful about it."

"You didn't think anything more of it? I mean that perhaps someone had hurt her, just not who she accused?"

"She never said any such thing to me. And I remained

treating her for many months after the incident. She did admit to being promiscuous. It could have been a matter of guilt for her actions and needing someone to blame. If she'd said anything that made me suspect an assault, I would have reported it to the authorities."

David absorbed that nugget of insight, feeling something wasn't quite right. "All right, thank you Doctor. If you think of anything else, please call me."

He hung up the phone. While swiveling back and forth on his chair, David tried to force the pieces of the puzzle into a coherent picture. Had Stella witnessed her father in some kind of encounter with another woman, causing a girl already in a fragile emotional state to become so hysterical that she would blindly run out into traffic?

Something had happened, maybe a series of things, which would eventually culminate in the emotional and physical deterioration of one young woman. Like peeling an onion, David seemed to be stripping back years of betrayal and abuse, each contributor desperate to hide their participation, no matter how large or small their specific role had been. In a way, the investigation was doing the same to him. Like Stella, he'd been hiding his pain. His weapon of avoidance being work, hers drugs, yet neither one could contain the pain forever.

He tried Raven's number again, getting voicemail for the second time. He left another message. He tried Marcy Anderson, who also wasn't answering. He left both his cell and office number, stressing how important it was that she get back to him. Whether that was true he didn't know yet, but it certainly wouldn't hurt to talk with the woman.

A few items left over from previous cases took up the remaining hours of the morning. Once the work was completed his time was officially freed up to focus on Stella's case. As such he deposited the check from Marjory, making a mental note to work on an itemized report of all the time he'd spent on the case and all the expenses he'd incurred so far.

While on his way back to his office he passed the turnoff for the street where Elaine's dance studio was located. On impulse he doubled back. As he drove down the street, Elaine herself came out of the front door. He continued past, pulling along the sidewalk at a position where he could still clearly see the building. She got in her car and pulled out onto the road, driving right past him. He waited a few moments then followed.

She drove through a twisted maze of streets, before finally stopping in an area of the city that David had never been to. It was just before the edge of the city limits, where construction was still underway on a series of elaborate, and very expensive, condominiums. Two units were complete, and this was where Elaine turned in. She pulled into the visitors parking and got out. David could see her from the road, where he waited about a hundred yards from the entrance to the lot. She approached a parked car, getting into the passenger side.

David had a small set of binoculars in the glove box, which he used to read the license plate of the parked car. He'd run it by Jimmy later, along with the address. Less than five minutes later she got out, a small package in her hand, and returned to her own car. The other car also pulled out, heading in the opposite direction. The windows of the car were tinted so darkly it was impossible to see who was at the wheel.

As he started to pull out from the curb his phone rang. He didn't recognize the number, but considering the numbers of calls he was waiting for, it was in his best interest to answer. When he identified the owner of the car he'd decide the next steps with Elaine.

"Hello."

"Hi, can I speak with David please?"

It was as young woman, a voice David didn't think he'd heard before. "This is David."

"Hi David, it's Marcy Anderson. Sorry I missed you earlier, I was taking my son to nursery school and then I ran a few errands."

"No worries. Thanks for getting back to me so quickly."

"You said it was important. And Dr. Garfield has already let me know about what's going on with Stella."

"Is there any chance we can chat right now? I can meet you wherever you like."

"Sure. You can come by my place."

"Great, can you tell me the address again? I'm not at the office right now."

She relayed the information, and he pulled away from the curb. Twenty minutes later he pulled up in front of a nice, two-story brick home. The driveway was neatly shovelled, as were the walk and front steps. He pressed the bell, waiting.

The door opened, revealing an attractive young woman with honey-coloured hair. Dressed in the yoga-pants, long-sleeved t-shirt style of many modern young mothers, she gave off the picture of contented middle-class. She ushered him in with a smile.

"I'm Marcy," she said and offered her hand.

"David." He handed her a card after shaking her hand, which she dutifully read.

"Come back to the kitchen. I'm working on some cupcakes for Simon's school."

"Is Simon your son?"

"Yes." She led him down a short hallway, past an earth-tone decorated family room, and a small dining room crowded with too much furniture. The set looked like something either she or her husband had inherited from a grandparent, out of sync with the style of the rest of the house. Framed pictures of family and friends lined the walls.

The counters of the kitchen were covered with several bowls of icing and all types of decorating materials. Several dozen cupcakes were cooling on stainless steel racks.

"Have a seat at the table. Hope you don't mind if I work while we chat?"

"No, go ahead." David took off his coat, pulling his notepad from the pocket. "So you met Stella at the Davenport Clinic?"

"Yes, that's right. We were both seventeen. Stella was there for her drug and mental health issues. I had severe depression. Started as soon as I hit adolescence. I was a mess, I'll tell you that. I didn't eat or sleep, I felt like the whole world was against me." Her hand hesitated over the cupcake she was icing.

David didn't want to dwell on the woman's problems. "And you and Stella became friends?"

"Right from the get go. We had rooms next door to each

other and shared some group activities. I'd never met anyone like her before. She was so beautiful and so defiant. I was a mouse, an empty shell, but she saw something in me."

"I understand that the two of you ran away together."

Emotion flickered across her face, something dark. "Yes, we did. A stupid move obviously, as neither one of us was well, but we were kids." Again her busy hands came to a standstill. She licked her lips and sighed. "Listen, there is stuff from my past I'm not proud of, things I've worked very hard to overcome. My husband doesn't know about this stuff, and I'd like to keep it that way."

"Of course, anything we discuss is between you and me."

She came around and sat at the table with him. "Stella and I had a thing. I don't know what else you'd call it."

"You mean like a sexual thing?"

"Yes and no. It was weird, neither one of us had ever been with another girl before, and I don't consider myself a lesbian or bisexual or whatever. It was a comfort, a connection that we shared." Her tense body language and lack of eye contact made it clear how uncomfortable she was in discussing the relationship. "I don't know if I can make you understand."

"It's not for me to understand, that was something private between the two of you."

"We had a bond. We'd both been...abused by people close to us. I know I felt like she was the only one who could really understand how I felt, because she'd been through it too."

Bingo. "Did she tell you who it was?"

"No, she never did. I asked her a few times, and she always said it wasn't worth getting into it because no one would believe her anyway. I told her I believed her, but that only seemed to make her more sad."

Marcy fiddled with her hands on the table top. Her face was that strange mixture of embarrassment and relief that many people wear when talking about painful times in their life. David imagined he'd had a similar look on his face during sessions with his counsellor, or even during the many heart-to-heart conversations he'd had with his grandmother over the past few years.

"Did you ever suspect anyone?"

"No, but I often wondered about it."

"Did she talk with you about her relationship with her family?"

"Yes. She loved her mother a lot, but I don't think she thought her mother could protect her. She said she wasn't close to her dad and brother. I guess her dad worked a lot and was often away from home. Her brother was older and away at university then." Another one who didn't see Christian as having any bearing on Stella's disappearance. *Maybe I am off track with him.*

"Did she talk about Sasha?"

"Oh, yes. She was crazy about that guy. She didn't think she was good enough for him."

"Why is that?"

She shrugged. "She thought she was damaged goods. I get where she was coming from. I mean I still have moments where I feel like I don't belong here." She indicated the house about her with a sweep of her hand. "I was lucky 'cause I didn't have the drug issues on top of everything else. I was such an introvert, I wouldn't have had the courage to ask anyone to get them for me. You know it's weird, but in a lot of ways Stella was the reason I finally had the courage to admit what had happened to me and to deal with it."

"Did you stay in touch after you left the clinic?"

"Yeah, we used to hang out sometimes. But the better my life seemed to get, the worse hers became. I did summer school, got my high school diploma. I went to college and did an Admin Assistant course. I got a job in an injury rehab office where I met my husband. We got married, and now I have a beautiful little boy. Stella just got deeper into the drug scene, hanging around some real lowlifes. I tried to help, I really did, but once the baby came..." Her words trailed off and she stared at her fidgety hands.

"You have nothing to feel bad about, Marcy. Stella's problems obviously ran very deep. Others have tried to help her, including professionals, with the same results."

"Do you think she's dead?" she asked, eyes brimming with tears.

"It's a possibility. Certainly one I have to consider."

"I really hope she's not. I'd like to see her again."

"Is there anyone you can think of that might help me?"

"Besides Sasha, I don't think she had any other real friends. She did get really close with Roberta, the lady who teaches art there. I know she told me that Roberta let her call sometimes. Have you talked with her?"

"Yeah, I have, but it can't hurt to try again."

"I'm sorry, I haven't been any help, have I?"

"Actually you've been a big help. I was sure that something was going on with Stella besides the obvious problems. Even if you don't have a name, you've definitely filled in some of the blanks. Do you know if she ever told Dr. Garfield about any of this?"

"No. She didn't want anyone to know. She just told him what she thought he wanted to hear."

Well, that meant Dr. Garfield had been telling the truth, one of the few of all the people who'd been interviewed on the case.

"I'm glad things turned out well for you."

"They did. I'm lucky, I know that. My mom was a rock. She fought for me, made sure the person who hurt me paid for it. I wouldn't have survived without her. Stella told me she'd believe me and that she'd help. She was right, and I'll never forget it."

"Okay, look, I don't want to take up any more of your time. You obviously have things to do."

"Will you let me know if you find her?" Her eyes searched his face, sad and guilty.

"Of course. I'm sure she'll need all the friendly faces she can find."

She walked him to the door, waving as he followed the walk back to his car. It struck him how profoundly different things could have been for Stella if someone had known the truth, and helped her through the aftermath of letting such a truth come to light.

He took another swing by the dance studio, finding the lot empty. Whatever errand Elaine had been on, she wasn't finished yet. Back at the office, David tried Raven's number, slamming the phone down after getting her voicemail once again. He decided to try a different avenue.

He dialled a number, about to give up after several rings. "Hello," a male voice said, slightly breathless.

"Sasha?"

"Yes. Who's this?"

"It's David. I'm hoping you can help me out with something."

"What's that?" His voice became tight, guarded.

"Can you help me connect with Raven True? She's left me a message, but I can't get through to her even though I've tried several times."

"Why do you think I can help you?"

"Because I saw you with her last night." There was a muffled scraping on the other end, and he was sure that Sasha had said something rude. "What is going on here, man? I'm trying to help."

"The best thing you can do is back off now. I mean someone shot at you last night. Do you want that to happen to Stella?"

"Do you know where she is?"

"Leave me out of this."

"Sasha? Sasha?" It was no use, he'd hung up.

Now David let out a string of profanity which made him feel better for about thirty seconds. *Think!* He pulled his notepad out, flipping through until he found the license plate and address he'd written down. He put a call through to Jimmy, catching the guy on the way out. He took down the information and promised to run it as soon as he could. He let David know that Leland Makowski was on his radar, and if anything turned up he'd pass it on.

His phone rang and he just about fell off his chair. It took two swipes at the receiver before he could get the thing to connect with his hand properly. "David Lloyd."

"Hi David, it's Sheila. I can't talk long, but I wanted to let you know that Christian was in earlier and he didn't look pleased."

"Well that's interesting. Thanks for the tip."

"George will be here for at least another hour."

"Right. On my way."

Good thing he got paid for mileage, especially after a day like the one he'd had. Traffic was relatively light, no accidents or roads closed despite the weather. He pulled into the lot of George

Barrowman's building, where Sheila had thoughtfully sent a pass down to the attendant to let him through. He remembered his way, this time feeling an anger tightening about his heart like a vise as he approached the man's office. If he had any part in his daughter's abuse, then the man was a monster. David wasn't certain he could keep it together if something really terrible came out of the conversation he was about to have.

Sheila nodded as he entered the office. He followed as she knocked at the interior door. "Your appointment," she said, returning to her desk.

David entered George's personal space before he even had a chance to respond to his secretary. He blanched when he saw whom his appointment was with.

"Mr. Lloyd, I'm surprised to see you again so soon. Aren't you supposed to be out looking for my daughter?"

"Well, I might have more success finding the girl if people would stop lying to me."

That caught his attention. "Surely you're not referring to me. If I had any idea where you could find my daughter, I'd tell you."

"Just like you told me about the affair with Elaine Gemmet's mother?"

"Excuse me?" He looked unnerved, lips pulling in a tight line.

"Don't try and deny it. I've heard about it from a few different places now. That in addition to your other escapades, shall we call them?"

"How dare you come in here and speak to me like this!" The man stood, veins in his neck standing out like strips of cord under his ruddy skin.

"Speak to you like what? The truth? While you were running around screwing anything you could get your hands on, did you once think about what it was doing to your daughter? Or your wife and son for that matter?"

"Get out of here. I'm not listening to this."

"It seems in addition to messing up your emotionally fragile daughter, you've also set the bar for your son. Did you know Christian likes to go out cruising for hookers? Is that something you taught him?"

"That's enough."

"Or are your urges so bad, you couldn't keep your hands to yourself, even in your own gene pool?"

The colour drained from his face, making him age a decade in the blink of an eye. "Are you accusing me of molesting my own daughter?"

David didn't respond.

"I have never heard anything so disgusting in my life. I love my daughter. Despite all her problems and all the crap she's put my family through, I love her. I would never do such a thing."

"Why was Christian here earlier?"

"Perhaps he's worried about just the type of thing that's happening right now. We want Stella back, but we don't need to have our names smeared in the process. Have you brought these accusations of yours to my wife yet?"

"I've let her know some of the things I've been told, including the information about your affairs. I happened to see Christian's actions with my own eyes."

"Whatever I may or may not have done in the past it has nothing to do with Stella being missing now."

"And your son?"

"I will speak with Christian."

"Do you think he knows something?"

George Barrowman frowned, fingers gripped around the edge of his desk. "Of course not. He's barely had any contact with his sister in years. He's busy working, she's been off doing God knows what. You really have your wires crossed here." He put a lot of effort into his performance, but he wasn't quite selling it.

"We'll see."

The cool persona came back. "You better watch what you're getting yourself into. Crossing the wrong person can have serious consequences."

"Are you threatening me?"

"No, simply offering some advice. Now I suggest you leave my office. I have more important things to do than sit here and be insulted."

David didn't see the point of asking more questions, not that George had answered any. He closed the door behind him. Sheila looked up, giving a knowing look. He nodded his thanks as he passed her desk.

He sat in his car, seething with anger. His skin was uncomfortable, his scalp tight and itchy. He decided he needed food, and a long drive to clear his head. An hour later, with the greasy proceeds of his meal slowly digesting in his stomach, he decided on a desperate course of action. A quick turn-around had him heading in the direction of downtown, specifically to the area where he'd run into Jenny the night he'd tailed Christian. Her presence there that night had convinced David she lived nearby, like many of the other working girls did.

He visited motel after sleazy motel before hitting pay dirt. The Highland was nothing more than a long strip of rooms and a cigarette-butt littered parking lot. The flashing neon advertised rooms for reasonable rates, but David suspected that wouldn't be the only thing you'd encounter during a night spent at such an establishment. Crabs, hepatitis, and all manner of transmittable infections undoubtedly kept permanent residence, waiting for fresh, warm hosts.

The woman minding the front desk had a two-inch-wide strip of grey along the part in her otherwise dull brown hair, which could be seen from the door. Her skin was yellow and pockmarked, saggy around her mouth and chin. She was easily two hundred pounds, having poured herself into a hot pink tracksuit that accentuated every gelatinous roll. Despite the coolness of the lobby interior, large rings of sweat stained the underarms of her top.

David strode over to the desk, only to discover the woman's smell matched her appearance. Bile crept up the back of his throat, but he forced himself to keep smiling. His attentive stare unnerved the woman. She ran her fat, stubby fingers through her hair, blinking her eyes.

"Hello there, I'm wondering if you might be able to help me?" It was the same spiel he'd tried at five such places already.

"Depends what you need." She gave a wide grin in return, showing the dark hole where her two front teeth should have been.

It was probably a lost cause considering he didn't have a last name or even a picture, but his options in finding Stella were rapidly vanishing. "I'm looking for a girl who might be renting a room here. Her name is Jenny. She has long blonde hair, she's very thin, um…"

"I think I know who ya mean," the woman cut in.

"You do?"

"Yeah, but I ain't seen her for a few days now. Actually I cleaned out her room earlier cause she was only paid up till Saturday."

"What did you do with her stuff?"

"There was a suitcase in there, so I just threw everything in it. If you want it, it's yours. Just a pain for me to throw out anyway."

"Great, yeah I'll take it off your hands."

With some effort she got to her feet and waddled to a room out of David's line of sight. She brought the battered case around to David's side of the desk on her return. With her fingers still wrapped about the handle she stopped, looking at him expectantly.

"Oh, right." He fished a twenty from his wallet. "Thank you."

She looked at the bill, then snatched it from his hand. "Uh-huh."

"Listen do you know a woman named Stella? She's another working girl."

"Yeah, sure. Haven't seen her for a long time though. Few months anyway. Used to see her and Jenny together some."

"Anyone else they used to be seen with?"

"Why?"

"Stella's missing. Her family's concerned about what might have happened to her."

Her face screwed up as though the thought process took a tremendous amount of effort. "Well, there was that guy with the nice car and some of his buddies. I guess he was their pimp, or whatever the hookers call those guys nowadays. Think his name is Lee. He's a real dick, always parking where he's not s'pose to and cussing out the girls right in front of the motel. Not good for business you know?"

"I guess not."

"You know he's been in a few times too, asking 'bout her. Seems real pissed that she's took off."

"You ever talk to Stella one on one?"

"Not really. Lee paid the bill. I might say a hello once in a while or take a message every now and again."

Messages? "You ever take a message from anyone named Sasha or Raven?"

She shook her head. It had been worth a try.

"No one else stand out to you? Like any customer ever get rough with her or anything like that?"

"Look, unless they've stiffed the bill or they're doing some damage to their room, I try and mind my own business."

"Of course. All right, thanks for the suitcase."

He placed the suitcase in his trunk, the sky already full with darkness. It was past six and about time he called it a day. He'd known already that Jenny and Stella were acquainted, and had suspected Lee of controlling their business activities, so he didn't see how the conversation had put him any further ahead. The lack of progress was maddening.

A surprise waited for him at home. Jamie's car sat in his driveway, and lights had been turned on inside the house. He came in the back door, which opened into a small mudroom off the kitchen. The scent of garlic made his mouth water.

Jamie was cooking, still in his dress shirt with his tie loosened around his neck. He was putting the finishing touches on his famous tomato sauce, a package of fresh pasta waiting on the counter. David placed the suitcase by the table.

"To what do I owe the pleasure?" David asked before snatching a slice of yellow pepper from the board where Jamie had cut vegetables for a salad.

"Well I hope it's a pleasure, 'cause you might be stuck with me for a while."

"What do you mean?"

"Someone broke into my place today and trashed it. As in, it's totally not livable."

David's blood turned to ice. "You're not shitting me?"

"Nope. I've spent the afternoon with the police and then an insurance adjuster. It's bad."

"This isn't a coincidence. I mean two days ago someone's taking shots at me, and now my boyfriend's house gets trashed. Come on."

"That's what I figured too. I passed the thought along to the police, so don't be surprised if someone wants to speak with you again."

"Right. Listen, I talked with someone today who may have given me the answer to the why of all of this. Well at least set me in the right direction, I think."

"Details please."

"That's just it, I don't know the details, so I'm still not able to even point a finger at anyone."

"What's with the suitcase?"

"Oh, it's Jenny's. I took a chance and went looking for her place. I figured she was renting a room down at one of the motels, you know where I mean?" Jamie nodded, all too familiar with the details of Toronto's prime crime areas. "Anyway, the manager was going to toss her stuff because she was overdue, so I took it. I can't imagine she's got much, but she still might want her stuff when she comes to."

"That was nice of you."

"That's just the type of guy I am," David said sarcastically.

"So really, is it okay that I stay with you for a bit?"

He gave Jamie a kiss. "More than okay. That way I can keep an eye on you, and maybe we can spend the holidays together. I assume you will be taking at least a few days of for Christmas?"

"I'm sure I can arrange that."

"Cool. Mind if I hit the shower?"

"Nope, dinner won't be ready for another fifteen minutes or so."

He left his partner to his cooking and went to stand under a scalding hot stream of water. He was so close to the truth, he could taste it.

CHAPTER 12

David awoke to the sound of the shower running, momentarily confusing him. Jamie almost never stayed over during the week, being very regimented and dedicated to a job that never had enough hours to complete all that was expected of him. He lay there in the soft darkness, the warmth from the other side of the bed not yet faded. His eyelids closed again, and he lingered in the comforting limbo between sleep and wakefulness until Jamie came back into the room.

He watched as he dressed in a modern yet still conservative suit and splashed on some cologne. He was tightening his tie when he came to David's side of the bed.

"I have to go." He pulled on his shoes then gave David a quick kiss on the forehead.

"Okay. I'll see you later."

He heard Jamie's footsteps going down the stairs, then a brief pause before the door opened and a car engine started. He needed to get his butt in gear also. A hot shower beckoned.

Once dressed he hit the closest donut shop, ordering the largest coffee they had. He sipped as he navigated the busy morning traffic, running over an action plan in his mind. Elaine, Christian, and Roberta all required another talking to, and he needed to make another attempt to connect with the ever-illusive Raven. Lee's goings-on would have to be put under watch. Ritchie too for that matter, as he would be the one most likely to be hands-on in any illegal or questionable activities.

This time his message light was dim. *Crap*. He'd hoped that at least Jimmy would have gotten back to him, but the guy did have his own job after all. He'd have to work out exactly how he wanted to treat the next interactions with Elaine and Christian. He expected both to either lie or simply evade him. Probably best to show up when they couldn't make a quick getaway.

David tried the Davenport Clinic, asking for Roberta. The secretary informed him that she was taking some personal time, and anticipated that she wouldn't be back for at least a couple of weeks. Well that didn't help, but life often didn't like to play by the rules.

He called the hospital to check on Jenny. She was stable, but had not regained consciousness. Her mother had not been found yet. After the update he called a florist shop, ordering a large bouquet to be sent to the girl's room. Not practical or necessary, but he hated the thought of the poor girl waking up alone, with no indication that anyone cared or even knew about her predicament.

Feeling frustrated and antsy, he took a trip to the gym. With muscles burning and sweat dripping down his face he started to attain a level of peace. A forty-five-minute run on the treadmill helped even more, the endorphin rush lifting his mood and sharpening his thinking process. Once redressed, he felt ready to meet the roadblocks in the case head-on.

His phone rang as he stepped from the gym out onto the icy parking lot. "David Lloyd."

"Hey Dave, Jimmy. I think you're gonna like the info I got for you."

"I could use some good news."

"The plate belongs to our dear friend Leland Makowski. Newly registered, expensive car. A condo at the address you gave me also comes back to him. Seems a bit steep for someone who lists his occupation as a courier and supposedly didn't clear more than forty grand last year."

"Hmm, interesting. So Leland is maybe dipping his fingers in a few different pockets. Thanks Jimmy, I appreciate the help."

"Listen I gotta tell you something else. Jeremy Black's been making some noise about your case."

He stopped mid-stride. "How so?"

"He says he got a call from the girl's dad. Says he isn't happy with your work on the case and wants the police to step in. Could be bullshit."

Not likely, considering his last conversation with the man. "Right, thanks for the head's..." A car was suddenly speeding through the parking lot, gunning right for him. He took a dive to get out of the way, hitting the asphalt hard. His phone slipped from his hand, sliding out of reach. The car didn't even slow down, continuing on at a dangerous speed until it reached the street, where it took a sharp left.

David's heart felt as though it had jumped into his throat. For a few moments the shock of the incident drained away all sound and feeling, his mind blank. Then with a rush, a throb started in his arm where he'd slammed it against the ground, and several excited voices closed in about him. The ground under him was damp and cold.

"Jesus, buddy. You okay?"

He looked up at two men standing over him. One dropped his gym bag and knelt beside David. "Seriously, are you all right? It didn't hit you did it?"

The man standing offered his hand and helped David back onto his feet. They were both looking at him like he'd grown another head, making him realize he'd yet to answer. "I'm good. Thanks for the help."

He spied his phone resting against the tire of a nearby car. He snatched it up, not surprised that the call had been dropped.

"You gonna call the police? We can give a statement if you want."

David shook his head. "No, I'm fine. Don't worry about it." He walked to his car with the two men staring after him.

Once inside his vehicle he started to shake. He gripped the steering wheel so tightly his knuckles turned white, and concentrated on getting his breathing to resume a normal state. The coffee and donut he'd eaten earlier churned in his stomach, wanting to make a reappearance, but he swallowed several times until the feeling passed.

When his heart had stopped hammering and he could breathe without sounding like Darth Vader, he put the car in reverse and peeled out of the lot. Someone had to talk with him.

Without realizing he had a destination in mind, he found himself pulling up in front of the dance company's rehearsal building for the third time in the past few weeks. The mousy secretary waved as he passed.

He found Marcus watching the rehearsal in progress, sitting where an audience would be with the same two women he'd been with the first time they'd talked. As soon as he saw David standing in the doorway he excused himself, coming to meet him. They stepped out into the relative privacy of the hallway.

"I'm looking for Sasha." No time for niceties.

"That would be both of us then," Marcus answered.

"He's not here?"

"Nope, I came in this morning to find a message on my machine from him, saying he'd be gone for a few weeks. That was it, no why, nothing. We're rehearsing for our Christmas performance, one of our biggest of the year. He can't pull this kind of shit right now."

"He must be protecting Stella."

"At the expense of his career?" The director was incredulous at the thought.

"Maybe. Look, please don't hold back now. If you have any idea what is going on here, tell me. I've already had shots taken at me and someone just tried to run me over. Another girl is in the hospital. Something serious is going on."

"I have no idea. I can't believe Sasha is involved in something like this. He's such a straight arrow."

"I don't think he's involved by choice. He's scared."

"I'm scared for him after hearing this. Listen, I'll keep trying to get him, and if I have any luck I'll let you know."

"If you talk to him, try and convince him to go to the police."

"I will."

David returned to his car. He'd never felt so close to a solution and yet so in the dark on a case before. He was sure the mother was guilty of nothing more than passivity and fear of losing her lifestyle, though undoubtedly her attitude had left its mark on her daughter. Janice, Sinclair, and Roberta, possibly even Sasha, seemed to know bits of the puzzle, but probably not the complete picture. So many people were orbiting about this girl, aware of trouble and traumatic incidents, watching her deteriorate before their eyes. He so desperately wanted to lay blame, but even if he found that one person or persons responsible for Stella's descent into despair, would it be enough to save her? Without confirmation that she still lived, the idea of her redemption could be moot.

The gnawing frustration had returned, this time holding tight. He grabbed a bite to eat at a greasy spoon two blocks from his office before returning. Again his answering machine was silent. Like he'd hit a brick wall, everything had come to a maddening standstill.

So what to do? Start at the beginning. He printed out all his notes from the interviews, police reports, and observations. He had still to dig deeper into the warehouse angle, which might have nothing to do with Stella, but with Lee and Ritchie involved was most likely the site of some kind of illegal activity. Bringing something serious against Lee would be a big coup, if only as revenge for using Stella as he had. Obviously, Lee and Ritchie, and the lifestyle they supported, played some aspect in Stella's downfall. The two had access to drugs, which would only have assisted in breaking down her resistance to further degradation, like prostitution. Her father's attitude toward women and sex must have muddied the waters for the girl's morality and willingness to accept such behaviour even further. So was she running from her family or her current associates? Or both?

The cycle of unanswerable questions circled in David's mind like sharks in a feeding frenzy. He needed coffee. As the water filled the carafe a knock sounded. He left it on the counter to answer the door. Instinctively he touched the gun resting in his shoulder holster. It was broad daylight in a heavily occupied building, but someone had just tried to run him down.

When he opened the door Roberta stood in the hallway, looking behind her. She gave a small jump when she found herself in David's presence. There were bags under her eyes, and her long hair was hidden by a dark, knitted cap. A large, bulky coat swallowed her slim frame.

"Hi David. Sorry to show up like this. Can I come in?" She

darted another nervous look behind her.

"Sure." He opened the door even wider, allowing her entrance to his office.

"Can you lock the door?" she asked, removing her hat to let long locks fall over her shoulders.

He did without comment. He'd been having his own paranoid moments lately, so indulging someone else's wasn't a stretch. They both sat.

"So this is convenient. I tried you earlier and was told you had taken some time off."

She took a deep breath. "Yeah, well, things have gotten a bit out of hand."

"Okay. How so?"

"Well when we chatted a few weeks back I wasn't entirely honest with you."

"Seems to be a recurring theme on this case."

She gave him a puzzled look but didn't ask for clarity. "Well, I'm here to clear the air, as much as I can anyway. Listen, I have heard from Stella recently. I spoke with her today actually. She's okay, for now."

David was so happy to hear the girl was alive he could have cheered. "Her mother will be so relieved to hear this."

"Oh, you can't tell her right now."

"What? Why not?"

"Because, there's still things going on, stuff I can't get into. Let's just say Stella is taking care of some business that's going to affect a lot of people. And some people really don't want the truth to come out. I think you know that already though." She met his gaze.

"I'm not following you."

She rubbed at her eyes, an anxious reaction. "This is not going to make any sense until I explain something to you. I'm Raven. I was at the club the other night when someone shot at you. My relationship with Stella is a lot more involved than you know."

That was the last thing he expected to hear. "A wig?"

She smiled. "Yes, Raven is someone completely separate form Roberta. I like it that way."

"Wait. So are you the one who got Stella into dancing?"

"Yes." She shook a hand as he started to protest. "Look before you say anything, I can honestly tell you that stripping was a positive alternative to some of the stuff that Stella had gotten herself mixed up in. It was safer, and it made the girl a decent income. That's how I put myself through school."

She had a point about the safety issue. There was nothing more dangerous than turning tricks, and there was always the chance of getting a bad hit when doing drugs or just plain overdosing. "What about the drugs?"

"I don't touch that stuff. Never did. I just didn't have a lot of alternatives when it came to money. My dad was killed in a car accident when I was a young girl, and my mom died from cancer during my first year at university."

"That's a tough break, but stripping?"

"I made enough money stripping to not have to take any student loans. I paid all my own tuition, books, rent, everything, and I came out debt free. I see no problem with that, but as your own reservations point out, some people have assumptions about women who do this kind of thing."

"So is this why you didn't say anything earlier?"

"The Davenport Clinic has an excellent reputation for high quality care and long-term success with clients. If Dr. Garfield and the Board of Directors knew that I worked as a stripper, I'd be let go in a heartbeat. That's not the type of image they would want associated with their organization." She fiddled in her chair.

"Okay, I can understand that. By why are you still doing it?"

"The money mostly. I make twice as much a year dancing two nights a week as I do at the clinic. Plus it's kinda fun."

"So let me get this straight. You met Stella at the clinic, when she was in care?" Roberta nodded. "And then after she left you two stayed in touch. So when did Stella start at the club?"

"She'd done it on and off but started on a steady basis about a year ago. She'd hit an all-time low, was taken to the hospital for OD'ing for the third time. She called me and asked for my help. She didn't want to go back to the clinic, she didn't want me to call her parents, so I took her in. I got her enrolled in an NA program and found some free counseling. She really seemed like she was trying, then about six months ago she started using again. She cut me out. Whenever I tried to talk with her she didn't answer my calls, or she'd tell me to leave her alone."

"And you have no idea what happened? Wait, didn't you say you spoke with her today."

"Lee happened. He has something on her, I'm sure of it. And I'm getting to how I know where she is."

"Does this have anything to do with her father?"

Roberta reacted as though he'd slapped her. "This has everything to do with that asshole, but not in the way you think."

"Enlighten me."

"George Barrowman is a dog. All that man thinks about is sex. He'll screw anything he can get his hands on."

"I've heard as much from other people."

"So, you can imagine how it would be on a girl like Stella, who does have legitimate emotional issues. She learned about his activities at an early age. Her mother always had her nose in the air, pretending nothing was going on. You know she caught him screwing one of her friend's mothers once? Can you imagine how disgusting and disturbing that would be for a young girl?"

"You're talking about Elaine?"

"Oh, don't even get me started about that bitch."

"Okay, we're going to side-step that one for a minute. Finish what you were going to tell me about George."

"George knows me from back in my college days. He was a regular at the club I worked at then. He really liked me and used to buy me gifts, even hired me for a couple of private performances." She caught David's look. "Not those kinds of performances. Strictly stripping, though believe me he asked for more. It eventually got to be too much. I changed clubs and stage names. The Letter is pretty high-end as far as these places go. No one bothers me there."

"So Stella found out about this?"

"I had to tell her. Her dad recognized me when he saw me at the clinic. He threatened to tell Dr. Garfield about my past if I didn't sleep with him. The thing is, I did...sleep with him, and I took his money for it. But when Stella and I became friends I couldn't keep doing it. She stood up to her dad for me, threatened to tell people about what he was doing. After that I couldn't turn my back on the girl."

"So you're Bobby?"

She smiled, and a tear slid down her cheek. "That's what Stella calls me."

"So I have to ask, did George molest Stella?"

"No. She told me he didn't, but that what he did do was just as bad. But she never explained what she meant by that."

"What about Christian?"

"Don't really know him. We've only crossed paths a few times."

"I caught him picking up a prostitute last week."

"Really? That surprises me. I always got the impression that he was very conservative. Stella always refers to him as her perfect brother. It pissed her off how much her dad loved him, being the hypocrite that he was. You know he was so proud of his straight A son, his social worker son, and there he was doing the crap he was."

"I also saw him at the Letter."

"Yeah, he's been in a couple of times lately, asking about his sister. He seems very concerned about what's happened to her, but until a few days ago, I didn't know anything. "

"Did Stella think her dad didn't care about her? Is that what set off all this stuff with her?"

"I don't know. In many ways the girl is an open book, but there are some things I know she hasn't told me about. I wouldn't judge her, you know. I'm sure no matter how bad it was, I could have found a way to help her."

"Do you have any idea what really happened the day she had her accident?"

"When she got hit by the car?"

"Yes."

"I don't know what you mean. I thought it was simply an accident."

"The more I've looked into Stella's background, the more

obvious it's become that something set the girl off. I think something really traumatic happened to her that day, and she was running for help."

She slouched down in her chair, thoughtful before speaking again. "Is this why you thought her dad was molesting her?"

David nodded. "So, how did you reconnect?"

"Stella called me, right out of the blue. I hadn't talked to her in weeks, and she told me she needed to talk to me. I went to see her. All I can get out of her is that Lee is involved. And she's scared that he's going to kill her or someone close to her. She'd been hiding from him for the past few months."

"Does she know something about his dealing, or something like that?"

"Could be, but it must be a huge deal. I've never seen anyone so scared in my life."

"Another of Lee's prostitutes was beaten very badly over the weekend. She might have known something too, so I think Stella has good reason to be scared."

"This is messed up."

"Where is she now?"

"She's with Sasha, somewhere safe. She's been getting clean and trying to figure out exactly what she wants to do before she tells us what's going on. Really that's all I know."

"So what does Elaine have to do with this?"

He eyes narrowed, bringing a dark, hostile edge to her disposition. "The girl is a snake. After all the crap with her mother, you know what she did? She slept with George too. Stella saw a tape of them together."

"But Stella stayed friends with the girl. Sasha told me that."

"I don't think he knew about that stuff. Honestly I never understood why she still talked to her. Again I think there's more to the story then she's told me."

"Stella sounds like a very troubled, desperate woman. Everywhere she turns people are stabbing her in the back."

"Not me."

"Good, she needs someone she can rely on. Whenever the truth comes out, I have a feeling it's going to be really bad. People have been shot at and threatened, you don't do that unless something major is on the line."

"Well she has me, and Sasha. That guy loves her so much it's ridiculous. I hope she can believe that some day. He'd be good for her."

"Well, I don't know what to do now. I'm actually Marjory's client, so I owe her something."

"Please just wait a bit longer. I'll be in touch, I promise."

David agreed, not without some distinct reservations. Maybe he wouldn't be looking for Stella directly, but there was no harm in trying to tie up some loose ends from her past and figure out what Lee was up to. In the process he might stumble across who had hurt Jenny and find some charges that would stick against the guy. Stella obviously needed back-up, or evidence to help her, but for what?

He watched Roberta leave with reluctance, but he didn't have much of a choice. It was late in the afternoon by then. He took a drive over to the hospital to check in on Jenny. The nurse told him that she'd briefly woken up earlier in the day but had not spoken. He sat by her bed for about thirty minutes, silently promising to find the bastard who'd hurt her. The bouquet had already arrived, a bright splotch of colour amidst the otherwise drab decor of the room. When he couldn't stand it anymore he took a trip to another part of the building. Jean wasn't in her office, so there was no news on that front either.

When he arrived home, Jamie's car was in the driveway, along with a vehicle he didn't recognize. He parked behind his partner so as not to block their guest.

Inside he found Jamie and his mother at the kitchen table, a pot of tea sitting between them. She looked up as David entered, her eyes puffy and red. He bent down and kissed Jamie on the cheek, an automatic action, only realizing what he'd done when he felt Jamie tense. David needed to remember he was still adjusting.

"Jamie, don't be self-conscious, please." Susan patted her son's hand before turning to David. "Sorry you have to walk in on this. Jamie said it would be all right if I came by."

"No problem. You're more than welcome here."

He took a seat at the table.

"That's very nice of you, something I don't feel particularly deserving of right at the moment." She took a shaky sip of her tea.

"My dad didn't take it very well," Jamie said.

"Ah." The news didn't come as a surprise.

"Which isn't your fault, Mom, and you shouldn't feel bad for whatever he may choose to do or say."

"So what happened?" David asked.

"I called Jamie's sisters over and sat them down with Sam, Jamie's dad. I told them outright, just like Jamie had done with me. Sam went ballistic. I've never seen him so angry. He was yelling and swearing. Jesus, he started spouting scripture at me, though we are hardly a religious bunch. Eventually he stormed out and went for a drive."

David noticed the muscles tightening along Jamie's jaw line. "Well, you did expect him to have issues with this right?"

Jamie let out a bitter laugh, bringing a pained look to his mother's face. "Yep."

"Well the good news is your sisters are on your side. They have no problem with this. In fact they'd like to meet David." Her teary gaze flittered between the two men, looking for some reassurance.

"That's great. We would love to have to the group of you over. Right, Jamie?"

"Sure."

"In fact, would you and your daughters like to join us for a holiday get-together I've planned?" The words started pouring out of his mouth despite the expression of alarm spreading across Jamie's face. "It's just a small gathering, but my parents and brother would be here. Maybe a few friends."

A genuine smile broke though Susan's look of despair. "I would love that. Thank you, David. I'm sure the girls will say yes too, so count on the three of us."

"This may be cold comfort, but my father acted in a similar way when I came out a few years back. We didn't speak for six months. I know my mother would be more than happy to talk with you about what she went through and how she handled everything."

"I don't want to be a pain."

"She wouldn't think of it that way, believe me. She's a pretty amazing lady."

"She really is, Mom, she's always treated me like one of the family."

"Look, I have taken up enough of your time. I know you're both busy men. Listen, I will call you in a few days, Jamie, and give you an update." She slipped on her coat and pulled her keys from the pocket.

Jamie stood to walk her out. As she passed she touched David's shoulder. "Thank you for being so understanding. I may take you up on the offer to talk with your mother."

"Anytime. Goodbye, Susan."

They disappeared into the mudroom, talking quietly for a few moments before the sound of the door opening could be heard. Jamie came back into the kitchen.

"Let's talk about anything but that," he said.

David nodded. "Okay, you want to help me sort out this mess of a case I have?"

"Sounds like a wonderful distraction."

"You must really not want to talk about..." David took a cue from the hard expression on Jamie's face. "Sit down and let me bring you up to speed."

Jamie had the same reaction he did to the news about Raven True's identity, shock.

"So Stella's alive."

"Yes, but someone obviously doesn't want her to stay that way."

"And this has nothing to do with that asshole father or the brother. What's his name?"

"Christian. Now Roberta says it has nothing to do with George or Christian, but she also said that Stella is not always completely honest with her. Maybe she's lying, maybe she's not. Either way, the dad's a creep and the stuff she witnessed and heard about had to have affected her. Christian too. Doesn't seem like the apple fell too far from the tree there."

"Is this just coincidence, and separate from what's she's gotten mixed up in with Lee?"

"I don't know, and that's what's driving me crazy. It seems at the very least the stuff going on at home, added to her emotional problems and the accident, all made her turn to drugs. And she kept using the drugs to block out pain, I think both physical and emotional."

"Wow, seems like everyone's family has their issues."

"Yeah, and if that wasn't bad enough, Elaine, the dancer friend I told you about whose mother George had an affair with." He gave Jamie a look, to make sure he was following. "Turns out she slept with the guy too."

"What? As a teenager? That's not only disgusting, but illegal." Ever the lawyer, he picked up on the implications right out of the gate.

"Yep, like I told you the guy's a dirtbag. Doesn't matter if he has lots of money or a fancy job, he's still scum."

"Okay, but why would Elaine do something like that? It doesn't make much sense."

"Who knows? If I've learned anything from this case, it's that people are fucked up. I mean what the hell could be so important that a person would be willing to shoot someone. Or beat a poor girl almost to death?"

"There has to be a reason for all of this, I just can't make it mesh right now. My brain's going in a hundred different directions. Can we try and work on something easier?"

"Like what?"

Jamie flicked a look at Jenny's suitcase, which still sat where David had left it the night before. "Like Jenny's stuff. You should look inside and make sure the motel lady didn't just throw stuff in that wasn't done up properly, like her makeup. Her clothes could be ruined, or whatever she has in there. The least we can do is make sure her belongings are in decent repair and she has some clean clothes when she wakes up."

David smiled. "See, you're getting a soft spot for her too, and you haven't even met her yet."

Jamie ignored him, putting the case on the table top. A loud snapping sound accompanied the latches opening. Inside was a jumble of clothing, shoes, makeup, and a few personal items. The well-worn stuffed dog with a missing eye caught both their attention, Jamie pulled it free of the other mess and raised an eyebrow in David's direction.

Putting the toy aside, he began to sort through the mess. He pulled clothing free from the other items, laying them to one side. David grabbed the pile and took it to the laundry room. After their removal the rest of Jenny's worldly goods seemed pretty sparse. She had a nice black leather jacket, with a pair of furry mitts stuffed in the pockets, but that was the only thing of any real value. A small bag held cosmetics, another her toiletries. David was surprised to find a few books, a couple of mysteries and a novel he remembered from his childhood days. Magazines, a wallet and a few loose pictures littered the bottom of the case.

Jamie removed the pictures, sitting to sort through them while David put the girl's clothes into the washing machine. When he came back the small pile of photos sat on the table, which he took a quick perusal of. The clothing and setting put most of the photos back at least a decade, and predominantly featured Jenny and another woman, who David guessed was her mother.

Next he grabbed her wallet, finding an expired health card from her home province, some change and a couple of condoms. He took a peek inside the toiletry bag, finding a partially used ring of birth control.

"Did she have a purse when she was found? This could be an extra wallet," Jamie said.

"No one mentioned anything to me."

"Seems strange that she doesn't have a cell phone. Everyone and their brother has one these days."

"I guess. We still don't know where she was attacked, so maybe whoever hurt her took the purse or the phone and ditched it. I really think the intent was to kill the girl, and taking anything that would help identify her would be a smart move on the perp's end."

"You're probably right."

Seeing that Jamie was working through something in his mind he sat. "What are you thinking?"

"I don't know. I'm just trying to imagine what this girl could know or have seen to make someone want to kill her. It's pretty extreme considering it was known that you'd already spoken with her."

"Yep. Then again hooking's risky business. Could be she was just in the wrong place at the wrong time."

"You don't believe that any more than I do."

He shook his head. "Nope."

"You have any thoughts about what you're going to do when she wakes up?"

"Nothing concrete, but I want to help her. I'd like to see her get off the streets permanently."

Jamie reached in and pulled the books from the case. He leafed through them absentmindedly, before pushing them aside. As he did, a few more photos slipped out of the back of one of the books. Jamie picked them up, lingering on one. "Isn't this Stella?"

David looked at the photo held out to him. In it, Stella, Jenny, Lee, and a small group of others sat on some folding chairs with what looked like filming equipment in the background. Stella was too thin, her eyes glazed. Lee was turned away from the camera, as though caught in mid-conversation with one of the people behind him.

"Yeah, that's Stella. Jesus, she looks like shit. I wonder when this was taken?"

Unfortunately the date was not recorded on the photo, but Jenny looked pretty much the same as the last time he had seen her pre-attack. It must have been taken in the recent past. As he flipped the photo over to check for any identifying marks something caught his eye. He searched the photo again, scanning every inch until he realized what it was.

Standing behind Lee, partially blocked by a large piece of equipment, was a person that had no business being recorded with a group of prostitutes and drug dealers.

"I think I'm having an a-ha moment," David said, unable to stop the smile spreading across his face.

"Don't keep me in suspense."

"See that man?" he said, pointing out the figure. "That's Stella's brother, Christian Barrowman."

CHAPTER 13

As with most recent nights, it took a long time for David's brain to settle down enough for sleep to come. The hospital had called to let him know that Jenny had woken again for a longer time than previously, but that she hadn't been coherent when spoken with. After less than thirty minutes she'd been unconscious again. The nurse did tell him that her waking at all was an excellent sign, and that tests performed earlier in the day had shown improvement.

He called Christian's work the minute he arrived at the office, only to be told that he didn't come in until noon on Wednesdays. Since his focus was temporarily off locating Stella, finding out what was going on with Lee had become his top priority. With the connection between him and Christian thrown into the mix, David's need to uncover the truth had hit a manic level. Both men disgusted him; Lee for his outward behaviour and Christian for his pretence at being any better than the scum who prostituted his sister.

If Christian wasn't available, maybe Lee was. He checked his gun, then hit a coffee shop on his way to Lee's condo. He parked down the block, circling about the area until he found a back way to access the parking area. Lee's car was in the same spot as before, cold to the touch. He returned to his car and waited with binoculars in hand. More than an hour passed without any activity. He sipped at his now cold coffee, internally cursing.

A pair of men exited the building through a side door, approaching Lee's car. David whipped up the binoculars, not surprised when Lee and Ritchie filled the field of vision. They pulled out, with David following at a casual distance. They made a few innocuous stops before heading to a twenty-four-hour diner, going inside together. David discovered with a guarded peek in the restaurant's window that they'd come to meet a couple of other men already seated at a booth. Though the waiting men were both dressed nicely, they seemed rough to David. He couldn't pinpoint any one thing in particular that made him jump to such a conclusion, but he felt certain they weren't there to talk real estate or life insurance.

He returned to his car and waited the forty-five minutes until they exited. The two unknown men shook Lee's hand as they left. He walked back to his car with Ritchie trailing like an eager puppy behind him. When he opened the back door to his car, David realized he now had a gym bag slung over one shoulder.

The next jaunt in the car took them back to the warehouse. They parked out front again, though this time the parking lot held a good number of vehicles. The building beside the one Lee was connected to looked as though it housed a paper product company, judging by the logo on several vans and delivery trucks parked in proximity. Lee gave a quick look about before heading to the front door. He took the bag with him.

Thirty minutes later a car pulled up, dropping off two very young women. They knocked at the door, waiting until Ritchie answered and ushered them inside. David waited another hour, alternating between freezing and running his car heater before he decided to head back to the office. He really needed a peek at the warehouse when no one else was around.

His phone was ringing as he opened the office door. He caught it before the other party hung up, to be told his car was ready for pick up. Another hour was wasted returning the rental and having them drive him over to the garage to pick up his own vehicle. It was after one o'clock when he was on his way again, an hour past when Christian was supposed to have started work.

Second Chances didn't look any less grim than it had on David's previous visit. The second-hand furniture was still worn and sagging, the so-called inspirational messages posted about the space even more depressing than the drab beige paint.

Two of the three computer stations were occupied, and a plump, cherub-faced woman sat at the reception desk.

All of the office doors were closed, three in all, only allowing muffled sound to filter out into the main area. A large room, which David guessed would be used for group activities, was open to show a small assembly of young people sitting on the floor. They had papers and a laptop in the centre of their gathering, attention fixed on some project or presentation.

David went to the reception desk, smiling. The young woman looked up, and as soon as she made eye contact a flush of red began to creep up her neck. She grinned, revealing braces. "Hi there. Can I help you?" Her words were breathy and rushed. David's appearance couldn't have caused the woman to be more flustered if the situation had been written into a comedy.

He decided to go with the effect he was having on her. "I bet you can." She beamed back, unconsciously raising a hand to her chest. "I need to speak with Christian."

"Do you have an appointment?"

"I'm afraid I don't. Is that a problem?"

She flashed him another nervous grin before turning her attention to the computer. "Ah, no, not really. I mean, he doesn't have an appointment booked right now. Let me go knock on his door." She stood up, smoothing her non-flattering knee-length skirt against her legs. She walked hurriedly, giving a timid tap at Christian's door. After sticking her head in the door and conversing briefly she turned back in David's direction. She then realized she'd have to retrace her steps while facing him, a fact that seemed to cause her some duress. The flush jumped into her cheeks as she gave her best shot at a smooth, feminine saunter back to her seat.

David gave her a flirty wink. "Thanks."

He knocked at the door before entering. Christian was seated at his desk, several client files in a haphazard pile on the desk. They were pushed aside as David entered.

"This is a surprise."

"Not as much as the one I got the other night."

"Sorry?" The smile faltered. His eyes widened slightly as David took his time sitting. He wanted the guy to squirm.

David pretended that he didn't notice Christian's reaction. "You know a girl named Jenny?"

"I know a lot of Jennys or Jennifers. Can you be more specific?"

"This Jenny is a prostitute."

Christian's smile widened, the look of pure innocence, but David knew better. "In this line of work I meet people from all segments of society, you must understand that."

He played along. "Of course. It's a sad fact that addictions can often lead to poor choices, like criminal behaviour. You would know that on a personal front as well, what with Stella's history."

Again a crack in Christian's perfected act of sincerity. "Unfortunately, that's true. So. I'm sorry, you were asking about someone named Jenny? Is this a friend of Stella's?"

"I guess you could say that. They both had the same pimp, a man named Lee. I asked you about the guy the last time I was here, and you said you didn't know him. Is that still your recollection, nothing you've remembered since that conversation?" He kept his gaze and voice steady, a bland expression on his face.

"Nope, I don't know anyone named Lee."

"You're positive?"

"That's hardly the crowd I would choose to be associated with." The smile had completely faded. His hands, clasped on the desk, began to twitch.

"That's funny, because I came across this picture in Jenny's belongings. Sorry, should backtrack here. Jenny was beaten within an inch of her life on Saturday night, she's now in the hospital. The doctors say it's a miracle she lived."

He blinked a few times, a classic tell when someone wasn't being truthful. "That's terrible. Who would do such a thing?"

"A piece of shit, obviously. Someone who had something to hide." He smiled. "So back to the picture. You want to tell me where this was taken?" He pulled the photo from his pocket and handed it across the desk.

Christian hesitated before taking it from David's grasp. When he did his hand trembled. He looked down onto the irrefutable evidence and the colour drained from his face. He took a long pause before he spoke. "I'd forgotten about this. It was one of those times Stella had called me, wanting to be rescued from whatever crap she'd gotten herself into that time. When I got there she was totally stoned, and had forgotten she'd even called me. This is part of the reason I distanced myself from her." He handed the picture back, seeming perked up by his blatant lie. "I didn't know anyone was taking pictures. You can see why I wouldn't want to be around these types of people. Someone might jump to the wrong conclusion after seeing something like that."

David nodded thoughtfully, and he could tell by the return of Christian's smile that he thought David was buying his story. "Well this is Lee." He pointed to the man's image in the photo. "It does look suspect. Sort of like you taking a drive down to hooker central the other night. But I guess that was just a bit of outreach right? You were trying to help those girls get off the streets, not looking for a piece of ass?"

"Did you follow me?" He frowned.

"I did. I find that the things people do and say when they aren't aware of being watched is much more telling than what I get in interviews."

"And what is it you think you saw?"

"I think I saw you cruise into a favourite haunt of yours and pick up a paid companion."

"You're wrong." He was still smiling, but the vein in the side of his neck throbbed. David would bet money that the guy's heart was racing a mile a minute.

"Glad to hear it. So this isn't something you've picked up from your dad?"

"Excuse me?"

David leaned forward. "Cut the crap. I know about your dad's activities. He also likes hookers, and apparently mothers of his kid's friends. Don't bother pretending you don't know about it. I have it on good authority, from a few different sources actually, that this stuff has been going on for a long time."

Christian looked like he was gauging his options. "Yes, I am aware that my dad has strayed a few times, but I'm not sure I get what you're trying to imply here."

"I'm not implying, I'm straight out telling you that your father's behaviour, and who knows, maybe yours, had a direct effect on Stella's emotional health. She knew about things no young girl should have, maybe even witnessed a few disgusting episodes."

"You know this or you believe this."

"What happened the day Stella had her accident? Did she come home and find your dad in bed with someone? Maybe he had some woman bent over his desk?"

Christian swallowed hard, and his Adam's apple bobbed about like a buoy in choppy waters. The blinking came back, a faster and longer episode. "I don't know what you're talking about."

"I think you do."

"You're barking up the wrong tree here. My father may have made his mistakes, but he never brought women back to our house. He would never be so tacky and insensitive. I have no idea what set Stella off that day. She's always been a messed-up girl, it could have been anything."

The first part of his statement rang surprisingly true, but a waver that came into his voice when denying knowledge of the events surrounding Stella's accident indicated another lie.

"So you're still sticking to your story that you think Stella's just gone on a bender or has taken off with some guy."

"Either one of those scenarios seems plausible with her history."

"Sure they do. It could also be that Stella's erratic behaviour and drug use is the effect of abuse she'd suffered over the years, and not just a symptom or unfortunate consequence of her emotional problems. You ever think of that?"

"Stella abuses herself." His words lacked conviction. David was hitting a nerve.

"I think she tries to cope. With exactly what, I don't know yet. But if you know about someone abusing your sister and you haven't come forward then you're just as guilty as they are."

"All I know is Stella has problems. She refuses to take the proper medication, instead she likes to do drugs and drink and thumb her nose at everyone who's ever tried to help her."

"Like you."

"Yes, like me."

David stood. "Oh, just one last question. Did you know about Elaine and your dad?"

Christian jumped to his feet. "That's enough. Just do your job and find my sister."

"Lovely chatting with you again Christian. I'll be in touch."

He gave the secretary a wave on his way out, to her obvious pleasure. Once in his car he didn't have to wait even fifteen minutes before Christian stormed out, engaged in an animated discussion with someone on the other end of his cell phone. He walked around the corner to the parking lot and pulled out onto the street a few minutes later.

That he ended up at Elaine's dance studio hardly came as a shock. David continued by, going around the corner to park. He cut through a small apartment building's property, which he gathered by its location backed onto the lot at the side of Elaine's studio. He followed the back edge of the yard to the rear of the building. He tried to visualize the layout of the building in his mind, remembering the main studio as running across the full width of the structure. If so, then the door he was looking at should enter right near it, possibly behind it.

He cautiously took the steps up to a small deck, where there was access to a door and a high-set window, perhaps in a bathroom. He tried the knob, finding the door unlocked. Slowly he opened it, peering into a small room with a wall directly in front and doors to either side. The wall he believed was the back of the studio. The door to the left did in fact lead to a bathroom; to the right was an L-shaped hallway leading to the changing room where he and Elaine had chatted, and if he continued farther he would come to the side entrance to the main studio.

He crept along, picking up voices the closer he got to the door. Music played, muffling some of the conversation. The door was slightly ajar, opening in the direction that offered him some camouflage.

"...I don't know, Christian. I didn't tell him anything."

"Well he fucking knows about you and my dad! And he was asking all kinds of questions about Lee. He had a fucking picture of me and Lee together, with a bunch of the whores we use."

"Where the hell did he get a picture?"

"From that stupid Jenny bitch. Remember we used her a couple of times? She's got a nice body, but she's a fucking whiner. I told Lee to cut her, and just keep her for hooking."

"Relax. The worst thing you can do is fly off the handle. Just lie low and see what happens. Even if Stella hasn't knocked herself off, she's not going to talk. She's not exactly innocent here."

"Neither are you. Remember that."

Footsteps pounded across the wooden floor, the sound dimming with each step. David turned around and let himself out the way he'd come in. He peeked around the corner, seeing Christian getting into his car. He bolted across the lot, into the apartment's yard, praying that he hadn't been seen. Christian drove down the street in the direction of where David'd parked. As he got in his car, he could see that Christian had been stopped by a red light. He pulled an illegal U-turn and continued to follow him.

Next stop: the warehouse. For the second time that day he pulled up in front of the innocuous-looking building, even more puzzled by the odd cast of characters accessing the place. A drug dealer and numbered business entity, a social worker, and a couple of trashy looking young women were all associated with the place, which made no sense to David. He knew a punch line was in the mess somewhere, but he hadn't quite fleshed it out yet. It had to be a front, some kind of shell business, most likely for distributing drugs. Without some kind of evidence, a hunch was hardly something he could call the authorities about.

He drove farther down the block, pulling into a lot unattached to the series of buildings where Christian had parked. The space seemed to service the vehicles of the building, piquing David's interest, and the ones directly to either side of it. The whole road was set up with similar groupings, a few buildings with a common lot sectioned off with concrete dividers. A chain-link fence ran for miles, fronting the entire strip of buildings, meaning you either had to go through one of the gates or travel to one end of the fence's length to bypass a legitimate entry. The end he'd driven by turned the corner, running the length of the property all the way to the lake, quite a hike. He made a mental note of practical places to park.

Christian was admitted into the building. David didn't think it would be a good idea to hang around, since he had already been there once that day and also because vehicles were moving about. He couldn't be sure which people belonged with which buildings, and he didn't need to tip off Lee and company to the one lead he had. He'd have to take a closer look at the place at a more convenient time.

Before returning home, he stopped at the hospital. Jenny looked much better, and several of the machines she'd been attached too had been removed. A nurse was taking her vitals as David came in.

The nurse looked up. "Hi there."

"Hello. How's the patient?"

"Doing well. She's been in and out for the last few hours. If you're lucky she might open her eyes for you."

David pulled up a chair to the side of Jenny's bed, quietly waiting until the nurse was done with her check-in. When the door shut he leaned his elbows on the edge of the bed and took Jenny's small hand in his. Her eyelids fluttered but did not open. Her face was so swollen he imagined it would be difficult to move any of the muscles under her mottled skin. He gently squeezed her hand, waiting for a response. Several minutes passed before she managed a small movement in return.

He stood then, leaning over her so his mouth was close to her ear. "It's David."

A small sound came from her, then a hard swallow that turned into a bout of coughing. She licked her lips when the spasm resided and turned her head toward the sound of his voice. She tried again to open her eyes, but couldn't quite manage it. "Handsome," she murmured.

David laughed. Even as injured as she was, the girl still had a sense of humour. "I have to say I've seen you looking better."

Her lips turned up in an attempt at a smile. Her chest rose shakily. "Funny."

"Listen, I know you're not quite with it yet, but I need to ask you something. Do Christian Barrowman and Lee know each other?"

For a moment she was so still David thought she'd passed out again. Slowly she nodded. *Yes, they did.*

"Does this have something to do with why Stella's hiding?"

Another nod.

"She knows something they don't want getting out, right?"

"Yes." Her voice was nothing more than a whisper. She started to cough again.

"Okay, that's all. Please, don't push it. I'm going to need you to help me put these bastards behind bars."

There was no response. She had fallen asleep. David kissed the girl on the cheek, leaving her to rest. He couldn't really count on her knowing anything more than she'd just told him, and it was likely she'd have no memory of the attack, but he had to keep hope. Someone was responsible and they needed to pay.

He took another wander through the hospital, this time catching Jean in her office. Her purse sat on the desk, and she was pulling on her jacket as he walked in. She sat down without comment, reaching for a stack of files to the side of her computer. Like Jean, everything in the office was neat and in its place. She deftly flicked through the paperwork until she found what she needed.

David took a seat as she opened the file and scanned the contents. After a few moments she pushed a few papers in his direction. He looked over the documents, all too familiar with the accident report template from his police force days. There was the write-up from the EMTs and the treatment notes from the emergency room doctors. Several referrals were included for orthopaedics and physiotherapy, and strangely one for social work, just as Jean had seen in the electronic file.

Unlike the notes seen on the computer, this version had an actual report attached. Sharon N. Milks, MSW, had seen Stella two days after the accident. In her report she indicated that the attending doctor had heard Stella make a number of statements that led him to believe that Stella had been assaulted in some way before the accident. When questioned by the social worker,

Stella flatly denied any such occurrence. Mrs. Barrowman also refuted that anything other than the accident had happened. There was no choice but to close the file, with a suggestion that counselling would be helpful.

"So what do you think?"

Jean considered the question. "Hard to say. Sometimes when people are in shock they say all kinds of strange things. As far as the hospital is concerned they followed up as requested. But you wouldn't be asking these questions if you thought this was nothing, right?"

"I can't dismiss anything at this point. This girl is troubled, there's no doubt about that, and she hasn't done herself any favours by getting involved with the type of people she has. I just can't believe that all of her problems are only in her head. It's become pretty obvious that someone hurt her, and more than once."

"I hope you get the bastard." David handed back the papers, which Jean tucked neatly back in the folder. "Walk me out."

"Love to."

They chitchatted about plans for the holidays and the endless cutbacks at the hospital until they reached Jean's car in the hospital's underground lot. As she pulled out David waved, but his mind was far away, full of unproven theories and an anger-filled need for answers.

Over dinner, David caught Jamie up to speed on everything going on with his case. He didn't know if Jamie was deliberately leaving work earlier than he usually did or had just hit a slower time at work, but he didn't care. It was nice to come home to someone who was happy to see him and wanted to talk about his day. Having someone who cooked dinner and understood where he was coming from as far as the nature of his work was concerned was even better. They made a good team.

So good in fact that when he made a decision about his next course of action, he knew he wanted Jamie to accompany him.

Jamie took a bit of persuading, but in the end agreed it was best for David not to attempt what he was about to alone. The least he could do was be a lookout for David, considering that someone had already shot at him and tried to run him over. He promised to throw aside all his moral objections, including the fact that trespassing and breaking and entering were the types of things he prosecuted people for.

It was past ten when they reached the area of town where the warehouse was located. The streets were deserted; the buildings nothing more than shadowy humps in the darkness. Both had dressed in warm, dark clothing. They parked a few blocks away; a soft crunching from a layer of snow atop the street could be heard as they walked to their intended location. A cold wind came across the lake, turning their breath to smoke.

Unlike during the day, at night the parking area's fence was closed and protected with a substantial padlock. They tried the next closest gate as an alternate way to gain access, and finding it locked had no choice but to scale the ten-foot chain-link.

"Do you know how much trouble I could get into for this?" Jamie whispered.

"Yep. So let's get this done quickly. There has to be something going on here."

They stole across the lot, which was empty except for an older, delivery-style truck sitting close to the building's front door. They avoided the few lights dotting the property, making their way along the side of the building. David remembered a set of stairs near the back that had led to a second-story exit. The area was so quiet the wind seemed to howl as it made its way across the slow-moving lake, an unnerving sound. Despite the cold, David was warm. His heart was pumping, adrenalin surging. He forced himself to breathe deeply as he needed to keep his focus sharp.

They crept up the stairs, where once at the landing David investigated the door and an adjacent window. The door had the telltale wires of an alarm system, an immediate deterrent, but the window proved another matter. Not only was it unwired, but the latch was broken. It took some manoeuvring to get the window open, as it sat several feet past the rail of the landing, meaning that David had to hang out over the concrete below, with one hand braced against the building for support and the other stretched to push the pane along its resistant track.

Once open he pulled himself inside, scraping his torso over

the jagged frame. The space underneath proved to be much lower than he gauged; he landed with a heavy thud. His knee gave a shriek of pain, but he held his breath, listening for any reaction to his sudden intrusion. After a full minute of silence he stood, squinting in the darkness to try and get his bearings. When he saw and heard nothing he dared to pull a small penlight from his pocket and turn it on. A set of stairs leading up to another platform, which he guessed led to the inner side of the door he had just checked, was just in front of him.

On the landing he reviewed the panel for the alarm system, finding that it hadn't been activated. He slid the length of wood barring the door out of its position and opened it to allow Jamie entrance. His partner gave a brief expression of surprise then ducked inside. David re-locked it and headed to the lower level.

The flashlight offered little illumination beyond a three-foot radius, but it was better than nothing. Once on the main floor, David cast the light about, taking in several sets of staircases leading to different areas, some open, some with enclosed divisions. Most of the upper area was bare, no boxes, furniture, or stock of any kind. A bit strange for a company that claimed to be in imports.

The main floor was a cavernous space several hundred feet long. At the rear of the building, the space was a maze of boxes and other discarded items. Their footsteps hit the silence like gunshots. Several glass-front offices lined the far wall of the room, all empty except for one that had been set up with a large desk and an abundance of electronic equipment. The door was locked, but David had it open in less than a minute. He'd refined his lock-picking skills over the last few years, sometimes a necessity of the job.

"Obviously not the first time you've done that," Jamie commented after the satisfying click of the lock releasing.

"I have many skills you probably don't know about."

Crammed inside the room were several large monitors, recording and lighting equipment, canisters of film, and a rack of questionable costumes. Jamie pulled out several hangers, finding bustiers, G-strings, even a nurse's uniform. He gave David a look that made him chuckle.

On the desk sat a stack of papers, which upon closer inspection turned out to be scripts for several different projects. Titles like *Daddy's Bad Little Girl* and *High School Gangbang* let the men know the type of movies being made on the premises.

David sat on the chair at the desk. "Okay, so they're making porn films here. So maybe Jenny and Stella are involved somehow?"

"I would guess. So aside from the legality of it, I mean I'm assuming an operation like this doesn't have the proper licenses to make and distribute their products, what is so important that someone is willing to kill over it?" Jamie leaned back on the desk then wiped his hands along his coat as though he'd touched something icky.

"So the fines wouldn't be enough to get their panties in a bunch?"

"Not really. I mean they can be substantial, and there is even a possibility of jail time, but these are hard cases to prosecute. I wouldn't want to take it on, I'll tell you that. They tend to drag on, and the end result is not usually worth the effort."

"Let me try the computer."

David opened the laptop he'd spied under a pile of film notes. Unfortunately it was password protected.

"Let's look out in the other room again."

Jamie wandered out, having adjusted to the near-total darkness. David put the papers back as he'd found them and took a few minutes to look about the room. Stashed under a chair covered in additional costumes David found the bag he'd seen Lee pick up from the men at the diner. Inside was more money than he'd ever laid eyes on before. The discovery gave him pause, but he didn't quite see what the significance was.

He locked the office when he left, catching up with Jamie. Closer to the front doors, under large canvas sheets, were several sets, including a hospital-type bed, another space decked out in an overly-done-little-girl's-room theme, and several others that the men weren't too sure about. After running a few scenarios over in his mind, David decided he didn't want to know what kind of acts had been performed there.

"David, come here," Jamie called from behind him.

He followed the sharp rustling sound to its source, his flashlight sliding over Jamie standing beside a newly uncovered pile of packages of white powder. The stack was taller than his partner, easily eight feet high. He couldn't even guess at the street value of the drugs they'd just uncovered.

"We need to call the police." It wasn't a question.

"Fuck."

David helped Jamie recover the mountain of illegal substance, trying to figure a way to get to Lee before the police did. Since the alarm wasn't employed the men decided it would be easier to leave through one of the main floor exits. They found one that could be locked on the way out without leaving an interior bar out of place. They stepped out to the side of the building, the corner to the front within arm's reach, to find several cars pulling into the lot. The closest one parked, and Lee, Ritchie, and two other men stepped out.

David stomped on Jamie's foot in his hurry to get back inside. He pulled the door shut as quietly as he could, but took the chance on leaving it unlocked. "We have company."

Jamie's look told him he understood. He grabbed Jamie's hand, yanking him along behind him as he made a hurried retreat to the back recesses of the building. The front door opened and several voices could be heard. They'd just passed out of the area that seemed to have the most use when a series of overhead lights came on. They moved into a section filled with flattened boxes and other discarded items from several incarnations of the building's past use. The light made the unlit parts of the building appear even darker, a welcome effect in the current circumstance.

Several forms filtered past, moving about the open space, but it was difficult to see any particular person's features clearly. Lee stepped up, surveying the activity. His back was to the area where David and Jamie stood peering through a crack in the piles of junk, but his profile was front and centre of their line of sight.

"That's Lee," David whispered right against Jamie's ear.

He could feel Jamie's fear, making his own pulse run even faster. He had to get them out.

It looked as though the men were moving the drugs out, an unfortunate turn of events as far as getting the police's help would go, but a focused activity that could work to their advantage. David looked about, judging the distance to the stairs leading to the second-floor landing where they'd entered. Except for a brief stretch of open space, the majority of the distance they needed to cover would be blocked by support walls, debris, and darkness. It was worth the chance. If all else failed, he did have his gun.

He whispered his plan to Jamie, who nodded his agreement. They moved with deliberate care, eyes locked on the position of Lee's men. David held his breath as Jamie passed across the section without cover. His heart slammed against his ribcage as he followed, shoes whispering across the gritty floor. A cool stream of sweat trickled down his back, and his winter coat felt irrationally restrictive and cumbersome.

At the stairs he took the lead, pressing his back against the wall as he ascended. The third step from the top gave a sharp creak. Both men immediately froze. From his position he was looking down onto the activity on the main floor, and no one seemed to have noticed the sound. He continued to the top. Jamie joined him without incident, his breath against his neck as he fumbled with the wooden bar positioned across the door.

"Holy shit! There's people up there," an excited male suddenly called out.

David didn't have to look to know that several men were now running in their direction. At last the latch lifted free, and he tossed it down the stairs with a resounding thud. The door opened just as a shot whizzed past his ear. He grabbed Jamie's coat and thrust him out onto the landing as another shot passed harmlessly through the bulky texture on the arm of his coat. He followed, pulling the door shut behind him.

They were halfway down the stairs when the group from inside reopened the door and spilled out onto the landing. Two of them men had guns, opening fire as soon as they spotted their targets. David pushed Jamie off the side of the stairs and jumped. He hit the ground on his side, pulse racing and breath tight. Two more shots sounded. He rolled out of the way, partly under the landing and out sight of the pursuers.

Jamie reached out his hand, pulling David to his feet. David yanked the gun from his shoulder holster as they started to run. A succession of thuds indicated that the men had hit the ground, but he didn't look back. More shots sounded as they turned the corner, heading to the back of the building. They came onto a narrow, paved area that led to a large, unoccupied dock, and farther on a strip of hilly ground.

Another shot rang out, hitting the building close to where they passed. David turned, firing several times at the rapidly approaching men. One gave a strangled yelp and fell to his knees. The other two kept coming.

"Keep going around the far side of the next building. We can cut through the lot to the fence. The car is right there." His voice sounded strange, panic tightening about his throat like a noose.

"Got it," Jamie responded without even looking at him.

Off in the distance several voices could be heard, the words indistinct with the distance and the heightened anxiety. The men giving chase began to slow, obviously not in the top physical shape that David and Jamie were. His knee was throbbing, but David refused to let it slow him down, not with so much at stake. He'd worry about the damage later.

They hit the far edge of the second building, skidding around the corner without slowing their pace. Snow had accumulated against the building, as deep as mid-calf in several places. As they neared the front lot the snow thinned, but their boots were still slick. Several motion lights snapped on as they ran by, alerting a small group of men standing at the front door of the building they'd fled. They looked up as Jamie and David bolted across the lot, not stopping until they hit the chain-link fence. More shots sounded, too far way to cause any harm.

They clambered over the fence like a couple of terrified monkeys, dropping into a run on the other side. The car was about a hundred yards away, a beacon of safety. David pulled the keys from his pocket as he ran, hitting the lock release. He could barely make out the sound of angry voices and a distant engine starting over his painful, ragged breathing.

Once inside he started the engine, peeling away without stopping to fasten his seatbelt. A car was in pursuit, high beams flashing as it raced after them. David took a corner way too fast, back end spinning out. He got control, then slammed the gas pedal to the floor. He didn't slow until they hit a more active area of town, where both cars and pedestrians were out despite the time of night. He moved through the traffic, changing lanes and turning down streets at random until he was sure he'd lost their followers.

He pulled into the lot of a fast-food restaurant and parked. "Holy shit."

"You can say that again. I don't know how you deal with this stuff."

"Ninety-nine percent of the time it's not like this. It's usually a lot of interviews, computer searches, and some surveillance, nothing like it's been this past week."

"You really do need some back-up." Jamie touched his arm.

"You offering, 'cause I'd be more than happy to take you up on that."

"Let's discuss it later." David had only been kidding, but Jamie sounded serious. "We need to go to the police and tell them what happened."

The closest station happened to be the one that David had once worked at, an ironic kick in the ass. They parked, but as soon as David's feet touched the bottom step of the entrance he was overcome with a violent urge to vomit. His hand went to his ear before he could stop himself. Jamie frowned as David touched the cool plastic of his hearing aid.

"Come on, you can do this."

"Yep."

Together they climbed the stairs, silently taking in the hustle and bustle of the place, still in effect at almost one in the morning. Inside the front doors was a large reception desk, where a uniformed officer that David knew but whose name he could not recall sat, a phone receiver clamped between his shoulder and the side of his head. He raised his hand in greeting as they passed.

David knew the building like the back of his hand. He

walked with purpose, forcing a stronger outward appearance than he felt. On the way in he'd called Jimmy, who, luckily, was working, and luckier still was actually in the building. He needed someone in the Narcotics and Organized Crime division, not Jimmy's assignment at present, but he thought working with an ally was the best route to go. Jimmy had agreed after hearing the condensed version of the night's events.

As they passed by a section of the building divided by a waist-height wall topped with glass panes, David caught sight of Jeremy Black sitting at a desk. He was speaking with another officer and referring to a file in his hand. He stopped, suddenly so full of rage he started to sweat. The chaos around him became nothing more than white noise, the only distinctive sound his pounding heart. He knew Jamie had stopped beside him, he could feel his presence, but had become blind to anything but the focus of his hatred. His hands clenched into fists.

Jeremy turned, as though he'd felt himself being watched. When he saw David there was a brief moment of surprise, then an arrogant sneer appeared. Jeremy tapped the arm of the man he was speaking to, who looked in David's direction. As the other man made eye contact with David, Jeremy made a distinctive slicing motion across his throat. Of course no one else in the room caught the threat, Jeremy was too smart for that. David put a protective arm across Jamie's chest, a move that brought a massive grin to Jeremy's face. Bastard.

Jamie shuffled beside him. "David. Let's go."

Snap. Like a movie being released from pause the station was alive with voices and movement. He started walking again. Jamie fell into step with him, taking the corner where an arrow pointed out the way to Sex Crimes. The glass door was closed, blocking out some of the noise from the officers and the barrage of phone calls, but it did nothing to hide the actions of a division that sadly never seemed to rest. Jimmy saw them and motioned for them to come in.

Walking through the door was excruciating, a sucker punch that just about knocked the wind out of him, yet in a way also exhilarated him. Sex Crimes had been the department he'd worked when he was attacked, and walking into the space was a bittersweet homecoming. He and Jimmy had never been partners, but had worked closely together for the better part of two years before he'd been hurt and subsequently forced to resign. The man had also been one of the very few who'd been on his side, going so far as to make an official statement about the harassment and threatening behaviour he'd witnessed by Jeremy against David. It hadn't won him many fans.

"Well now, this kind of thing I expect David to get mixed up in, but Jamie, I'm surprised to hear you were tagging along." He offered his hand to David, then Jamie in turn.

"I guess you can say he's rubbing off on me."

"Well, just be careful. We like our favourite prosecutors on this side of the law."

"Hilarious," Jamie answered.

They followed Jimmy to the back of the department, where the door to the meeting room stood ajar. A couple of the officers at their desks cast an inquisitive glace as they passed, some David recognized and others he'd never laid eyes on before. They sat around the oval shaped table, chipped and marked with scores of overlapping condensation rings from the copious amount of coffee consumed in the room over the years.

David removed his coat, feeling overheated and constricted. "I saw Black on the way in."

"Yeah that one's like a cockroach. Just can't seem to get rid of him. Let's not waste our time on a dickhead like him. Tell me what the hell is going on."

"It's the same case I've been on for the past few weeks."

"The same one you've been having me run names and addresses for?"

"Yes. It started out as a missing person's case, but my girl has been found, more or less. But in digging into her past and trying to figure where or who she might have gone away with, I've managed to step on a few toes."

"You always were good at pissing people off. Glad to see that some things never change."

Jamie gave a low chuckle. "Thanks for that."

Jimmy smirked, and David shook his head at the both of them. "Can we cut the digs, please. This has to do with our boy

Lee, who you had the pleasure of meeting the other night. You told me he's been suspected of moving drugs, and Jamie and I can verify that for you now. He's also got his fingers in some kind of porn operation. We're not clear on what's going on, or who's all involved, but you can bet it's not legit."

"Give me specifics, whatever you've got. We'll worry about how you got the info later."

"We found a huge shipment of what I'm going to guess was cocaine. I mean tens of thousands of dollars' worth. And there were sets and film equipment, scripts, everything to make your own homemade pornos," Jamie said.

"If you don't act now, you'll be lucky if anything's left. I'm sure they're sweeping the place as we speak." David gave Jimmy a hard look. He knew he was putting a friend on the spot.

"If anyone else had come to me with this I'd have told them where they could stick it. You know that."

"I do, I know you're going to be sticking your neck out."

Jimmy gave a sigh and pushed away from the table. He left the room to put the legal wheels into motion so a proper raid on the warehouse could be undertaken. What seemed like hours passed while David and Jamie sat, not speaking. He didn't realize he was drumming his fingers against the table until he felt Jamie's warm hand on top of his, pressing down to stop the grating action.

"Well, isn't this an interesting turn of events." The voice came from the doorway, and David didn't even have to look to know who it was. The way his skin crawled made it obvious that it could only be one person.

"Jeremy," he said, turning to meet the man's gaze dead-on. He wouldn't be intimidated by him, not ever again.

Jeremy and two other men entered the room, taking a seat at the table. His gaze flicked down to where David's and Jamie's hands were touching. David fought the urge to snatch his hand away, knowing he had nothing to be ashamed about, but that one look made him feel inferior. Jamie moved his hand away, as though reading his thoughts. David leaned back in his chair.

"I see you've brought your lawyer," Jeremy said, his attention moving to Jamie, who didn't even blink under his blatant scrutiny. "Isn't that convenient. He can help you get out of your legal messes, then you can take him home and thank him in your own *private* way."

Jeremy's ear-to-ear grin was met by a stony gaze from the man on his right, and a snort of laughter from the one on his left. David looked at the man who had laughed, remembering him as being one of the younger officers who'd been completely in awe of Jeremy when he'd been active, eager for any attention the more experienced officer might give him. It was easy to see how pleased the young man was to be working with Jeremy, obviously all too happy to follow the asshole's lead in the offensive and inappropriate way he would conduct the investigation.

"You know Black, a harassment suit filed by an employee of the Attorney General's office wouldn't be a good thing for an officer who already has a few transgressions on their record." Jamie's voice was smooth and authoritative. In his lawyer mode, the man was a force to be reckoned with, having the brains and the savvy to take down the most hardened criminal. He'd managed to break down even the toughest of the tough in court, and Jeremy Black didn't stand a chance if things came to a verbal sparring match.

"I beg your pardon. You two just seemed very cozy in here. Maybe I've jumped to conclusions." The mocking smile didn't waver.

"Leave him alone. His personal life has nothing to do with this."

"I'll have to disagree with you there, David. You should know as well as I do that people do and say things they might not say under other circumstances, when loved ones are involved. I am here to establish the facts, so I need to ask, are you two romantically involved?"

Jamie gave David a sideways look, one that tugged at his heartstrings. He knew how hard this was for Jamie. Once the words were out, it would be all over the police station and back to the Ministry Office in no time.

"Yes. We're a couple, have been for several years," David answered. Jamie looked as shocked as David felt when the words left his lips, but he quickly regained his cool.

Black jotted something down in his notepad. Jimmy and a few more officers came into the room as the interview continued. David told them everything he knew about Lee, Ritchie, Elaine, and Christian, including the connection to Jenny. The photograph was handed over, and he pointed out all the parties that he could identify. He passed along his suspicions about George Barrowman and Stella's possible sexual assault, which Jeremy recorded without comment, even though David knew the man had already been in touch. He told them he suspected the shooting at the Scarlett Letter and the attempt to run him over were tied to his nosing into whatever activities Lee and company were involved in. Lastly, he explained what he'd seen in the warehouse, leaving out the fact that Jamie had actually entered the premises with him.

"Well at the very least we have drug trafficking and possible illegal production and distribution of pornographic films. Who knows what else these clowns might be involved in," Jeremy said after hearing David's entire story.

"What about the girl?" one of the other officers asked.

"Yeah, have you located Stella?" Jeremy asked.

"No," David answered. "Not yet." Jimmy squinted at his response, but didn't challenge him.

"Okay, let's get our butts in gear." Jeremy started barking out orders, laying the outline for the team to check out the warehouse.

The proper paperwork changed hands, and the group was off. The room cleared, leaving only Jamie, David, and Jimmy.

"You know, the possible assault on Stella and the films gives me an angle here. I can take a deeper look into this for you," Jimmy said.

"Good. I know the others will get to it, but see if you can dig deeper on the warehouse. Find out who the business is actually connected to. There has to be a person attached to it somewhere."

"Will do. I'll connect with you tomorrow. You guys should head out. It's really late, or early depending on how you look at it."

David offered his hand across the table which Jimmy shook. "I appreciate your help Jimmy. You're always a class act."

"Hey now, don't go spreading that around, you'll ruin my rep."

By the time David and Jamie made it home, four o'clock loomed. Jamie called his secretary's voicemail, leaving a message that he was taking a personal day and wouldn't be in to the office. They were both physically and emotionally exhausted, but too keyed up to fall asleep. They took a long hot bath while knocking back a couple of glasses of wine. The horizon had begun turning purple, the sun threatening its appearance, when they finally crashed.

CHAPTER 14

The next day started with a bang. Literally.

A sharp crashing sound startled the men awake. David ran downstairs, with Jamie on his heels, to find that someone had tossed a rock through his living room window. Shattered glass littered the ground, and a bitter wind made the curtains dance.

"Motherfucker!" David yelled.

"I'll call someone to come fix the window," Jamie said, knowing it would be a good idea to give David a moment to cool down before trying to talk with him

He paced the room, cursing. A knock sounded at the front door. He came around the corner into the front hall, bypassing Jamie who had peeked around the doorway from the kitchen with the phone pressed to one ear. A quick look out the window alongside the door alerted him to the visitor's identity.

"Hi, Mr. Albert," he said, opening the door wide enough to let the man in.

Jamie waved, then returned to the kitchen to finish his call.

"More trouble I see," the older man said by way of greeting.

"Yeah, sorry about this."

"Don't be sorry, son. Have to say, I hope this isn't a personal thing." He eyes were watery from the cold outside, giving the impression of vulnerability.

"Nope, not personal. Just some trouble from a case I'm working on."

They had been neighbours long enough for him to know that David was a private investigator.

"John, please. I told you that last time."

"Right, John. Come on in and have a cup of coffee. It's the least I can do."

He followed David into the kitchen, where Jamie was just hanging up the phone. "Someone will be here within the hour. Hi Mr. Albert."

"Like I told David here, call me John. No need for formalities."

Jamie smiled. "Right."

David pulled the coffee from the fridge and set about making a pot. They made polite noises about how John took his coffee and how much he though the window repair would cost. Belatedly David realized that he and Jamie were dressed for bed, he in sweats and Jamie in a pair of Toronto Maple Leaf pajama pants and a t-shirt.

"Your insurance will cover it."

"Thank goodness," Jamie said, bringing the mugs to the table.

There was an awkward pause.

"So did you see anyone?" David asked.

"Yeah, a dark car. Could have been the same one as the other night, but I really can't say for sure. A guy in a big coat got out, threw the rock, and jumped back in, drove away. Took about thirty seconds."

It wasn't even worth calling the police for. They finished up the coffee, and David thanked he man for his attentiveness. He walked him to the door.

"Listen, I'm going to be having a small Christmas get-together next weekend. I'd love it if you could come," he said.

John smiled, looking touched. "Sounds good. Let me know the time." He shuffled back across the road to his own place, giving a last wave before going inside.

The window repair guy arrived about thirty minutes later. He boarded up the space, and took the measurements for the replacement glass. He promised to be back the next day to finish the job.

While in the shower David realized that he hadn't gone to his grandmother's place for dinner the night before, something he never missed. He was sure she'd understand that he'd been busy, but it had been terribly rude to not have even called. As soon as he stepped out of the tub he grabbed his cell phone to make an apology. When he flipped it open the message screen popped up, letting him know he had four missed calls. He'd forgotten he'd turned the ringer off before going to sleep. Looking at the clock he realized it was nearly one o'clock, and any number of things could have happened in the previous few hours.

The first caller was Susan, wanting his mother's number. He let Jamie know and asked him to call her back with the information. Jimmy had called next; he had news about the raid and the warehouse ownership. He asked for a call back. The hospital left a message that Jenny had been up for several hours, even managed to take a few bites of solid food. He made a mental note to go and see her later. The last call was from Roberta, made only thirty minutes before. She sounded very upset, her message jumbled and confusing.

He called Jimmy back at work, getting his voicemail. He next tried his cell, which was picked up after several rings. His friend sounded tired and irritated.

"Jimmy, Dave. I got your message."

"Well hello, sleeping beauty. Got some news for ya."

"Hit me."

"First, like you suspected the building had been cleared. No drugs or video equipment. No films, but they did leave behind the sets you mentioned, so some circumstantial evidence anyway. Lee and company are being collected as we speak. I expect he'll lawyer up, but I guess it depends how bad a mess he's got himself in if he'll talk or not."

"And the warehouse."

"There, you were right on the money. After some digging, not too easy a feat either mind you, its turns out that the company who owns the building and who supposedly runs this importing business can be traced back to one George Barrowman. He set the company up and makes a nice profit from it each month. There seems to be other investors and other legal BS, but that still needs to be sorted out."

"So what does George have to say about this?"

"Nothing yet. The guy's out of the country on business until sometime next week. The wife says she knows nothing."

Was he into something as sleazy as making a profit off his own daughter's pornography career? It made David sick to even consider such a thing. "What about Christian?"

"He came in voluntarily this morning. Gave a statement. Says he knew nothing about it. When asked about the photo you gave us, he stuck to the same story he'd told you. There's nothing to even hint he's involved."

David didn't believe that for a second. "He knows. There's something not right about that guy."

"Could be, the trick is proving it. Look, I gotta hit the hay. I've been up since yester morning."

"Right, thanks for the info."

"No problem. We'll talk again soon."

He tried Roberta next, but his call wasn't answered. No voicemail picked up either, which worried him.

Jamie came back into the room as he stood there, phone clasped in his hand.

"Everything all right?"

"I don't think so," Davis answered. He explained what Jimmy had uncovered and told him about not being able to reach Roberta.

"So what do you want to do?"

"Find someone who'll talk."

They pulled into the dance studio's lot a short time later. There were no other cars in attendance, and his earlier call hadn't been answered, but David had a hunch that Elaine was there. He pounded on the front door and waited. Silence answered them.

He motioned toward the back of the building, and Jamie followed as he approached the back entrance. This time it was locked. He gave a quick look around, then kicked the door in.

"Holy shit, David. Warn a guy."

He followed the hallway to the studio, hearing a quick scurry of footsteps as he reached the door. Elaine was trying to make a break for it. David raced across the wood floor, damp shoes squeaking. He caught her arm and yanked her back from her flight to the front door.

She was crying. Her bottom lip had been split, a seal of dried blood holding the two sides together. One eye was swollen, beginning a rainbow of bruising. She swatted at his hand clamped on her arm, but he didn't let go.

"Don't hurt me," she begged.

"David," Jamie said and he let go of her arm.

"I'm not going to hurt you. I just want to ask you some questions and I want the truth this time."

"Lee will kill me if I say anything."

"Yeah, well you'll probably be going to jail if you don't." He had no idea if that were true since he didn't know exactly what part she'd played in the whole fiasco, but it was a good threat.

Fat tears welled up in her eyes, accompanied by heaving, wet sobs that made both men cringe. "Okay—I'll tell you. Can we sit down?"

They followed her to the lounge area, where she wrapped a coat around her shoulder and sat on a chair with her knees drawn up against her chest.

"I don't know where to start."

"Start with George Barrowman and your mom."

Here eyes flicked back and forth between the men. "Wait, who's this?"

"Jamie."

She paused, trying to recall where she'd heard the name before. "Your girlfriend?"

Jamie made a face, which David ignored. "I never said that."

"I guess you didn't. I just assumed. Very sneaky of you."

"Right, now back to you and George."

She wiped at her damp face with both hands and took a long, shaky breath. "That man is a piece of shit. He tore my family apart. I guess you know about the affair with my mom?" He nodded. "Well she thought he cared about her, that he wanted to be with her. What a joke. He just wanted to screw her and then move on to the next one. Problem was, my mom had fallen in love with the guy. My dad found out and left her. George dumped her soon after that. She started drinking and taking sleeping pills, she even overdosed once though she swore it was an accident. It fucked up everything. She couldn't afford to pay for my dance anymore. I was so pissed I went to tell him off."

She choked back some phlegm, her body language becoming defensive.

"What happened?"

"He offered to give me money if I slept with him. I was only sixteen years old. But it was a lot of money, and I really wanted to keep dancing."

"So you slept with him."

"Yep. It went on for a few months. Stella had no idea, but Christian found out about it. Apparently his dad had videotaped us, and Christian saw it. They have a very weird relationship, those two. George used to give Christian porno films when he was a teenager, and apparently took him to hookers and stuff when they travelled overseas, sometime even here." A look passed across her face that David couldn't read, but one he didn't like.

"Then what happened," Jamie prompted.

Elaine seemed to snap back to the conversation at the sound of his voice. "Then I got myself in a whole heap of trouble. Christian cooked up a plan to blackmail his dad with the tape, you know 'cause I was underage. It worked, we got a big chunk of money, even more than he'd been giving me to sleep with him, and he backed off me after the money changed hands. I used part of it to open this studio. Anyway, it also kept me tied to Christian, who despite his image is not a nice guy." She started to cry again. "He got me high a few times, and I agreed to make a couple of movies for him, you know what I mean? And he introduced me to Lee, who I run drugs for sometimes. He says he'll expose me for the stuff with his dad and the movies, and then no one will want their kids coming to me for dance lessons. So I just do what he asks and keep my mouth shut."

"So who roughed you up?"

"Lee and Ritchie came by earlier. Lee uses Ritchie to hurt his girls when they don't cooperate." She pointed to her face. "This was a warning to keep quiet."

"So what does this have to do with Stella?"

"She was knee-deep in it. It all started when she and I went to a party with Christian. She met Lee and everything just went to shit."

"Wait. Christian introduced Stella to Lee? I always thought it was the other way around," David said, totally caught off guard by the information.

"No, no. Christian met Lee when he was at university. Lee was a dealer then, I mean lower down than he is now, and he knew how to get prostitutes. We were about sixteen then, so Christian would have been about twenty, twenty-one. Anyway Stella had already been doing drugs, and had been having a bad time since the accident, and she just took to Lee like a moth to a flame. He kept her stoned and she did whatever he wanted."

"Which was what?"

"Hook and make movies."

"So Christian knows about this?"

"Yeah, he knows. He makes money off of it."

"What do you mean?"

"He and Lee organize the films, get them filmed and distributed. He makes a profit, so do Lee and a bunch of other people."

"What other people?"

She shook her head. "I don't know. Honestly."

"Mrs. Barrowman?"

"She doesn't have a clue. She knows George strays sometimes, but she ignores it, and she thinks Christian is perfect."

David had to take a few moments for everything she'd said to sink in. What a sick, twisted family the poor girl had come from. But it still didn't explain what had happened the day of her accident. David was certain that had been the beginning of her downward spiral, and everything to come after simply compounded the original pain, feeding her need to disappear through drugs.

"Why did she stay friends with you?"

"We weren't really friends, more like victims of the same people. I know I did a shitty thing, but I didn't realize that her brother was such a creep that he'd use his own sister. Anyway coming here was a chance for her to dance and be herself. I know dancing was the only time she felt free."

"Do you know what happened the day of the accident?"

Elaine seemed confused by the question. "She got hit by a car."

"I mean before that."

"I don't know what you're getting at. She never said anything to me about something happening."

"Maybe it was just an accident, David," Jamie said.

He couldn't explain why he was so certain something had happened, there had been absolutely no proof to indicate so, but he just couldn't shake the feeling.

"I don't think so."

"What's going to happen now?" Elaine asked.

"You need to talk with the police and give them every place that Lee and Christian might have gone."

"I can't!"

"You have to Elaine. There's no other way out of this."

"What will happen to me? This studio is my life."

"That's up to the police."

Jamie tried a softer approach. "If you cooperate, the police will most likely overlook the worst of your crimes. And you do have the law on your side here, if George Barrowman had sex with you when you were only sixteen."

"Come on, we'll take you down."

Seeing no other viable option, she agreed. David found a chair that could be wedged under the busted door until a proper repair could be made. The three made their exit out the main door at the front of the building. They were at the walk when Elaine realized she'd left her purse inside.

"Just give me a sec."

She raced back up the stairs. The sound came as she had her key in the door. Her gaze turned to the road, eyes wide. The bullet hit her in the chest, a second took her at the base of her throat. Blood sprayed against the doors and coated the snow-dusted landing. David had his gun out, getting off two shots at the car as it drove past. The shooter pulled his arm back inside, and the tinted window closed as the vehicle sped away.

Jamie went to Elaine. He had his hand clamped over the wound at her throat, blood pouring through his fingers. David called 911 and raced up the steps to help him. A terrible, gurgling sound escaped from her slack mouth. She gave a series of tight, short-lived convulsions and then went still.

She was dead before the ambulance arrived. They gave their statements to the EMTs and again to the police who arrived a few minutes later. David felt numb, not upset or angry, just blank. Jamie was shaken; he kept crossing and uncrossing his arms, and his face was very pale.

At last they were given permission to leave, after promising to come to the station to give formal statements. David led Jamie back to the car, where he finally broke down. He let his partner cry for several minutes, wrapping his arms about him. When he managed to get himself under control David took him back to his house.

He tried Roberta for a second time. As before it simply rang and rang, with no chance to leave a message.

Jamie sat at the kitchen table, hands wrapped around a mug of tea. The colour was starting to come back into his face, but he'd never seen him look so scared before. David did what he could to comfort him, not one of his best skills. He finally convinced him to lie down. He took him up to the bedroom and made sure he was comfortable.

"Listen I'm going to go out for a bit. I won't be long."

"Where are you going?" Jamie said so loudly that David winced.

He sat beside him and hugged him. "I'm going to go to the hospital. I just want to check on Jenny."

"You can call the hospital."

"I want to talk to her if I can. She woke up last time I was there. She might have an idea where we can find these guys."

"Don't go. Leave this to the police."

"Jamie, this is my job. I don't consider this finished until Stella is back with her mother and all these assholes have been rounded up and thrown in jail. You know that my job is risky sometimes, it was even more dangerous when I was a police officer."

"Yeah, but I never saw any of this stuff before. It's one thing to talk about it, but it's a totally different thing to see it firsthand."

David got up from the bed and went to the lockbox he kept in his closet. From inside he removed a small six-shot pistol and some ammunition. He loaded it and brought it to Jamie.

"Take this. You'll be safe until I get back. I will lock the doors, and I'll let John know I'm going, though he's probably already watching the place. I won't be long."

"Fine. I'm sorry. Go."

"I love you. I'll be back soon." He kissed him.

"Love you too. Watch your ass."

David gave his butt a wiggle, which made Jamie laugh. He tossed a pillow at him, which he easily caught.

"Go already."

Daily visits to the hospital had alerted him to the most likely places to find a decent parking spot. Two tours about the facility and he found one within a half-block of the entrance closest to the ICU. The wind stung his eyes as he walked to the door. He couldn't help but look behind him several times, finding nothing more sinister than a few environmental workers emptying the trash and an elderly couple also on their way in to visit someone. The woman carried a small bouquet of flowers.

Inside the smell of sickness and disinfectant hit him, mingling with the effects of the cold wind to make his eyes and nose run. He took a quick detour to a washroom to wipe his face. A young woman sat on one of the worn sofas in the family area of the ICU, her face down as she stared at hands clenched together on her lap. A knitted toque was pulled low, obscuring her features.

The closer he got to the woman the more familiar she seemed. His presence caught her attention and she looked up. He noticed a thin scrape ran along one cheek and soft bruising, which was the beginning of a black eye. Roberta jumped to her feet as she recognized David. A nurse looked up from the nearby desk at the suddenness of her movement. David smiled at the nurse, trying to give the impression that everything was hunky-dory. He motioned for Roberta to follow him.

Together they turned the corner to the small hallway where Jenny's room was located. A small monitoring desk was at the far end, where another nurse sat, keeping an eye on the various equipment servicing the patients under her care. David stopped, angled himself away from the nurse, and spoke in a low voice so as not to draw any suspicion.

"What happened to you?"

"Lee sent one of his goons after me. I don't know how, but he figured out I was Raven. The guy was waiting for me when I came home, and he jumped me. Luckily I've had some self-defense training. I managed to get a few hits in. I kicked him in the balls pretty hard, and it took him down long enough for me to get away. Lost my phone though." Which would explain why she hadn't been answering.

"Would Stella have told Christian about you?"

"I don't think so, but I guess it could have slipped out if she were stoned."

"Are you okay?"

"Yep, nothing that won't heal."

"Are you looking for me?"

"Yeah, I didn't know where else to go. I tried your office, but you weren't there. I remember you said something about Jenny, so I came here. I've been waiting for about an hour, but I figured it's pretty safe here."

"How do you know he knows you're Raven."

"'Cause that's what he called me. Thought he was pretty funny too."

"You're very lucky. These guys mean business. Elaine was shot today."

Her eyes grew as round as saucers. "Is she dead?"

"Yes. But not before she told me some of what's been going on." He glanced behind him, catching the nurse openly staring at them. "Let's go to Jenny's room, we're drawing attention here."

She followed him without comment. The nurse nodded as they passed. Jenny was awake and had been propped up in her bed. She tracked their movement, even the eye with the most swelling slightly open.

"Hey, gorgeous," David said.

"Funny." Her voice was scratchy and thick.

"This is Roberta. She's a friend of Stella's."

Jenny's gaze moved from David to Roberta, lingering for a few moments. "Hi."

"Hi Jenny. Sorry to barge in like this." She sounded sincerely concerned.

Jenny nodded, as best as her injuries would allow her to.

"Jenny, I know it's hard, but do you remember anything about the night you were attacked?"

"Ritchie," she answered, the word getting caught in her throat.

"Ritchie did this to you?"

She nodded.

"Was he alone?"

Another nod.

"Do you know why?"

Her eyes closed. David waited patiently, knowing he shouldn't be questioning her at all, but since people were being beaten and shot at it was worth the chance.

"Christian. Lee."

"Yes, what about them."

"Movies. Shouldn't be at the warehouse." She was struggling to make her answers clear, an effort that was clearly taking its toll.

"Why?"

"Supposed to be drop off. For Crimson Knights."

The name struck a chord with David. The Crimson Knights were a well-connected organized crime operation, with tentacles in drugs, prostitutes, stolen property, and any number of ever-changing scams. The group was notoriously well organized and had a reputation for evading detection and in many cases, prosecution. Their businesses surpassed not only laws but borders, reaching into the States and overseas.

"So the building was bought as a dumping ground?"

"Uh-huh."

"And Lee is one of several people responsible for moving the product once it's landed?"

She nodded and took a shaky breath.

"But he's using it for his own endeavours also, and the higher-ups in the Crimson Knights won't take kindly to that?"

"Yes."

David looked to Roberta, and he could almost see the wheels turning as she also put the pieces together.

"I don't think these guys would like being cut out of a lucrative deal, especially when it's being pulled off on their property," Roberta said, echoing exactly what David was thinking.

"I wonder if George Barrowman knows what the building is actually being used for?"

Roberta scrunched up her face. "What does he have to do with this?"

"Sorry, thinking out loud. There's a lot of things going on in the background that Stella may have become aware of. Sounds like Jenny stumbled onto some of it too."

"So Lee and his buddies are knocking off anyone who might know something that could land them in hot water with the Crimson Knights?"

"That's what it sounds like to me."

"And Stella's dad and brother are involved in this somehow?"

"I knew George was a piece of work, but Christian too? No wonder the girl's so messed up."

Jenny had fallen asleep again, but what she'd shared had been enormously helpful. *Now to find a way to put the knowledge to good use.*

"We should go. She needs her rest."

Roberta agreed with a pained smile, after giving the sleeping girl one last glance. They moved out into the hallway, closing the door behind them. The same nurse sat at the desk, giving them her undivided attention. David waved as they passed, feeling like a school boy being watched by the principal.

Movement ahead of them caught David's attention. Another man turned the corner into the short passage they occupied as he looked up. He returned his attention to Roberta before suddenly realizing he'd recognized the man. His head snapped up, locking eyes with the person coming right toward him. There was a brief moment of understanding where everything seemed to come to a standstill.

Ritchie.

Roberta let out a sound, half gasp, half scream, which startled David and alerted the nurse to the fact something was not right. In the split second his gaze wandered, Ritchie had charged them, knocking into David with his full weight, who in turn bumped into Roberta. She stumbled, hitting the wall, but managed to keep herself upright. The nurse was yelling, her footsteps pounding furiously up the squeaky-clean tile flooring.

David took several unsteady steps backward, connecting with the nurse. Ritchie came at him again, and his fist took David in the face. Roberta screamed again, then seemed to launch herself into the air, coming down on Ritchie's back as he attempted to retreat. He easily shook her off and kept going.

David took a moment to shake off the punch's effect, then also started running.

"Stay here!" he ordered.

His last glance behind him found the nurse bent over Roberta, who lay on the floor cradling the back of her head.

Ritchie was fast. He'd already passed the family waiting area by the time David rounded the corner, and was sprinting down another hallway that David knew would access a staircase leading to the ground floor. From there he could take off in any number of directions or get to the car he undoubtedly had parked nearby.

David threw all his energy behind his pursuit. Ritchie reached the door, and pried it open with barely a break in his stride. David was right behind him, but Ritchie had already cleared the first staircase. He looked up and grinned, showing his mouthful of rotten teeth. Then he vaulted over the stair's railing, in effect bypassing a whole set of stairs. David leaned over the railing as he descended, not wanting to lose sight of the man. He didn't dare attempt the same leap, not with his bad knee. He'd be down for the count, and Ritchie would surely get away.

Ritchie burst through the door located at the bottom of the final set of stairs. It swooshed shut behind him, leaving David in a thirty-second limbo where he couldn't track him. When he reached the door he ripped it open, erupting into the hectic main lobby, where people sat waiting for information, discharging, and accessed an open-air cafeteria. He spotted Ritchie at the revolving door that would take him to the street.

He bumped into someone as he ran but didn't stop. An angry female cursed him as he followed Ritchie. Outside the cold air hit him, shocking his overworked lungs. He scanned the large area, where people and cars moved about, looking for Ritchie. When at last he found him, the man had already passed the emergency lot, and was heading across the street to another parking area adjacent to the hospital's main building. David slipped as he started running again, almost falling.

He burst across the street, narrowly missing a yellow Volkswagen. On the other side he started up the slope, struggling over the snow-covered grass. At the top, the hustle and bustle of the hospital died out. A huge parking lot loomed, with a handful of people moving to and from their vehicles. A strange sound distracted him, which he came to realize was his own laboured breathing.

Ritchie had vanished.

"Fuck!" A college-aged girl looked at him as he swore, giggling as she passed him.

Up and down the rows he ran, looking for Ritchie. Everywhere he turned were empty cars, and faces he didn't recognize. He pulled his gun out, the heft of it in his hand giving some comfort. His heart began to slow, but still pounded like a drum in his chest. The sights and sounds around him touched his sense with hyperawareness, painful and intrusive.

His phone rang, startling him so much he almost dropped his gun. He pulled it out, the caller ID showing a blocked call.

"Hello?"

"It's Roberta."

"Where are you?"

"In the hospital. I gave the nurse the slip. She was demanding my name, and threatening to call the police."

"Listen, get a cab. Go to my place. Tell Jamie I told you to come there, and wait till I get back." He gave her the address and hung up before she could protest.

He passed another series of empty cars, feeling more discouraged with each passing second. A rustle of wind touched him, which he belatedly realized was not a natural event. A car door smashed into his back, knocking him to the asphalt. The gun and phone were both knocked from his grip. The door was pulled closed again as he scrambled onto his back, now peering up onto Ritchie's agitated expression.

"You won't fucking quit will you, you stupid shit. This has nothing to with you."

"But it does have something to do with Stella." He attempted to stand, but Ritchie caught him in the ribs with his boot. The wind left his lungs in a forced exhalation.

"That bitch got what's coming to her. What do you care about some junkie whore anyway?"

"She's someone's daughter," he said, while wrapping a protective arm about his mid-section.

Ritchie's fist came down, striking him in the ear, then the jaw. "That's too fucking bad. She crossed Lee, and she's going to pay for it."

There were footsteps and a shout from an unseen male. Ritchie's attention drifted, and David took the opportunity to punch the man as hard as he could between the legs. Ritchie howled, grabbing at his groin as he went down. David came at him, but he recovered impressively fast. They rolled, knocking against a parked car. An awkward series of blows was exchanged, confined by the space between two vehicles.

David spotted his gun lying about ten feet away. He scrambled toward it, but Ritchie grabbed one of his legs, yanking him back. He felt the other man's weight on his lower body, then was roughly turned onto his back. He tried to get his hands around Ritchie's neck, but he'd managed to pull his own weapon from his coat pocket. He pointed the gun at David's head.

Ritchie stood and started to back up. "Stay right where you are or I start shooting."

David took the threat seriously. Whether it was him or an innocent bystander, no one else needed to die. Ritchie got in the car whose door he'd hit David with. David pressed himself against the one beside it as Ritchie peeled out of the lot. He wasn't touched, but his cell phone became a casualty, having been crushed under one of the wheels.

As a small group of people gathered he trotted across the lot to retrieve his gun, which he tucked back in his holster. After assuring those who'd come to his aid that he was fine, he left the bewildered bunch behind. His heart was thrumming again by the time he'd reached his car, and he figured he'd had more than his fair share of exercise that day.

He made quick work of getting home, pulling into the driveway with a squeal from his tires. He made sure to lock the door, though it wouldn't be any kind of deterrent to the kinds of people whose feathers he'd ruffled. The side door was locked, and it seemed like hours before he could get his hands steady enough to get the key in the slot. By the time the lock clicked and he'd turned the knob, the door was being pulled open from the inside. Jamie waited on the other side.

He'd never been so glad to see anyone in his whole life. David made a strange chocking noise before giving him a crushing hug.

"Did Roberta get here okay?"

"Yes. She's in the kitchen."

He shrugged out of his coat and hung it on the rack by the door. Roberta sat at the table hunched over a cup of tea, a sight not dissimilar to Susan's visit earlier in the week. He really needed to get people over to his place under better circumstances.

"Did you get him?"

"No. I caught up to him and we had a bit of a fight, but he knocked my gun out of my hand and then pulled his on me. There were people about, and I had no choice but to let him go." He sat down, wincing as his back touched the upright part of the chair.

"Jesus, how hurt are you?" Jamie asked, concern making his eyes sparkle.

"Dunno, he hit me with a car door and got a couple of punches in."

"Take your shirt off," Roberta said, snapping out of her anxiety-induced timidity.

"'Scuse me?"

"Just do it." Her tone indicated she wasn't taking no for an answer. To Jamie she said, "Can you get some Tylenol, ice, a towel and maybe a tensor bandage if you have one. Oh, also a clean cloth."

Jamie left to get the supplies. David removed his shirt, wincing as he raised his arms. Roberta helped remove the shirt the rest of the way. In the front he had a well-defined red patch, starting to darken from the kick he'd taken. He imagined his back was even worse where he'd connected with the weight of the car door.

Roberta looked him over, fingers gently moving over the area on his face where Ritchie had punched him. She moved his head, looking at the other side of his face. She brushed aside his shaggy hair but didn't comment or ask about his hearing aid.

Jamie returned and placed everything but the ice on the table. Roberta ran the cloth under warm water and cleaned the cuts on David's face. Jamie had put some ice in a bag, which he brought to Roberta along with a cup of water. He handed the cup to David and shook out a couple of Tylenols for him to take. Roberta covered the bag of ice in the towel and wrapped the tensor bandage over it to hold it in place against his back injury.

"We have to keep up with our first aid for the centre," she said by way of explanation.

"You need to tell the police about this."

"I'm sure they've already been called. The nurse was pissed," Roberta said.

Jamie sat down. "What the hell was Ritchie doing there?"

"Trying to finish the job I suspect."

"That's pretty ballsy to do in a hospital, isn't it?"

"He isn't the sharpest tool in the shed. He just does what he's told," David answered.

"Still. It's risky to pull something like that."

"I guess the people involved figure it's better Jenny's dead, than them." He paused, realizing the bigger implication of what he just said. "We do need to call the police. They need to park a guard at Jenny's door until everyone is rounded up."

A knock sounded at the front door, the distinct bang-bang-bang variety that always announces some kind of authority. Red and blue lights flashed beyond the family room window, the telltale sign of a patrol car.

"Roberta, get out of sight," he called as he walked to the front door. David opened the door to two uniformed officers and the last person on earth he wanted to deal with.

"Hello there, David. We keep crossing paths these days," Jeremy said.

It wouldn't have taken a rocket scientist to put two and two together. No doubt the nurse had passed along his description, and his connection to Jenny had already been established.

"That didn't take long."

"Not with the force's finest on the case." Jeremy was enjoying himself far too much.

David had no choice but to let him in.

Jeremy and the other officers followed him back to the kitchen. Jamie's eyes narrowed as Jeremy entered.

"Can you get me something to put on? Something that does up in the front," David asked Jamie. He was too sore to pull the shirt he'd been wearing back over his head.

Jamie left without answering.

"If I didn't know the circumstances, I'd have to wonder about what was going on here?" Jeremy chuckled at his own innuendo. Nobody else found him amusing.

"Have you checked on Jenny?" David asked.

"Yes, the nurse on charge called security, and they were waiting when police arrived. There were multiple calls from her room and also a nearby parking lot."

Jamie returned and handed David a front-zip sweatshirt.

Jeremy continued. "After I heard a description of a man sounding like you, I came here, hoping I'd catch you. So you want to tell us what's going on? Seems everywhere you go people are getting hurt and killed."

David sat, feeling like absolute crap. Jamie moved to stand beside him.

"We went to question Elaine about what she might know, and we had convinced her to come and make a statement to the police. We were heading to the car when she was shot." David had a flash of Jamie covered in the woman's blood.

"Did you see who shot at you?"

"Not really. It was a dark car, tinted windows. I believe it was a man, wearing a dark winter coat. It happened too quickly."

Jeremy wrote something down. "And what happened at the hospital?"

"I went to check on Jenny. I've been going every day since she doesn't have any family. When I was leaving Ritchie was coming down the hall. He jumped us and took off. I chased him out to the parking lot where we got into a fight, and he pulled a gun on me. He drove off."

"The nurse said there was a woman with you."

"Just some friend of Jenny's. Said her name was Carla, but I can't be sure about that. I've never seen her before."

Jeremy didn't look convinced. "Anything else to add?"

Jamie gave David a questioning look, but remained silent.

"Jenny woke up briefly when I went to talk with her. She said Ritchie's the guy who hurt her. He's one of the guys I already told you about," David explained.

"Well that's something we can move on. We'll beef up the effort to find the guy."

"Good."

"Okay. Well here's what I'm going to suggest." His condescending tone made David want to punch the man in the face. "You guys stay put. You've already put yourself and others in the line of fire, and screwed up what could have been a major drug bust. If we turn up anything about your missing girl, we'll let the family know."

David was treading in murky waters. He did have a responsibility to Marjory, yet he had no authority to bypass a police investigation. His hatred for Jeremy made it even harder to think through his next actions in a rational manner. He'd love nothing better than to show the man up, taking the so-called glory for himself.

David made an understanding face. "Of course, we won't interfere with your investigation."

"Good. Nice place you have by the way." He turned as though dismissing David in his own home, leaving with the other officers trailing behind.

Once the door had closed Jamie sat down. Roberta returned

from the bathroom, where she'd obviously been listening.

"What an asshole," Roberta said.

David couldn't help but laugh at her quick, and spot-on, assessment. "Yep."

"You're not actually going to listen to him are you?" Jamie asked.

David's grin grew wider. "Are you actually telling me I should not follow orders from the police, Mr. Prosecutor?"

"You're a lawyer?" Roberta asked, clearly surprised.

"What did you think I was?"

She gave him a serious inspection, taking in the casual clothes and sleep-tousseled hair. "I don't know. You're very cute, though. You could be a model or something like that."

David laughed so hard it hurt his injured ribs. "Oh, that's priceless. Pretty-boy Jamie."

"Stop." He gave Roberta a smile. "Thanks for the compliment, but I really am a lawyer. I'm usually trying to talk sense into him, not encouraging him to do something reckless or illegal."

"Yeah, he's generally as straight as they come, if you pardon the pun."

"So you guys have bad blood with the dickhead?"

"You could say that."

The merriment died away quicker than the snap of a finger. Jeremy Black was suspect number one on both David's and Jamie's lists of who was responsible for his attack. He'd suffered endless harassment and at times outright hostility from the man in the months preceding the night at McBurney's Bar. He'd been the definite ringleader for a group of officers who had made it clear they weren't happy with his sexuality, or having to work with someone they deemed inferior. His being gay had embarrassed and infuriated Jeremy, but there had been nothing he could do through professional channels to get David to leave. David was sure he'd decided to take a different, more violent track to end his career.

It hadn't been a surprise when Jeremy had provided an alibi. He fully admitted being in the same bar as David, saying that he'd left before him. The buddies he'd been with that night all backed him up, saying they walked to another bar, where they were in fact recognized. Their timing had been fuzzier, but the group stuck fast to their story. There had been no witnesses of the actual incident. Sean had come looking for him after he'd been gone for a long period of time. He'd found him outside in the alleyway at the back of the bar, unconscious and covered in blood.

"Wow," was all Roberta could say after hearing the story.

"Yeah, that's how I got my bum knee and this," David said, pointing to his ear.

"Let's not talk about him. We need to figure out what to do. If Lee, Ritchie, and Christian haven't been picked up yet, we need to start looking for them. We also need to warn Stella about what's going on."

"You need to explain to me this bit about George and Christian and the warehouse," Roberta said.

Jamie made more tea while David filled her in on what he'd uncovered about George and Christian, his suspicions about the events surrounding Stella's accident, and what Elaine had told him before she was shot. They also discussed Jenny's brief but enlightening revelations.

Roberta got very quiet, concentrating on her cup as though it contained the answers to their situation.

"I knew about the movies," she said at last. "Well, that Stella had done some, but I didn't know about Christian being involved, and I don't know what Lee's role is either."

"Well he's involved, but whether it's under direction of the Crimson Knights, or a deal he's pulling on the side, we can't say for sure yet. We're assuming he's pulling a fast one on his bosses," Jamie said after thinking over the information that had been collected. "We don't know how she knows what she does, and she's in no shape to elaborate on what she does or doesn't know."

"And what's Stella's angle? I mean does she simply want to blow the whistle on some lowlifes, including her brother, or is there more to it?"

"You're still stuck on this accident thing aren't you?" Jamie asked.

"What do you think, Roberta? You know Stella pretty well.

Is it just a case of a girl with emotional problems who also likes to get high? Or do you think her emotional problems are the result of something, and she uses drugs to escape?"

"The stuff I told you in your office about Stella and her family is true. She's never told me more than the fact she thinks her dad is disgusting for the way he sleeps around on her mother. She hardly ever mentions Christian, and when she does it's always vague."

"Doesn't that seem strange in and of itself? I get that lots of times siblings aren't close, but with the stuff going on in her family, I don't know, it just seems weird."

"Maybe? Could be she just didn't like the guy if she knew he was like her father. That would be another reason to hate her dad more, if her brother had turned out like him."

"Yeah, I guess." David hung on to his suspicions stubbornly.

"Regardless of what, if anything, happened, Christian and Lee are involved in drugs and pornography, both of which will likely mean jail time. Ritchie will be wanted for assault, maybe even murder if he's the one who pulled the trigger on Elaine. Plus the shots taken at you and the vandalism. George Barrowman will be in hot water with the underage sex scandal and his involvement in the warehouse ownership. Enough crime's gone on in the past few weeks to keep these guys behind bars for a long time. Once they're all removed from the picture, Stella should have a decent chance to recover and get her life back on track."

"Always the lawyer," David said.

"Well, look, if something did happen, like you suspect, maybe Stella will talk about it once she's away from these men."

"I need to get hold of Jimmy, see what's turned up."

"I need to call Sasha and pass along the warning. You have a phone I can use?" asked Roberta.

Jamie grabbed the portable phone from its base and handed it over. "Voicemail," she said. "What's the number here?"

She repeated what David told her, and gave a brief explanation of what had happened and where she was.

"He rarely answers, but he'll call back soon." She handed over the phone to David. "Your turn."

Jimmy didn't have any new information. Elaine's body had been taken to the morgue, pending autopsy. There had been no witnesses other than David and Jamie. None of the wanted parties had turned up yet, despite an exhaustive ongoing search. All records for the warehouse were being pulled. He promised to call if he heard anything.

The three ordered pizza and decided over their meal that Roberta should stay with them for the time being. They didn't think any of the players involved would be stupid enough to come around again with the police involved, and as the popular theory stated, there was safety in numbers.

By the time they all headed to bed, armed and alarm system activated, Sasha had yet to return the call.

CHAPTER 15

When David came down to the kitchen the next morning, the always welcome aroma of freshly brewed coffee preceded him. The radio played, tuned to some pop station, and a female voice sang along to the current number. The sound stopped him in his tracks. It had been a long time since a woman had spent the night in his house, and the understanding brought a wave of guilt with it. He'd really done a number on his ex-wife, letting her believe in something that he'd never been able to feel for her in return. He had loved her, but the feeling had been and would always remain platonic. It would be nice to see her again, as she had agreed to come to the party the following weekend.

Roberta was at the table, coffee in hand and a newspaper before her. The singing came to an abrupt end as David appeared. He took down a mug and poured himself some coffee, taking the first wonderful sip before joining her at the table. Jamie had left earlier, needing to clear up some things at his office.

"Any calls yet?"

"Nope. I'm getting worried. I hope Lee or Christian hasn't gotten to them." She pushed a section of the paper to him. "Elaine's murder made the papers."

David skimmed the article, which was brief and vague. The reporter seemed to imply a random act of violence, an assumption far from the truth.

"Hmm. We need to get a hold of these guys before anyone else gets hurt."

"We need to find Stella and Sasha."

"Any ideas where they might have gone?"

"Not really. Sasha's life is dance, but I can't see him turning to anyone at his company with this situation. I mean what are a bunch of ballet dancers going to do to protect them?" She had a point.

"Can't hurt to ask. We should check with everyone we can think of. Feel like coming on a ride with me?"

"Sure, let me grab a shower."

"We should hit a mall too, get some new cell phones."

"Good idea."

About a half-hour later they were on the road. Snow fell like a heavy, wet blanket, slowing traffic and exciting tempers. They hit the nearest retail centre, forcing their way through the busy Christmas shoppers to a cell phone outlet. The employee helping them would just not get that they weren't a couple, and as such would not be needing a shared plan. At last they both emerged from the store, newly activated phones in hand. David immediately called Jamie and his mother to let them know the new number. Roberta tried Sasha again, leaving a second message.

They went by Lee's place, but his car was gone. A check-in with the site manager let them know that he hadn't been around in a few days. A call to Marcus confirmed that he hadn't heard from Sasha and wasn't aware that any of the other dancers had either. David even tried Janice, getting the expected answer. There'd been no contact.

Christian wasn't at work. He'd called in sick, expecting to be out for several days, which seemed suspicious considering the only evidence working against him was a statement from a now-dead witness. Having been seen speaking with prostitutes was circumstantial at best, and a good lawyer could have the situation with the warehouse working for his client with the right kind of spin. Everything else in his past screamed goodness and decency, a notion that caught in the back of David's throat like a lump of phlegm.

"What about his house?" Roberta asked as they stepped out onto the sidewalk. The wind howled and snapped, blowing icy wetness against their skin.

"I guess. I have it in my notes. I haven't gone by there since he'd been agreeable about meeting. A good snoop session might turn up something interesting though."

It turned out that Christian didn't live more than three blocks away from Marcy Anderson's house. It was a nice two-story home, the empty driveway neatly shoveled. David parked half a block away, and he and Roberta went to the front door. The bell and insistent knocking went unanswered for several minutes. Taking that to mean no one was at home David started around the side of the house, where a wooden gate led to the backyard. He let himself in after reaching over the top of the fence to release to latch. No dogs jumped out at him and no shots were fired. The backyard was silent and deserted.

Roberta came in behind him, shutting the gate to keep prying eyes away. The back door had a decent lock, but David managed to get it open in less than a minute. Tentatively he opened the door, checking for an alarm system. Finding nothing he started inside.

"You should probably go back to the car. Once you come in you're as guilty as I am."

"Let's just do this," she answered, stepping in.

Inside the house was nicely decorated and extremely clean but had all the charm of a generic storeroom display. Very few personal touches had been applied, leaving a cold, empty feeling to the space. They found nothing remarkable on the main level, and the basement held only a washer and dryer, and the regular assortment of little-used items like luggage and tools.

They were rewarded for their search of the second floor. One bedroom was a guest room with nothing but an empty dresser and a neatly made bed. The closet was bare. Another room had been turned into an office and showed the most use of any room in the house. Cabinets held files, both personal and work related. The desk was covered with professional articles and other benign documents. David tried the computer, which had been locked with a password he couldn't crack. On the desk sat an eight-by-ten framed photo of Stella as a teenager, dressed as though for a dance performance of some kind. For the first time in any photo he'd seen she was smiling, a look that brought an ache to David's chest.

Roberta picked up the photo and smiled sadly. "If only

things could have stayed this way for her."

In Christian's bedroom they searched the dresser, closet, and the attached bathroom. He liked name brand clothing and expensive cologne, and kept up a moisturizing routine that would have put most women to shame. Another picture of Stella sat on his bedside table, this one of the both of them frozen in pre-adolescence. It was a posed picture, brother and sister dressed up and looking slightly uncomfortable.

Underneath the bed, David found a shoebox and a large photo album. He pulled them out and sat on the bed to take a look. Roberta joined him. They flipped through the pages of the album, which held countless photos of Christian and Stella as they grew up together. There were pictures of holidays and birthday parties, and several family vacations. As Stella aged through the procession of photos, the more obvious it became that her happiness and vitality was being drained from her, so that by the time she hit her early teenage years she'd become a pale ghost of the girl she'd once been.

Yet despite the obvious loss of vivaciousness and the deadness slowly taking permanent residence in her eyes, Stella's beauty could not be denied. Apparently her brother had noticed too, as the pictures began to take on a dark and inappropriate nature, moving from ordinary snapshots of times passed to an intrusive, voyeuristic analysis of the girl's physical attributes.

Lost were the other people in Stella's life as the photo diary progressed, all the remaining photos focusing solely on the girl herself. She was caught in bathing suits, wrapped in towels as though coming from the shower, and photo after photo of her in various dance performances and rehearsals. When caught stretching or posed for performance the pictures had taken on a decidedly lewd tone, often closing in on her chest, the curve of her buttocks, or her private area.

"This is disgusting," Roberta said after viewing several pages of disturbing photographs, which clearly displayed an unnatural lust.

"Yep," David agreed. He slammed the book shut when they came to a section of nude photos.

"What's in the box?"

After what he'd just seen David wasn't sure he wanted to know. He pulled off the lid, finding a handful of loose photos and several DVDs. He gave Roberta a look that she mirrored: repulsion. A television with DVD player sat on a small stand near the bed. David popped in one of the discs, not surprised to find a pornographic film appear on the screen. When the camera focused on Stella, he turned it off.

"This guy is a sick fucker." David's stomach churned. His blood boiled, yet the understanding of what they'd uncovered chilled him.

"Oh my God, Stella."

David put the items back where he'd found them and they returned to his car. As they drove Roberta tried Sasha again.

"Hi, Sasha?" She paused while listening to his end of the conversation. She turned to David, placing her hand over the phone. "They heard about Elaine's murder. They read it in the paper."

There was a jolting, anxious conversation, ending when they agreed to meet David and Roberta in a restaurant of their choosing. He didn't know the place but was familiar with the area.

The restaurant was a smaller mom-and-pop type place, low on ambience, but looked like a place that would offer a menu full of comfort food. Inside, the place was half full, the hour middling between lunch and dinner. David spotted Sasha in a booth near the back. A woman sat with him, her back to the door. The long sandy hair had been pulled into a low ponytail.

David felt an indescribable anticipation seize him, burning like a tough case of indigestion. Though he'd only been on the case a few weeks, he felt close to Stella, protective of her, and yet he'd still hadn't met the woman face to face.

With each step closer his heart pounded more forcefully. His scalp tightened, running a spidery, tingling sensation down his neck. Time slowed as he stepped alongside the table. He was unable to breathe as she turned her attention to him, eyes wide and suspicious. Only when he offered his hand in greeting did her shoulders relax, and a hesitant smile appeared.

"Stella? I'm David Lloyd."

She took his hand, the skin warm and soft. "Hi David. It's nice to meet you."

Sasha and Roberta made noises of greeting with each other, but David couldn't take his eyes off of Stella. He didn't know exactly what he'd expected, but he was pleasantly surprised. The young woman was clean, well-dressed, and impossibly attractive in no makeup and hair pulled back from her face. Unlike many drug addicts David had been around, she didn't shake or have a sallow sheen to her complexion.

"You have no idea how glad I am to have finally tracked you down. You've had people worried."

"Roberta said my mother hired you?" David nodded. "She's the only one I care about who might have been looking for me. Despite everything, I know she loves me, and she did try and help me as best she could. I can't say the same about anyone else. Present company excluded of course."

Both Sasha and Roberta smiled at the comment. The waitress came to their table. They all ordered coffee, and Stella asked for a piece of blueberry pie.

"Sorry, I have such an appetite now that I'm not doing drugs."

David let the admission pass. "So where do we start with this mess?"

"It has become an unbelievable mess hasn't it? I still can't quite believe that Elaine's dead. She was a back-stabbing bitch, but still, I didn't want her to die." Stella gave Sasha a knowing look, and he sighed.

"Lee and Ritchie are still on the loose, and as of right now your brother's missing as well. We don't know who's responsible for what, but they're all tied up in this somehow. We know about the warehouse, and the...movies." David resisted the urge to squirm, remembering what he'd seen earlier at Christian's house.

"Right," was all she had to say about that.

The waitress brought their order, scurrying away after observing the collective grim expressions of her customers.

"Are you okay, Stella? I mean you look great." Roberta jumped in, filling the awkward silence that had taken over.

"I'm good. I've been clean for eight weeks now. I've been dancing again. I mean, I'm in terrible shape, but I'm trying."

"Where have you been?" David asked.

She was quiet for a few minutes, pushing the remains of her pie about the plate with her fork. "I stole some money from Lee and rented a house out of the city. I wanted to get clean and focused before I dealt with some stuff."

"What stuff?" David asked, even though he already had a good idea what she was talking about.

"I need to face the truth about how I got to this point, no matter how painful it may be for me and my mom. I need to get off the drugs for good and take control of my life."

"Go on," David prompted gently.

"Well, you know about the movies, right? Those have been going on for a few years now, maybe four or five. They started back when Elaine and Christian pulled a fast one on my dad."

"You mean when they blackmailed him about sleeping with Elaine while underage?"

"Yeah. Christian found out about it. They got one of the encounters between Elaine and my dad on tape and threatened to go public with it. He would have lost his job, and he could have gone to jail, so he paid them off. Well, he paid Elaine off; he didn't realize that Christian had set the whole thing up. Anyway that gave Christian an idea. He went to Lee, who he knew had access to girls who would do the kinds of things he wanted, and they went into business together."

"They told you about this?"

"Not in so many words. Christian got me hooked up with Lee for the drugs. They both liked when I was stoned, 'cause I was easier to control. They just didn't always watch what they said around me, you know, thinking I was nothing to worry about. I figured out they were using some of the drug money to fund the films, and the warehouse became their headquarters, even though it belonged to the people Lee works for."

"The Crimson Knights?"

"Right."

"I'm guessing they not only don't know about any of this, but that they're not getting a cut of the profits?" David asked.

"That's right, and if they ever found out, Lee and Christian would have been in a lot of trouble. Like the kind that gets your legs broken or worse."

David thought of Elaine, her blood so bright against the snow. "Did you know your dad set up the business that officially owns the warehouse?"

Stella shook her head. "No, but it doesn't surprise me. He and my brother are very tight. He always overlooks any of the bad stuff my brother does, especially if it gets him women or money."

"Do you think he knows about the movies and the drugs being shipped there?"

"Probably not. He likes to maintain his image so the less he knew the better. When it comes down to the wire, I'm sure he'll say he didn't realize anything illegal was going on, you know, he was just trying to help out one of his son's friends. He wouldn't have known the details, but he would have had to suspect."

"So let's be clear here, you say he knows about Christian and his activities?"

"Oh yeah. Absolutely."

"Your mom?"

The question brought a strange expression to Stella's face. "No. I can't believe she didn't know that my dad cheated on her, but she pretended she didn't. I don't think she knew anything about Christian. I never told her, and I'm sure he didn't."

"So are you planning to blow the whistle on Lee and Christian's operation? Is that what's going on here? 'Cause I feel like there's more to the story."

"There is. Much more. I mean, I guess you know I was in some of the movies? Lee always threatened to hurt my mom and anyone close to me if I didn't do what he wanted. That's why I kept using. When I was stoned I didn't feel, and it kept everyone else safe. One night I just wanted it to stop, I was so sick of it. I went looking for Roberta. We'd kept in contact after I was at the clinic, but this time I really wanted to stop. She took me home, got me some help to get sober. I lasted most of a year until Lee found me again. Someone told him I was dancing at the Letter and he waited for me. He took me back with him and beat the crap out of me." She'd started to cry, but continued with the story. "This was last spring. He shot me up, and it was like I'd never left."

"So this is around the time you had the fight with Sasha?"

"I showed up at his place and made a total ass of myself. I left again and went back to Lee. I stayed there, not knowing what to do. When I saw Ritchie and another guy beat one of the girls…to death, because she refused to do something they wanted her to do for one of the movies, I just couldn't take it anymore. I took some money and I ran. I ended up at Sasha's and he's been helping me ever since. When Jenny got hurt I called Roberta." Her face was red and blotchy from crying, and it was getting harder for her to speak. David handed her a few napkins from the container on the table.

"So Ritchie's already killed someone. He's the one who put Jenny in the hospital too, but I think that was just luck. I'm sure he thought she was dead when he left her."

Stella took a shaky breath. "Is she going to be okay?"

"Seems like it. She's woken up, but I think it's still too early to know the extent of her damages."

"I'm sorry for that. She's really an okay girl, she just comes from a rough past."

David tried to sort out the information against everything else he'd already uncovered. Stella was holding back, she had to be. Some things just didn't add up, like the accusation against Marcus, the drug use before meeting Lee, and the car accident.

"What aren't you telling me?" David asked.

Stella had regained her composure. She flicked a look in Roberta and Sasha's direction. "Can we talk, just you and I?"

"Of course."

The two left, agreeing to wait in Sasha's car until they were finished. Stella was fidgeting, clearly distressed, but David knew he had to get the truth from her no matter how difficult it would be. The people who'd hurt her had to pay, but without her voice they may never receive the punishment they deserved.

When she remained silent David asked, "This is about Christian, isn't it?"

A single tear slipped down her cheek. "It's always about Christian."

"He hurt you, didn't he?"

She stared intently at the plate before her. "Yes." Her voice was barely a whisper.

"What happened?"

"He raped me."

David took the admission like a sledgehammer to the gut. "The day of the accident?"

"Uh-huh. I came home from school. He was at university then, and had a room on campus. But he'd come home for something, I don't even know what, so he was there when I got home from school. He'd done things to me before, touched me and stuff. I tried to stay away from him, but sooner or later he'd find a way to get me alone."

Though he'd suspected something like what she'd just admitted, hearing the words out loud were surreal. How could anyone do such a thing?

"Did you tell your parents?"

"I talked to my dad once. Big mistake. He got really angry and told me not to say anything to anyone else. He must have talked with Christian, because he stayed away from me for a while, then he went to school."

"So after he assaulted you, you ran over to Sinclair's house?"

"Yes, I didn't know what to do. He'd hurt me then made me take a shower and put clean clothes on. When he went to get rid of the other things I'd been wearing I took off. I didn't even have shoes or anything. I don't remember what I was thinking, just that I had to get away from there. Sinclair and Janice brushed me off. I'd already been having problems because of what Christian had been doing to me. I ran away from the house and I got hit by the car. When I came to in the hospital and my mom and dad were there, I just couldn't say anything. I don't know why, I was just so scared."

"Stella, you were just a kid. And your dad had already let you down once."

"I never told him anything, well, not till much later, but I think he suspected. He had Christian transferred to another school, one where he'd be far away from me, and things were okay, except for when he came home for holidays and stuff."

"Why did you accuse Marcus of raping you?"

"It happened again, with Christian. I'd made such a mess of things by then with drugs and having sex with other guys. I didn't think anyone would believe me if I told what he'd done, but I wanted someone to pay, you know? I don't know why I choose Marcus, I just did, the words came out of my mouth and I couldn't take them back. But I knew it was wrong so I wouldn't give a statement to the police."

"Then you went to the Davenport Clinic?"

"No this happened before I went. The second time with Christian happened right before the start of my last year of high school. I participated in a few workshops, but I just couldn't keep it together. I kept having flashbacks of the attacks, I had nightmares. I started doing drugs again. I ended up at the clinic. I met a girl there, and she told me about what she was going through with her stepdad. It triggered something in me, a rage that I'd never let myself feel before. The first time I saw Christian after I returned home I snapped."

"And accused Marcus."

"Yes. Around the same time I found out about Elaine and my dad, and I just felt like I couldn't trust anyone. I confronted him, and he told me that Elaine had blackmailed him about it. That was it, I just lost it. I didn't care anymore. I let Christian and Elaine use me. I took all the drugs I could get my hands on so I wouldn't have to think or feel anything. I wanted to die."

"Why didn't you ask Sasha or Roberta for help?"

"I was messed up. I was ashamed, and I didn't think anyone would believe me."

"But you stood up to your dad for Roberta, didn't you? Don't you think she would have returned the favour?"

"Maybe. Look it's bad enough what they do know about me with the drugs and the movies. I don't want this getting out, I'm going to have a hard enough time as it is reclaiming my life."

Every awful, disgusting fact that Stella had unveiled clawed at his tightly held emotions, threatening to throw open the floodgates. As she spoke, not only could he feel her pain and shame, he was also filled with a burning remorse for his own tragedies. He felt anger for being tossed aside like a second-class citizen, and even worse for not having fought harder for someone to have been brought to justice for his attack. He knew part of the reason he'd walked away had been embarrassment. He'd wanted to push the incident away as though it had never happened, save face any way he could. When it felt like no matter how hard he tried or how justified he was, that no one would stay with him to the end, sometimes it was just easier to walk away. He could understand Stella's need to keep her past private and the pain locked away.

"You know, Roberta is already aware of some of this."

She tensed visibly. "What do you mean?"

"We were at your brother's house earlier, and found a photo album he keeps of you and some videos. Not the kind of stuff any brother should have of his sister."

"Jesus." She started to cry again, silent tears of shame.

"It's not your fault Stella. It's Christian's. He's sick."

"That doesn't make me feel better."

"Will letting him get away with this make it better? Do you want him to continue hurting girls like he does? Unless you make a statement to the police, there's really nothing to go on. The stuff at his house is circumstantial at best. I'm quite sure your father will deny knowing anything, otherwise he risks looking like a monster for not protecting you."

"I can't do this." The fork dropped from her shaking fingers.

"Yes, you can. You're strong, otherwise you wouldn't have made it this far."

"You said yourself he's gone somewhere. Maybe he won't come back."

"You and I both know that's not likely. There's no evidence against him except a connection to the warehouse. Spun the right way he'll get out of that, claiming he didn't know there was anything illegal going on. He's squeaky clean on paper, you know that."

"So what can I do?"

"Call him. I have an idea."

CHAPTER 16

The four regrouped at David's house, where he put a call through to Marjory. They had a meeting planned, which he begged off with an excuse of having had some new information come to light that would hopefully lead him to Stella. A convenient twist of the truth. He didn't tell her the information would most likely put her daughter's drug dealer and woman-beating sicko in jail, along with her twisted son, and would at best smear her husband's reputation. Since Jamie already knew about George Barrowman sleeping with Elaine when she was under age, he would have bet money his partner wouldn't let go until he made charges against the man stick. In one fell swoop the woman would learn the shattering truth about her son and husband, and be forced to face the abuse her daughter had long suffered. Not a happy experience for anyone to go through.

They'd decided on an uncomplicated, classic sting. It had the best chance for success and the least potential for unwanted surprises. Sitting around the kitchen table, which had become the unofficial meeting spot for the case, Stella put a call through to her brother. Her hands trembled as she dialed the number.

"Hello." Christian's voice came from the phone, set to speaker mode, like a demon from the pit of hell. In David's book he rated even lower.

"Hi Christian," Stella said, her discomfort impossible to ignore.

"Stella? Where the hell are you?"

"Doesn't matter. Look I know what's going on. I heard about Elaine and Jenny. I don't want anyone else to get hurt, so...I'll come back."

There was a pause. "Well things are a bit complicated now Stella. The police are involved, and Mom's hired some asshole detective who's snooping into everyone's business. We have to shut down production for a while, wait till stuff blows over."

"Do you want me to come back or not Christian?"

"Of course I do. It's sucked the last few months not having you around. I just need to figure out what to do about Lee."

"What do you mean?"

"He's pissed. For me, it's just a cut in money, but him, if his bosses find out, well he'll be in some deep shit. He blames you. I think if he sees you any time soon he'll sic Ritchie on you, and we both know how that turns out."

"Then meet me somewhere that he doesn't know about."

"Yeah, I can do that. Somewhere private, 'cause you have a lot to make up to me."

The implication of his words could not be misunderstood, and the thought of what he wanted from Stella made David sick to his stomach.

Stella met David's eyes as she answered. "Yes, there's lots to make up for. Where and when?"

He gave her the address of a second building in the same vicinity as the warehouse. She promised to be there by seven o'clock.

The next few hours were impossibly long, both with dread for the interaction about to happen and with hope that the entire miserable ordeal would finally come to an end. They decided to go early, park away from the site and make their way in on foot. David wanted to scope the layout of the building and surrounding area. It was always best to know the location of all possible exits and escape routes.

The address turned out to be a small building, out of place amongst the many larger warehouses and processing facilities. They all found positions in sight of an exit and had cell phones in hand to report any suspicious activity. Stella was wired, which David monitored. While he stood watching the door that opened onto a private, rear parking area his phone rang. He flipped it open mid-ring after recognizing the number.

"Hey Jamie."

"Hi. Why are you whispering?"

"Stella's meeting with Christian. We're in place to catch the bastard."

"Who's we?"

"It's a long story."

"You need more back-up?'

"I think you'll be cutting it too close. He's supposed to arrive any time now."

"Give me the address, David. I can at least drive by and make sure things are kosher. He won't be looking for my car."

David didn't have the time to argue. He passed along the information and said goodbye.

"David? Check, check." Stella's voice came on, speaking directly into David's good ear.

"I hear you loud and clear," he answered.

He could only imagine the fear and revulsion churning about in her mind. The only consolation in having her go through such an ordeal was the fact that Christian would be apprehended and turned over to the authorities, who would make sure he wouldn't hurt anyone else.

Stella suddenly took a deep inhalation of breath. David felt himself mimicking the action, muscles tensing.

"Hi Christian," Stella said.

"Good, you came alone. I wondered if you weren't trying to trick me, but I guess a whore like you would know better."

Christian's insult and condescending tone made David so angry he saw red. He'd never felt such an absolute hatred for another human being except Jeremy Black. The cold night around him evaporated. At that moment there was nothing else but the need to squash the piece of shit under his shoe like the worm that he was. He had a feeling that Christian might have a serious *accident* before he made it to the police station.

There came a sound like someone being struck and then Stella gave a gasp of surprise. "What the hell Christian? I came didn't I?"

"Yeah, you also fucked everything up. Lee's pissed, the movies are shut down, at least for the time being. Dad's been up my ass for dragging him into this, with the building and everything. And that detective's turned up a lot of stuff that doesn't need to get out."

"I didn't have to come here. I could have gone to the police."

"For what? You're a junkie, Stella. You fuck people for money. Who's going to believe anything you have to say?"

"Then why are you so worried, huh? Why'd you take time off work? Aren't you Mr. Perfect, where everyone just thinks the sun shines right out of your ass?"

"Shut up, Stella."

"Are you worried that someone might believe that you fuck your own sister? That you raped me when I was fourteen yours old? How perfect would you seem, when people knew that you and that sick fuck Lee kept me in drugs so you could send me out as a prostitute and so I'd make your fucking movies?" Stella's voice was becoming shrill, so loud it made David's ear ache.

"You liked it. Just as much as I do." At last, a confession.

"Keep your fucking hands off me."

A scuffle started, and then Stella screamed.

David burst through the door. "Let go of her, you little shit!"

He found the two of them on the floor, Stella struggling against her brother's strength. Christian took the full force of David's tackle, getting knocked a few feet away. Stella was immediately on her feet, running for the door. A shot rang out.

David looked up into the muzzle of a small pistol. Christian rose to his feet while keeping the weapon pointed at his sister. She started to run again and he fired, the shot barley missing her.

"Get back here. I should have known you'd be stupid enough to try something like this."

Stella slowly turned and walked to her brother. He grabbed her arm and wrenched it up behind her back.

"Don't do this Christian. It can't end well for you," David said.

"You think I'm going to let some has-been cop and my stupid, fucking sister ruin everything for me? No way." He started backing toward the door, using Stella as a shield.

"Where are you going to go?"

"Who says I'm going anywhere? I think it's Stella who needs to go on a little trip. And you, sit your ass back down."

David did as he was told. His fingers twitched, wanting to reach for the gun at his shoulder, but he knew he'd never reach it in time.

"With Stella out of the picture, the rest of this stuff will just blow over. Elaine's dead, so there are no witnesses to anything she might have told you. My dad has a whole team of lawyers who'll get him out of the warehouse mess with no problems. My stupid mother will just believe everything we tell her like she always does. And Lee and I will find somewhere else to shoot the movies."

"You'd really kill your own sister? How twisted are you?"

"Not twisted, smart."

"You're a disgusting, perverted waste of skin."

"Watch it. I'm the one with the gun."

"Right. So if you're so smart what do you plan to do about me and the other people Stella's told? You going to kill all of us?"

A look of uncertainty settled on Christian's face, wiping away the smirk. "Anyone who my sister might have told will have to be dealt with. As for you, I guess it depends on how stupid you want to be."

"Come again?"

"Well you can walk away from this with your life and some money in your pocket, or you can take a trip like the one Stella's going on."

Stella's eyes had become enormous pools of fear, shining with tears. She didn't struggle or cry out, but silently pleaded with David to save her. His gaze darted about the small space, seeing nothing to help them.

"I understand you like to take payouts, David. Like you did with the police force." The smirk returned.

"What the hell are you talking about?"

"You took money with your tail tucked between your legs so you could be with your boyfriend."

David's stomach turned to stone. As he struggled to contain himself, a blur of motion passed by the open doorway. Christian had himself angled toward David, his back to the door. Jamie's face appeared out of the darkness, with a finger raised to his lips. David could have cheered, despite being angry with him for not listening to his directions.

Jamie grabbed at the arm holding the gun, and wrapped his other arm about Christian's neck. The surprise was enough to knock Christian off balance, letting Stella escape. She turned around and punched her brother in the face with every bit of strength she could muster. He threw Jamie off and lunged at her.

"Run!" David jumped to his feet.

Stella ducked out of the way and bolted for the door. David crashed into Christian, taking them both to the floor. Christian kept a firm grip on the gun while he managed to wriggle out from under David. As he stood he caught David under the jaw with his foot. He took a wild shot back at the two men, then followed Stella into the night.

The sound of further gunshots preceded Jamie and David out of the door. They ran after the two, hitting the darkness like a wall. It was difficult to see more than a few feet ahead, but a sudden scream alerted them to the direction they should take. David pulled his own gun free as they ran, but he didn't dare fire without the intended target in sight. Stella could be hurt, and no doubt the commotion had alerted Sasha and Roberta.

At last two figures could be seen heading toward the water. Another shot rang out. Footsteps pounded along a wooden deck, voices carried over the wind coming off the lake. David pulled ahead of Jamie, and despite the screaming agony in his knee he raced toward Stella and her brother. A loud splash touched his ears, then Christian let out a string of curse words. A second splash followed, and he had no doubt what had happened.

"Jamie, Jamie, hurry." David passed over his gun when Jamie caught up. "If you get a clear shot at Christian take it."

David pulled off his coat and jumped into the icy water, ignoring Jamie's cries of protest. The connection took his breath away, the cold so intense it burned. The shock made it impossible to see for several seconds, but the sound of screams reeled him back to reality. Not more than ten feet from him Christian was attempting to drown his sister, her head intermittently disappearing beneath the choppy surface of the lake. David swam over, wrapping his strong arms around Christian's torso. He could hear several voices yelling, but none of the words were distinct enough to catch his attention. The ear with his hearing aid became foggy, adding to his disorientation, but he held fast to Christian's thrashing form.

Another body knocked into him, but the darkness and the intensity of his need to control Christian made it impossible to tell who it was. A sudden, hot pain took him in the side, a sensation that fought with the hypothermia overtaking his body. Bile burned up his throat. His arms started to go slack, though he knew he had to hang on. Soon the darkness was no longer an entity he struggled with, but one that consumed him.

"Stella," David said, not hearing an answer if one was returned.

The next thing he saw was a strange face peering down at him. The noises about him sounded contained, as though he were inside, but his eyes would not focus on anything past the man who regarded him. His limbs were heavy.

"Hey, nice to see you," the man said before flashing a light into his eyes. "Pupils reacting." David had no idea if he were speaking to him or someone else he could not see.

There was only muffled sound from his left side, so he knew his hearing aid had been removed. He tried to speak, but his tongue would not cooperate. His throat felt like it had been lined with tree bark. At last the space about him began to makes sense, telltale objects registering with his lagging brain. An IV line ran to his left arm, a defibrillator was attached to the wall. He was in an ambulance.

Voices sounded just past the edge of his visual ability, and then the stranger stood, allowing another person to take his spot. David tried to track the movement, but it made his head ache terribly. He closed his eyes to ward off an attack of dizziness. When he opened them again Jamie was smiling at him.

"Stella," he managed to say.

"She's okay. A bit beat up and frozen from the water. She didn't get shot like you did."

"Shot?" The word didn't make sense.

"Yeah, Christian still had his gun. I jumped in after I saw Stella go under. You were fighting with Christian, and I thought she might drown. Sasha and Roberta came too, and Sasha jumped in to help. Roberta called 911 and went to the road to flag down the ambulance. We got Stella out, and I came back to get you. You're a tough bugger you know, you were still holding on to Christian even though you were starting to pass out."

"Christian?"

"The police have him. He's going to jail."

Jamie's face started to fade away, and David surrendered to the darkness.

Jamie was walking toward him, smiling, with his hand outstretched. He took a step forward to meet him, but instead of closing the space between them the movement forced his partner farther away. An insistent, angry throbbing filled the air around him, a heartbeat louder than a jet engine. Jamie suddenly clutched his hands to his chest, smile faltering. A crimson stain began to seep out from beneath his fingers, soaking his pale blue shirt. He crumpled to his knees, revealing Christian standing behind him, gun raised. David screamed, but the sound could not be heard over the unnatural heartbeat.

With a start he sat up. His heart pounded, blood rushing with a painful hiss in his ears. He took a bewildered look around, realizing he was in a hospital room. Jamie dozed in a chair beside his bed. At the sight of him alive and unharmed, David lay back on the pillow, releasing a breath he hadn't known he was holding.

A soft shuffle of footsteps sounded. He looked up, expecting a nurse or family member, but finding Jeremy Black instead. He came to David's bed, giving Jamie a glance before speaking.

"See, this is what happens when you don't leave the dangerous stuff to the professionals."

"Christian was caught, wasn't he?"

"You got lucky this time."

He hated being in the man's presence when the playing field was somewhat equal, but injured in bed was not a position he would ever want to be in again.

"If that's all, you know where the door is."

Jeremy smiled. "You got balls, I'll give you that. You certainly showed more guts than I thought someone like you could."

"Someone like me? A fag you mean?"

"Tsk, tsk David. That's not very PC language, now is it?"

"Whatever, Black. You've had your fun, now get out of here."

Jeremy looked him right in the eye. He leaned down over David, so close he could feel the other man's breath. "No, I had that fun in the alley by McBurney's grill."

David forced himself not to twitch or give any outward sign of how badly those words affected him. His blood pressure shot into the stratosphere, but he did not crack. Jeremy waited a few moments, and when no outburst came he left the room.

"Motherfucker, cock-sucking son of a bitch."

"I heard what he said."

David jumped, so angry that he'd forgotten that Jamie was there. He looked into his cool green eyes.

"Yeah, and he'll just deny it."

"Sure he will, but now you know the truth. What do you want to do about it?"

"I want to make him pay."

"The best way to hurt him is going to be through his career. Without his job, the man's nothing."

"Yep. Fuck!" He slammed his fist down against the mattress.

"We're a couple of pretty smart guys. We'll think of something."

THE FOLLOWING SATURDAY NIGHT

The doorbell rang again. David answered, opening the door to reveal John standing on the step with an enormous vegetable platter in his hands.

"Let me take that," David said. The man stepped inside.

David deposited the platter on the kitchen table, along with the other food. Surveying the impressive collection, David figured he and Jamie would be eating finger food for the next week. Despite his protest everyone thus far had brought something with them. His mother had arrived with enough food to feed twenty.

Susan came into the kitchen and handed him a beer. "Compliments of the bartender."

Despite the dull ache in his side from where the gunshot wound was healing, David felt pretty good. While in the hospital he'd touched base with Jenny's primary doctor to find that she was doing well and was expected to be released within a few weeks, as long as she had a place to go to. As her mother had not been contacted yet, David assured the man he'd take care of it. When he'd spoken with her, she'd clarified a few shaky details for him. The man she'd seen Stella with had been Sasha, confirmed after David had shown her a number of photographs. The car she'd gotten into, it turned out, had belonged to Roberta.

He wandered into the family room where a table had been set up in one corner to act as a makeshift bar. Jamie was pouring drinks and chatting with Dana, David's ex-wife, and her new fiancé, Keith. It was a sight he never thought he'd see, yet one that brought a warmth to his chest. Jamie caught him looking and waved him over.

"So Jamie was just catching us up all the excitement of the past few weeks," Dana said.

"I'm sure he's exaggerating."

The doorbell rang again. "You stay and chat. I'll get it." Jamie left.

Dana gave Keith a look, and he wandered off to speak with David's mother and Jamie's sisters, who were having an animated conversation at one of the sofas.

"So, really, you doing all right?"

He looked at Dana, feeling a jumble of emotions stirring inside him. He did love her, and always would, as a dear friend, He also felt a terrible shame for the deceit he'd used against her. "I'm okay. The wound's not bad."

"Glad to hear it. I just thought maybe there might be more to it, you know with Jeremy being involved in the case. I'm sure it wasn't easy to deal with him."

"Nope. I hate the bastard with every atom of my being."

She laughed. "Don't hold back or anything."

Jamie came back into the room, escorting Stella and Marjory. David and Stella made eye contact, and an unspoken message passed between them: *I'm okay.*

His eyes felt hot. "You know Dana, I'm really sorry for everything I put you through."

She had a moment of being caught off guard, then smoothly regained her composure. "I know you are. Believe me, I was really frigging mad at you, but after that passed I realized how hard it must have been for you too. And everything's worked out for the best right? We're both with people we love. Let's let the past alone." She offered her hand.

David ignored the hand and gave her a tight hug. "Let's do something soon, the four of us."

"Sure, sounds good."

He excused himself and went to speak with Stella. "Hi ladies. So glad you could come."

He meant it. After the events of the past week, he didn't figure either one of them would feel much like celebrating. Christian had been charged with rape and a number of related charges, as well as being linked to illegal film production and distribution. During a sweep of his house, another cache of items had been found in a hidden compartment at the back of his bedroom closet, containing, among other things, the film of his father having sex with an underage Elaine. As a result George had also been arrested. He'd admitted that Christian had told him about the movies, and Stella's involvement in them, during the recent conversation overheard by Sheila. He adamantly refused knowledge of the drug running or Christian's abuse of his daughter.

The proverbial silver lining had been the location of Lee and Ritchie. The former's body had been found in a remote area outside of town. He'd been beaten and shot several times, making it impossible for him to implicate anyone else in either the films or his drug racket. Ritchie had turned himself into the police, probably the only smart thing he'd ever done in his life. A life behind bars was still a life, and knowing what he did would have made him a target for the same people who'd dealt with Lee.

He admitted to being the gunman in the incident at the Scarlett Letter and the attempt to run David down, as well as trashing Jamie's house. He also took the blame for Jenny, but would not admit to killing Elaine. He blamed Lee pulling the trigger in Elaine's murder, facts which could not be disputed. Wisely, Christian wasn't implicating himself further in any of the incidents, though his presence at the club the night of the shooting was more than suspicious. It didn't matter in the eyes of the law, he'd still spend the remainder of his life in jail.

The arrests and shut down of the film production were great, but the real success in the case had been Stella. She'd come through it all with her head held high, refusing to slip back into her old ways of coping. Standing before him, smiling and looking healthy and calm, was all the thanks David needed. She did look fantastic. She'd obviously had her hair done, and she wore some makeup and a shimmery, emerald green dress. Marjory stood proudly at her side dressed in a red skirt and a dark blouse with a sash tied about her waist.

"Hi, David. Thank you for the invitation."

"I didn't know if you'd feel like a party, after everything."

Marjory smiled. "On the contrary, I think this is just what we need."

"Can I get you a drink?"

"A ginger ale for me," Stella answered. "Wine for you, Mom?"

Marjory nodded. He retrieved their drinks and then introduced them to the odd assembly of guests. David's parents, his brother and his girlfriend had come, and his aunt and uncle, along with Jamie's mom and sisters. His grandmother sat with John on a loveseat, and as he surveyed the room, he wondered why he hadn't thought of putting the two together before. Both were widowers and could have benefitted from the friendship.

Jean had come with her husband, as had Jimmy and his wife Shawna. There were a couple of guys from the gym, another neighbour, and three women from Jamie's office. To his pleasant surprise, most people hadn't batted an eye when the truth about his sexuality had come out, and those who may have had an issue kept it to themselves. Roberta and Sasha were also there, putting the touches on an assembly of people he could never have dreamed of having in his house. They passed the majority of their time with Stella, showing their friendship had survived the toughest of challenges.

The night went on with drinks and nibbles and a series of wonderful conversations. Before making her departure, his grandmother had agreed to take Jenny in after she was released from the hospital. He figured if anyone could straighten the girl out, it would be her. Home-cooked meals and compassion would weaken the hardest of hearts. David hoped that when she recovered he could convince her to become his secretary, but that had yet to be broached with the girl.

Stella and her mom stayed for about an hour. They chatted about her reconnection with Marcy and her ongoing health regimen, including a new therapist. With the revelation of her past abuse the Borderline Personality diagnosis needed to be reassessed. For sure, Stella had her emotional issues, but a new focus might finally give her the process she needed to heal and move on. With her relationship with her mother intact, the drugs removed from her life, and the option to dance available again,

Stella had the world wide open to her. Seeing her move on to the freedom of unhitching herself from the demons of her past reminded David that he had the opportunity to do the same.

Before they left Marjory had pulled David aside to thank him for everything he'd done and handed him a cheque for ten thousand dollars. He protested, but she insisted. He asked her to stay in touch, as he sincerely wanted to know how Stella made out. She had a lot of work ahead of her, to come to terms with years of abuse and self-loathing. He knew she'd make it with her mother, Sasha, and Roberta on her side. Through an ironic twist, Marjory had found a way to take over Elaine's studio, which she'd then registered in Stella's name. With a new lease on life and a career that she could take pride from, Stella had everything going for her recovery.

He and Jamie had a really nice visit with Jamie's mom and sisters. His dad was still not happy with things, but they assured the men that they were fully supportive. They stayed for quite a long while, even playing a few hands of cards.

All in all it had been a successful evening. As they lay in bed, the guests having returned home and the food stored in the refrigerator, they talked about the upcoming new year and what the future might have in store for them.

"I think I should move in here. Permanently," Jamie said.

"Really? You sure?"

"Yeah, I am. You were right. I've been hiding our relationship like it's something to be ashamed of, and you don't deserve to be treated like that. It just makes sense on so many levels. Maybe we can even get a dog."

"Don't get ahead of yourself. But seriously, I'd like you to be here with me."

"Then let's do it. I have a couple days off over Christmas. We can pack up my stuff and put the house on the market."

"You better be sure about this. It's a serious thing to sell a house."

"You getting cold feet now?"

"Not at all."

"Then it's settled."

"Now the only thing left is your dad."

"There's something even more important than that. We need to find a way to nail that asshole Jeremy Black to the wall."

David sighed. He looked forward to the new year. Like Stella, he'd entered a new phase of life, free of guilt and fear.

He felt like there was nothing he couldn't accomplish.

ABOUT THE AUTHOR

Liz Strange is the published author of ten novels and several short stories. She has also written multiple scripts for both film and television.

www.ingramcontent.com/pod-product-compliance
Lightning Source LLC
Chambersburg PA
CBHW021707180626
46816CB00012B/520